MINECRAFT™
MOB SQUAD

MINECRAFT™
MOB SQUAD

DELILAH S. DAWSON

NEW YORK

Copyright © 2021 Mojang AB. All Rights Reserved.
Minecraft, the MINECRAFT logo, and the MINECRAFT STUDIOS logo
are trademarks of the Microsoft group of companies.

Published in the United States by Del Rey,
an imprint of Random House, a division of
Penguin Random House LLC, New York.

DEL REY is a registered trademark and the CIRCLE colophon
is a trademark of Penguin Random House LLC.

LIBRARY OF CONGRESS CATALOGING-IN-PUBLICATION DATA
Names: Dawson, Delilah S., author.
Title: Minecraft: mob squad / Delilah S. Dawson.
Other titles: Mob squad
Description: New York: Del Rey, [2021]
Identifiers: LCCN 2021014046 (print) | LCCN 2021014047 (ebook) |
ISBN 9780593355770 (hardback) | ISBN 9780593355787 (ebook) |
ISBN 9780593496992 (international edition)
Subjects: CYAC: Adventure and adventurers—Fiction. | Villages—Fiction.
Classification: LCC PZ7.D323 Mk 2021 (print) |
LCC PZ7.D323 (ebook) | DDC [Fic]—dc23
LC record available at https://lccn.loc.gov/2021014046
LC ebook record available at https://lccn.loc.gov/2021014047

Endpaper art: M. S. Corley

Printed in the United States of America on acid-free paper

randomhousebooks.com

2 4 6 8 9 7 5 3 1

First Edition

Book design by Elizabeth A. D. Eno

For Rhys and Rex, always. Now you're canon in *Star Wars* *and* Minecraft.

And for the MCYT community and especially the cast of the Dream SMP. There's a disc in here for you.

MINECRAFT™
MOB SQUAD

1.

MAL

 So here's what you need to know: My name is Mal, I live in a town called Cornucopia, and I would do anything for my friends. Literally. Which is why they always come to me for help.

My family runs the biggest cattle ranch, which I've nicknamed Cornu-cow-pie-a as a joke. Most days, I wake up with the rooster and take the cows out to pasture, which isn't a very long journey, as our town is completely contained within impossibly tall walls. Still, we have to switch where the cows graze or they'll eat down to the dirt and possibly keep going. Cows aren't very smart. They are cute, though, and I like eating breakfast as they graze. Their crunching is very companionable.

"Mal!" a voice calls as I munch on my apple.

I look around—definitely not a cow. And anyway, I know that voice.

"Morning, Lenna!"

My friend Lenna jogs toward me, out of breath and frantic, her poufy brown hair bouncing and full of leaves. "Mal. You've got to come help. Jarro has Tok and Chug cornered in an alley!"

With Lenna, you have to stop and make sure you have all the details right.

"Okay, slow down. I know Tok couldn't fight a sick beetroot, but Chug can take on Jarro any day of the week. What's the problem?"

She cocks her head. "Chug has a hoe."

Ah.

See, Chug and Tok are the other two people in our friend group. They're brothers, but as different as two people can be. And, yes, they're almost always in trouble for something or other. Scrapping with Jarro is one thing, but if Chug is holding a hoe and Jarro goads him enough, especially in a hidden alley downtown, we might have a real problem. Plus, if Chug breaks the hoe over Jarro's head, he'll be in even worse trouble.

It's not like hoes grow on trees.

You can buy them only from Old Stu, and they're pretty expensive.

And Tok . . . kinda goes through a lot of tools. He's always trying to create interesting gadgets to help around their family's pumpkin farm—not that any of them seem to work. He's very smart and creative, but he gets so excited that he forgets about rules and safety.

Chug, on the other hand, is all fists and not a lot of calculations. We need to hurry—not to protect the boys from Jarro, but to protect Chug from Chug. He's my best friend, but I'm the first to admit that he doesn't know when to shut his mouth. He's the king of comebacks and is always ready to stand up against any bully. If he hurts Jarro, things will go badly for all of us.

"Seriously, Mal. Chug was turning red. We've got to hurry!"

Lenna turns around to run, looking back to make sure I'm with her. She's known for hyperbole and telling tall tales, so I'm pretty sure Chug isn't about to start bopping people on the head with a hoe. Still, I'm the one who has to make sure everyone is okay, so I sigh and toss my unfinished apple toward the nearest cow before standing to run after Lenna.

I end up outpacing her as we charge into the Hub, which is what we call the center of town. She leads me to a back alley in the warren of old shops and houses, and sure enough, there they are. Tok is up high, out of reach, perched on part of an ancient staircase that leads toward a second floor door nobody uses any-more. His cat, Candor, is by his side, her fur puffed up as she hisses at the scene below. No one knows if Candor is male or fe-male, but Tok decided that she is a she and she hasn't complained, and I respect that. She spends most of her time on his shoulder. I can't really picture Tok without an orange ball of fluff acting as his second head.

The scene below, though? That's the real problem. I'm glad we ran.

Chug does indeed have a brand-new hoe held in both hands, and he and Jarro are nearly chest to chest in the narrow alley. Jarro's two toadies, Remy and Edd, are just behind him, aching for a fight. I'm glad Lenna and I are here so the boys aren't out-numbered.

"Put down the hoe and put up your fists," Jarro growls. He's a foot taller than Chug with longer arms, but Chug's got more weight—and more reason to fight. He'll do anything to protect his brother.

"If I put down the hoe, one of your pet donkeys over there is going to steal it," Chug says. "Isn't that why you chased my brother into this alley to begin with? Because you're a thief? You certainly stole all the ugly around town for yourself."

Jarro doesn't know what to say to that, as he's not very smart. "Come on!" he shouts. "Quit yapping your trap and fight me!"

Chug notices Lenna and me standing behind Jarro and grins. "Okay, never mind. I'll put down the hoe. The odds just got much better. Hey, buddies!"

When Chug waves, Jarro and his friends turn around to look at us. Chug tosses the hoe up to Tok and takes advantage of Jarro's surprise, socking him in the belly. Jarro doubles over with a star-tled "Oof!"

"Aw, man. I put up my fists, and you totally missed it!" Chug says.

Remy and Edd are nervous now—this crew of bullies likes to find and corner weaklings, not go up against four friends.

His toadies stay focused on Chug, but Jarro recovers enough to turn around and face me.

"Oh, look. It's your fearless leader." Jarro's face screws up in disgust as he looks me up and down. "I'm not afraid to hit girls, you know."

He takes a step toward me and Lenna, and I don't flinch, but she skitters away.

"Wow, you're so open-minded," I say. Over his shoulder, I see Chug putting up both fists, and I make eye contact and shake my head. I want to stop the fight, not allow Chug to deepen his grudge with Jarro. "I'm not afraid to hit boys, either."

Jarro sneers and steps even closer, so close I have to step back or—ew!—touch him. "You've never hit anybody. You just get out of every situation by—"

"Doesn't your mom hate it when you start fights, Jarro?" I say, chin up so he won't notice my trembling knees. "Lenna, go check the Hub and see if she's standing around close by." Jarro's mom lives for gossip and is usually near Stu's Store this time every morning to keep tabs on everyone in our town. Lenna nods and disappears around the corner. For once, Jarro is right—as our group's unofficial leader, I prefer to resort to diplomacy. Or, in this case, threats.

The toadies turn around to see what Lenna and I are doing, and Chug being Chug, he steps between them and lands a kick right in Jarro's backside. I wince—if Chug will just let me handle it, we can all get out of here without bruises or lectures. Jarro whirls on him, hands in fists.

"I think I hear your mom, Jarro," I say warningly.

Even Jarro can do the math of four against three, plus factor in the looming concern of his mom. "You little babies can keep your hoe. But one day, I'm gonna catch Tok alone, and then . . ."

"No you won't." Chug shakes his head slowly. "But if you ever do, I think you'll be surprised at what he can do. Like, I dunno— basic math? All sorts of things you can't understand. He's tougher than he looks."

"Then why does he always run?" Jarro shoots back, trying to appear superior.

"Because he's afraid that whatever made you look like that is contagious."

Having lost both the verbal and physical duels, Jarro shakes his head. "You're not worth it." He jerks his chin at his toadies and bumps into my shoulder on his way out of the alley. Once they're gone, Lenna creeps out from where she was hiding behind an old, broken chest. She looks sheepish and is holding an interesting rock, so I'm guessing she got distracted and never even made it to Jarro's mom.

"So that went well," Tok says.

He tosses the hoe to me and scoots to the edge of the step. When he isn't sure how to get down, Chug gives him a hand. Candor leaps off the staircase like it's nothing, and then we're headed out of the alley and back toward the center of town.

"It went great!" Chug holds up a fist. "Any day I get to punch Jarro is a good day."

"It didn't go as well as you think," I remind them both. "Now Jarro's going to go tell his mom that you hit him, and everyone is going to give us dirty looks."

"If they bothered to ask us what happened, they'd call us heroes!" Chug wails.

"Yeah, but adults never really want to know what happened. They just want the problem to go away." Candor jumps onto Tok's shoulder, and he strokes her orange fur.

We do indeed see Jarro whispering to his mom, Dawna, so I take off at a run, and everyone else follows. We don't have to talk about where we're going—the boys' pumpkin farm is our unofficial base. At my farm, my parents will put us to work, and Lenna's parents are really strict about kids at the mine. The pumpkin farm is usually chill, but . . .

"I just don't understand how this keeps happening. Hoes aren't free, Tok," the boys' constantly exasperated dad says when Chug hands over the new hoe. "You can't just make one any day you want to. Tools are hard to come by—and expensive. We owe Stu ten of your mother's pumpkin pies because of this morning's accident! I know you meant well, but you've got to stop breaking things for your inventions."

"But breaking things is the first step to making better things!" Tok argues.

"As long as you're not breaking our bones," Chug adds.

Their dad is actually a very patient man, but then again, you'd have to be with a kid like Chug. And a kid like Tok.

"I would never—!" their dad starts.

"Oh, gimme a break!" Chug interrupts. "I don't find threats humerus!"

Their dad just shakes his head. "No more bone puns. You're both going to spend the rest of the morning weeding as punishment. The entire south field."

"That's not fair!" Chug barks. "We already did our chores, and—"

"We'd be happy to help," I say, stepping up with my best "Good Kid" smile. "We'll get the weeding done in no time if we all work together. Right, Lenna?" She nods, and the boys' dad looks out at the neat rows of pumpkins and sighs.

"That's very kind of you kids to pitch in, but make sure the boys do their share. And please, Tok—just don't break anything else today."

He trudges away, and as soon as he's gone, Tok walks over to another of his failed machines, a jumble of parts that don't quite fit together. He pokes at the head of the broken hoe, and it thunks onto the ground. "This machine was going to revolutionize weeding. I was so certain it would work this time. It's like I'm missing some important part of the formula."

Chug nudges his shoulder. "It's okay, bro. You'll get it. Dad just doesn't understand, but one day he will. All he can think about are pumpkins. He's out of his gourd."

We walk out to the south field, which is so far away from town that two of Cornucopia's walls meet in a corner. I'm already done with my morning chores, and Lenna's parents don't trust her to do any work anywhere near their mine because she's known for being a clumsy daydreamer, so we all settle in for a morning of weeding by hand.

Honestly, it's not terrible, and at least we're doing it together. We each take a row and chat as we pull up anything green that's not a pumpkin vine, toss the offending sapling away, and shove any seeds we find into our pockets. Their dad runs a tight farm, so there's not actually much to do. Still, Lenna falls behind, as she always does. One minute she's squatting down, yanking on a particularly tough sapling, and the next minute she's wandering away to follow a bee or staring off into space.

Tok is explaining an idea for harnessing sheep to wash dishes when we hear a scream. It sounds like Lenna, so all three of us take off running in the direction we last saw her.

Lenna had apparently wandered off quite a bit, and we find her standing in the far corner of the field. She's staring up at the wall and screaming, and even if she does often do weird stuff, this is pretty freaky.

I'm the fastest, so I get there first. "Lenna, what's wrong?"

Lenna turns to look at me, her eyes huge and her hands shaking as she points at something I can't quite explain. The pumpkins in this corner of the field are all a sick grayish green, with curling purple smoke rising off them like mist. As we watch, they cave in and turn into mush, their vines going black and hard.

"There was a thing," Lenna says, in almost a whisper. "A gray thing with wings. It poured a potion on the pumpkins and flew away—*straight through the wall.*"

"A gray thing with wings?" Chug snorts and kicks a collapsing pumpkin, making it splurt over on its side and melt. "Like an evil chicken, maybe?"

Lenna looks down. "It wasn't a chicken."

"Then maybe it's a new kind of bird? And maybe it looked like a potion, but it was, uh . . . not a potion?" Even creative Tok can't think of any excuse for why a bird would have a potion, since they're incredibly rare. Potions, not birds, that is.

I put my hands on my hips and stare up at the wall, which is so tall that I've never seen beyond it. No one has. The wall doesn't have any doors at all and is lit day and night by thousands and thousands of torches. We don't know what's on the other side, but we know one thing for sure:

The wall is there to protect us, and what lies beyond it is dangerous and terrifying.

Our grandparents have never been outside, our parents have never been outside, and we have never been outside. Not since our great-great-great-grandparents founded Cornucopia has anyone been beyond the wall.

Before now, looking at the wall always made me feel safe and secure. Our town has everything we need, and nothing bad ever really happens here. Sure, I'm curious about what's outside, but I know the town Founders built the wall for a reason.

Still, now, as I try to picture what Lenna has just described, a trickle of icy unease ripples down my spine.

Did Lenna really see something, and if so, what was it?

And why would it want to poison our crops?

2.

LENNA

 So here's what you should know: My name is Lenna, I'm the youngest and least reliable of ten kids, I'm a flibbertigibbet, and my friends are the only people who really see me. That's why it hurts so much when they look at me like this—like I'm just making stuff up. Because I'm not.

Okay, sometimes I am, but not on purpose. It's easy to get daydreams, dreams, and reality mixed up. I mean, who can remember which is which? And the daydreams are so much more interesting. But this time, I know what I saw, and I know it was real. And I'm going to keep telling them until they believe me.

"So it went through the wall?" Mal asks, her eyebrows drawn down.

I nod. "Yeah, like the wall didn't even exist."

"And how'd it get in?"

"I don't know. I was watching a bee. But then I heard this weird sound, like a horn, maybe? And it was just there. Smaller than a person, all gray, with wings. And it just . . . flew."

Mal and Chug do this thing where they talk with only their facial expressions, and I can't always read that sort of thing, but I can tell they're both very dubious. Tok is already on his knees, scraping a piece of rotting pumpkin into his pocket, probably to study back at home. Candor looks pretty grossed out and has her mouth open like she's going to heave.

I'm with Candor on this one.

"So what do we do?" Chug finally says.

Mal looks around the field. Hundreds of perfectly normal pumpkins, and then this one, gross corner where we stand, where I saw something impossible.

"Your dad was already mad, and Lenna has a reputation for . . ." She frowns. "I just don't think anyone will believe the current explanation. So let's wait and see if everything is fine to-morrow. Maybe there's just some weird pumpkin sickness going around. He's not going to harvest over here today, right?"

Chug walks a few rows over to where the pumpkins are perfectly cubical and orange, not black and mushy. "Nope. It'll be a few weeks until the stems are fully loaded and ready. Er, *were* ready. *Would've been* ready? I don't specialize in pumpkin grammar."

"Then we wait and see. I mean, have you guys ever heard of something like this before? Is it a . . . a known pumpkin ailment?"

"Liquefaction? Definitely not," Tok says, inspecting his sample.

"I've never heard of anything that happens this fast. Or maybe there wasn't . . ." Chug glances at me guiltily.

I am very accustomed to this glance, but at least my friends just wince and glance, whereas my parents and siblings have a whole host of unpleasant nicknames for me, ranging from Loony Lenna to Queen Hypatia of Hyperbole to my least favorite, the simple but hurtful *Liar*.

"Maybe it was a bit more gradual and we just didn't notice,"

Tok finishes for his brother. "There are some diseases—from bugs, or something that travels underground." He looks back toward the farmhouse and barn. "But I definitely don't want to bring my dad any more bad news today, especially the kind that I can't adequately explain."

"Lenna, what do you think?" Mal asks, and everyone focuses on me—not my favorite feeling.

I look at the high wall, at the ruined pumpkins still emitting odd purple smoke, at the place where I was standing when that thing showed up. There's another interesting bee, but my friends are waiting for me to respond.

What do I think?

I'm scared.

And I'm not really sure why.

I guess because this time, I know what I saw, and yet still no one believes me.

"Wait until morning," I agree. I walk over to a row of unmelted pumpkins, immediately attacking a green sapling that has no business here. My cheeks are hot, but if I focus on tearing out the sapling, hopefully they won't notice that I'm about to cry, even though I don't want to.

Mal pats my back, which is nice. "Don't worry. We'll figure it out. We always do, right?"

I nod. Normal people always figure it out, but I am always so full of questions. Why do some bees fly upside down? Why do some sheep have fleece that changes color? Why do I sometimes hear weird moaning under the floorboards of my room at night? Who decided to call cookies "cookies"?

It's a weird word, "cookies," especially when you whisper it to yourself ten times in a row.

We go back to weeding, and I try to stay focused. I stick near my friends—we all stick together this time, so maybe they do believe me, at least a little bit. We laugh and throw dirt and pumpkins at one another and share a pumpkin pie Chug brought along—his mom really does make the best pumpkin pies. In hindsight, we should've eaten the pie before we threw the dirt, but a little grit is probably good for the teeth.

We're done long before dinner and play a game of toss with a lopsided pumpkin and even poke around the old barn, looking for interesting things for Tok to fix. It would be a nice afternoon if not for the fact that I'm freaking out and everyone else is ill at ease and we're all pretending that everything is okay.

As the sun begins to set, Mal and I wave goodbye to the guys and head for our houses. We're both smeared with dirt and pumpkin seeds as we part at the cobblestone path that leads to my family's mine.

"See you tomorrow," Mal says.

"Yep."

She steps closer. "Are you okay? I know what happened earlier was weird, but I'm sure everything will end up fine."

"How do you know?"

"Because everything else up until now has ended up fine. Right?"

There are flaws in her logic. I mean, everything might be okay for us, but the meaning of "okay" is different for everyone, and that doesn't count the people for whom things are not okay, like Benn, who got hurt in the mine last week and had to be carried out on a stretcher with what looked like burn marks and maybe bites? My dad said he fell down a ladder, but I'm pretty sure ladders don't leave tooth marks.

"Right," I say, because sometimes you just have to agree with people to get along.

"Right." Mal pulls a chunk of pumpkin out of my hair and grins before heading down the road toward her farm, waving over her shoulder.

My heart sinks as I walk toward my house. It's a big, pretty house, with a variety of rare stones making elegant patterns between the large glass windows. Torches shine everywhere, because torches always shine everywhere in Cornucopia. The yard is oddly quiet, and that's how I know I'm late. My parents and all nine siblings are sitting at the long table in the dining room, and they all turn to me as I try to sneak in.

"What happened to you?" Mom asks.

"Well, I saw this weird thing—"

"She's asking why you're covered in dirt and pumpkin chunks," my dad explains.

I look down at my arms.

Oops.

"I'll go wash," I say, because honestly, they want a behavior and not an explanation. They hate explanations. They call them "excuses." There's a big difference, but explaining that only gets me into more trouble.

I hurry to the bathroom and wash off all the dirt and pick the leaves and twigs and orange rind out of my big, fluffy hair. Once I look more presentable, I take my seat at the table, where we're placed in order by age because my parents are very precise and logical. I'm the only one in the family who isn't that way, actually. But since I'm usually the last one to arrive, I always know which chair is mine, because it's empty.

My oldest sister, Letti, is a great cook, but I have a hard time enjoying meals. My parents make us do this thing where we go around the table and talk about our day, what we learned, and what we're grateful for. This is apparently very easy for most of my siblings—"I sorted ore and stone," "I learned about a new type of ore (or stone)," "I'm grateful for ore and stone"—because they all work around the mine, doing physical work or paperwork. But when it gets to me, I'm caught.

If I tell the truth, they'll think I'm lying.

But if I lie . . . then I actually am lying, which I hate.

"How about you, Lenna?" Mom prompts after everyone else has stated how much they enjoy stone and stone products.

All eleven of them look at me, and it's like my brain floats away. "Um."

"What's something you did today?"

That, at least, I can answer. "I helped Chug and Tok weed the garden after Tok broke a hoe and his dad joked about breaking his bones."

Eleven faces look annoyed, and I realize I should've left out the part about breaking bones.

"That sounds like an exaggeration," Dad says.

"I guess it was. He asked them not to break things, and it was Chug who made the jokes about breaking bones, now that I think about it," I agree quickly. I always get flustered when everyone is examining me like this and finding me wanting. So, to avoid getting yet another gentle reprimand about making up stories, I continue, talking fast to get my turn over with and let them go back to talking about ore. "I'm grateful for bees, and I learned that when flying gray things pour purple potions on pumpkins, the pumpkins immediately rot and smell like old fish."

There is a moment of silent incredulity, and then everyone breaks out laughing.

"Oh, Lenna. That's hilarious," Letti says.

"It's so funny how your mind works," Dad adds.

"But I would like to know something you actually learned." This from Mom, in that gentle but stern voice that brooks no refusal.

My head falls forward, heavy as a pumpkin. "I guess I learned . . . Well, Tok has this weird box he found in the old barn, and if you put it on top of a pumpkin, it plays a crazy kind of musical fart sound. So we decided to put all sorts of things under and on the box to make strange sounds, and we tried hay and clay and—"

My parents exchange a dark look, but all my siblings look either perplexed or embarrassed.

"You kids shouldn't mess with things if you don't know what they are. There are dangers you simply can't know about," my mom says.

"It was just an old, weird box that made sounds—" I start.

"Lenna, drop it. And don't play with things you can't identify. In fact, maybe just don't go into that barn again," my dad says before motioning for my mother to follow him into the kitchen. They both leave, and all my siblings stare at me.

"You always ruin dinner," my brother Lugh groans.

"Why can't you just be normal?" moans his twin, Lia.

Even though they're just a year older than I am and spend their time sweeping up rock dust, they think they're sooo superior.

For a moment, anger rages in my chest and my hands go to fists, and I almost tell them exactly where they can shove their "normal." But then I hear my other siblings snickering, and Letti murmurs to Lars, "Somebody's always got to be the baby of the family, huh?" and the rage drains out, leaving me as droopy as the rotten pumpkins.

No explanation can convince them that I saw what I saw and that I don't do this for attention—this is just the way I'm made. If they're all granite, I'm that weird purple crystal they keep under a cloth in the very back of the storehouse because no one knows what it is and they think the way it pulsates is unnerving.

I don't say anything else. My parents come back to the table with dessert, and we finish dinner in an uncomfortable silence. As I lie in my bed that night, I can hear Letti and Luci whispering about me across the room, about how my parents should give me a job just so I'll stay at home instead of running around with my friends.

"Everyone in town calls them the Bad Apples," Luci hisses. "So embarrassing."

I want to explain that my friends aren't bad apples at all—they're more kind, brave, and generous than my own blood. And I'm not bad, either. But again, my family would just hear whining, not an explanation. I turn my back to them and pull up my blanket.

On the other side of my bedroom wall, I know the town's tall stone wall stands between me and . . . whatever is outside. Well, except for the gray thing I saw today, which can apparently fly directly through walls. I shift a little away from the cold stone. What if it decides to come through this wall, too? What if it pours a purple potion on me and I shrivel up like a rotten pumpkin and my guts turn green and black and liquid and smell like old fish?

Long after Letti and Luci go to sleep, I'm still awake, staring at the wall and imagining all the terrible things outside that could get in. I shift off my bed and crawl under it with my blanket and pillows. It's chilly and dark, but it definitely feels cozier down here. Even if I have nothing else in common with my family, I, too, like the feeling of being in a cave.

The next morning, I wake up before everyone else and tidy up my bed as if I had slept on top of it like a normal person. As I hurry down the road to Mal's farm, eating my bread on the way so I don't have to take any more taunts from my siblings over breakfast, I notice something unusual.

There are people outside, talking—a lot more people than usual. Stu is outside his store, Jami has stopped with his flock of pitifully bleating sheep, Inka is holding a mushy black ball that smells familiar in the worst possible way.

"I can't explain it," she says, near tears. "The whole east field of melons is just . . . destroyed."

I hear it dozens of times as I run faster to meet my friends.

Everyone's fields have gone rotten, just like the pumpkins.

3.

CHUG

 So here's what you need to know: Don't mess with me, don't mess with my brother, Tok, and don't mess with my friends, or I'll mess you up. I don't want to get punchy, but if words won't work, fists will.

Unfortunately, whatever is destroying our family farm is beyond the reach of both words and fists. Whether it was Lenna's weird flying thing or some scary new plant disease, a quarter of our fields are now completely destroyed, the pumpkins greenish black and smoking slightly, their vines gone crispy and gray. I've never been that into pumpkins—they're not lovable, like Mal's cows—but it hurts to see that much destruction. And stomping the ruined pumpkins to get my anger out doesn't help. It just makes my boots smell like rotten fish.

When I woke up this morning, I had this nice, cozy moment in bed where everything felt normal. I figured Tok and I would do our chores and then meet up with Mal and Lenna, maybe attempt to ride some cows or try out Tok's latest invention, which is supposed to hurl pumpkins high in the air but mostly just flings them into the ground at a high rate of speed. I swear, he has such good ideas, but somehow they never quite work out.

So we headed outside to fetch our hoes, and neither of us mentioned the possibility that anything could be wrong because what's the point? Either things are good or bad, and me chewing the inside of my cheek won't change that.

At first, I actually thought things might be okay, but then we heard crying and followed the sound to where Mom and Dad were standing in the middle of the fields. From here, we can see the whole farm. Everything is properly green and orange until the south field, which is . . . just nasty. Caved-in pumpkins, sizzling vines, weird purple smoke, and that awful smell that reminds me of the fertilizer we get from the salmon farm.

"What did you boys do?" Dad asks, his face red with anger as he holds Mom and she cries on his shoulder.

"We weeded the field as commanded," I say quickly. "You'll notice there are no weeds."

"The field is destroyed!" he shouts, and though it used to make me want to run away when he raised his voice, now it just makes me mad.

"Well, we didn't do it! How could we? I didn't gain magical powers overnight!"

Dad looks at Tok, who is ignoring us as he kneels beside Candor to inspect a half-rotten pumpkin. "Tok, were you trying to mix up potions? Have you been playing with things you shouldn't?"

"Uh, I—" Tok starts.

He's no good at lying, but sometimes, he's not even good at telling the truth. It's like his brain is on some other level and it takes a lot of effort to come back down to earth with the rest of us.

If Lenna's head is in the clouds, Tok's head is on a one-way trip to the moon that he's happily planning in-flight.

So I answer for him.

"Potions? Seriously? How would he even do that? What goes into a potion? No one knows! It's forbidden."

Tok stands, looking hurt and sincere. "If I knew how to make potions, maybe I could fix this. Maybe it's a root issue. We could build walls that went underground to block off the dangerous areas and save the remaining—"

"Enough!" Dad barks. "I'm going into town to see what can be done. This family has been farming pumpkins since your great-great-great-grandparents claimed this land and planted the first seeds in this very field, and I'm not going to lose our livelihood to some . . . some . . . ." He stares at Tok, fuming. "To a kid messing with dangerous substances!"

"Tok didn't do this!" I shout back. "He was with me all day. Lenna saw something put a potion on the pumpkins. We thought she was just being Lenna, but now we know it's true! She said it was gray and had wings—"

Dad holds up a hand. "Wild stories won't change things. What you've just described is impossible—it doesn't exist. This is real life, and this is our farm, and this is our town. If we don't supply pumpkins, if we don't do our part, then there won't be enough food to feed the other families and their livestock. They depend on us. We have to fix this, or else . . . ." He looks far away, toward the wall.

"Or else?" Tok prompts.

Mom's crying has fallen off, and she smiles gently and puts a hand on Tok's shoulder. "Let the adults worry about that. Head out to the north field—"

"No! Just stay out of the fields today," Dad interrupts. "Go play. But don't get in any trouble."

He gives me a look that I hate, a look that reminds me that "not getting in trouble" means that if Jarro starts picking on Tok, I shouldn't make Jarro eat dirt. My parents just don't understand that force-feeding bullies a little of their own medicine is better than letting the bullies win. They haven't seen Tok after Jarro and his friends have found him alone, but I have, and . . . Well, like I said: Don't mess with my brother.

"C'mon, Tok. Let's go." I tug on his shirt to pull him away from examining the half-and-half pumpkin, and he reluctantly follows with Candor on his shoulder.

We head toward the center of town, which is the way to get to anyone else's house. When our great-great-great-grandparents helped found Cornucopia with six of their friends, they planned it really well so that there's a farm to meet every need. Pumpkins, melons, wheat, cows, sheep, chickens, salmon, beetroot—which I detest—all jutting out like spokes on a wheel. It's pretty convenient when I want to hang out with my friends because we can all meet in the center, which everyone calls the Hub.

We can tell there's something wrong as soon as we get near the Hub. Our neighbor Fredd is pushing a wheelbarrow full of black gunk that might've once been wheat from his fields. Beside him walks Krog, thankfully not pushing a wheelbarrow full of his farm's beetroots, which are equally disgusting whether in their usual state or mysteriously reduced to mush.

"And so there I was, writing a meditation on man's search for meaning, when I smelled the most loathsome odor!" Krog cries, waving his arms around dramatically. The guy loves attention, but weirdly enough, most people don't like listening to him. Poor Fredd, trapped behind his wheelbarrow, is stuck.

But Krog's not done. "I threw open my door and beheld a vision most gruesome: my beetroots, reduced to vile putridity!"

"I know," Fredd says. He gestures at his wheelbarrow. "Obviously."

During the brief moment that Krog is stunned and annoyed into silence, we take the opportunity to scurry around them. Fredd nods at us but Krog gives us a dirty look—he doesn't like us after we accidentally kind of almost sort of set one of his fields on fire trying to build a megatorch. (Yes, it was because we were trying to destroy as many beetroots as possible, but he wasn't moved by our philanthropy.) Before Krog can say something nasty and many-syllabled, Tok and I give each other a look and speed up. Candor leaps to the ground and paces alongside us.

"Bad apples," Krog mutters at a high volume. "Rapscallions! Scalawags!"

"They're just kids," Fredd says, sounding bored beyond belief.

Farther on we hear cows lowing mournfully from Mal's farm, and I can tell that Tok is thinking hard.

"Their fodder," he murmurs as we jog. "If the blight destroys vegetation, that includes everything cows eat. And sheep and chickens . . ."

I've never really thought about it before, but what do you do when you live behind high stone walls that have no doors—and you run out of food?

I run faster. Tok pulls ahead, and then we're racing. But not the kind of race where you want to beat the other person and rub it in their face—the kind where you're both grinning and enjoying the feel of the wind and the sun and how nice it is to have someone to run with. For a moment, I forget the looming threat of rot.

We're neck and neck as we enter the Hub and dart around

passersby, and I almost run over a deeply upset sheep, and Tok pulls ahead, and then he's flat on his back on the cobbles with Jarro standing over him, his meaty arm still out from clotheslining my brother.

I'm on my knees immediately. "Tok, you okay, bro?"

Tok can only wheeze, considering he's just had the breath knocked out of him by a much larger kid, but he nods as he sits up. Candor meows worriedly and rubs against him. I bolt to my feet.

"Oh, it's you again, Jarro. I thought maybe he'd run into a cow's behind."

Jarro is a foot taller than I am, and Remy and Edd are on either side of him. They're all grinning in that way that only bullies do, like they think they've already won and are the true heroes of the story.

It's my job to prove otherwise.

"You're a—" he starts, but I interrupt him with a punch to the belly, doubling him over.

"I'm sorry, I couldn't hear you," I say. "I'm a what?"

His toadies close in on either side, and I'm just about to give in and whoop some rumpus when a shadow looms over us all. It's Elder Stu, the owner of the general store and the eldest of our Elders, and we all freeze. Stu's a tough old geezer, and he does not suffer fools.

"What in tarnation are you young scofflaws fighting about? Stop that right now."

"He punched me, sir," Jarro wheedles loudly.

"He knocked my brother to the ground first, sir," I say, even loudlier.

Stu puts a hand down and helps Tok stand up. Anyone with

eyes in this town—which is everyone, because they're all nosy—
knows that Jarro has been picking on Tok since we were babies,
and yet no one ever steps in to do anything, probably because
Jarro's mom has the only sweet berry bushes in town and they
don't want to make her mad.

"You okay, kid?"

"Yes, sir," Tok whispers, still trying to breathe normally.

"Then run along, and your little cat, too. Whole town's in a
tizzy, all the plants are dying, and you kids are fighting. There's a
town meeting at noon, and nobody needs any more problems. Go
on. Get." He flaps his hands, shooing us away.

"Chug! Tok!"

I turn around and see Mal and Lenna hurrying toward us.

"Oh, look, it's your girlfr—" Jarro starts before I take a step
back and elbow him in the ribs to end that thought. Mal's my best
friend, not my girlfriend, and I don't care what Old Man Stu
says—Jarro is the problem, not us.

Tok and I meet Mal and Lenna on the other side of the fountain from where Jarro is still trying to recover his own capacity to
breathe.

"So it looks like we have a real problem," Mal says instead of
delivering our usual greeting.

"Our entire south field is trashed," I say. "And Fredd's wheat."

"And Inka's melons and Saya's carrots and Rhys's potatoes. All
the crops. We lost an entire pasture of grass," Mal confirms.

"The cows are so sad," Lenna says.

"Has anyone told their parents about what Lenna saw?" Mal
asks.

Lenna looks down. "My parents didn't believe me. My whole
family laughed at me."

"Our dad blamed Tok for it," I say. "Thought he might be mixing up potions. I mean, how would you even do that? Nobody but Elder Gabe knows where they come from!" I'm still angry from the Jarro incident, and it feels like smoke is going to come out of my ears. "What about you, Mal?"

"I asked my mom if she'd ever heard of a gray winged creature, and she kind of remembered something about a lullaby her grandmother sang when she was little, but she wasn't sure. She sang a little of it for me. *Beware the vex, all gray with wings, beware the night and what it brings.* But that's all she could remember. And she didn't know anything about what's killing the plants." Mal puts her hands on her hips, which is how you know she's thinking hard. She turns and looks out toward the forest, with all its trees planted in orderly rows. I already know what she has in mind.

"Do you think she'll know anything?" I ask.

"Maybe. I mean, what do we have to lose?"

Tok is making his perplexed face. "What are you guys talking about?"

"Mal's great-great-grandmother. She lives at the far side of the forest."

That surprises both Tok and Lenna.

"Wait, what?" Tok hates learning that there's something he doesn't know. "Mal's great-great-grandmother is *alive*?"

Mal gets a faraway look. "My Nan is the oldest person in Cornucopia, and she had my dad and uncle build her a little house way out at the end of the forest. She said she wanted to end her days alone and in the wild, like she started. Said the town was getting too crowded."

"And your dad actually did it?" I can imagine why Lenna

sounds envious. She'd probably love a life like that, where she could end her days alone and unbothered, out where it was quiet.

Mal nods. "He kind of had to. She's a force of nature."

"So should we—" I start, but I'm interrupted by shouting.

We all share a look before following Mal over to where the adults are gathered on the square. I say "the adults," but basically, it's everyone over eighteen in the town. There are wheelbarrows full of black mush everywhere, and the smell is terrible. We stand in the back to listen, a little behind a statue of the eight Founders.

"We can't wait until noon for the meeting!" Rhys shouts. "We're doing it now!"

"The sheep are going to starve!" Jami adds.

"There's no choice! We've got to leave!" Krog finishes.

Elder Stu steps up onto the stone stage the town uses for speeches, harvest festivals, and swap meets. The crowd quiets down a bit. "Fine, then," he grumbles. "Didn't want breakfast anyway. Is anyone's farm untouched—anyone growing food or fodder?"

The crowd answers him with one loud "NO!"

"Did anyone see anything happen, anything suspicious?"

Voices call out a variety of names—troublesome neighbors and even, much to my surprise, our names.

"It was those Bad Apples," Jarro's mom, Dawna, shouts. "Mal and her gang. They're always up to something!" Beside her, Jarro nods and grins.

"Our children didn't destroy over a dozen farms overnight! They're just kids! Both my boys were home all night behind a locked door!" my dad shouts, temporarily providing a wonderful sort of relief. Even if he blamed Tok at home, he's defending us now.

I don't know what Dawna is thinking—what kids would willingly destroy sweet berries? Krog's beetroots, maybe, but not sweet berries.

"Quiet now!" Stu waves his arms until the yelling calms to angry mutterings. "If there's no definitive proof and nobody saw the culprit, then we've got to talk about next steps. Right now, we can keep on, but if the blight spreads, we'll have to consider something drastic. No crops for us, no fodder for the animals . . ." He trails off, shakes his head. "We can't go on like that. We'll have to leave. Scatter in the four directions from which our Founders came, as they directed us in the original town commandments."

The adults murmur and shout, but me, Mal, Tok, and Lenna just stare at one another, barely able to breathe.

It's unthinkable—the thought of leaving Cornucopia. Ever since our great-great-great-grandparents founded the town, those walls have been up, protecting us from whatever horrors lay outside. We know everyone here, know every family. We're safe and cared for. And more important, I have my friends, who, let's be honest, are also family.

What if Mal's folks go in a different direction from ours? What will Lenna do without us there? What lies beyond the wall isn't nearly as scary as being anywhere without my best friends.

"What are we going to do?" Lenna asks in a tiny voice.

The adults have abandoned their orderly meeting to shout at one another at full volume, questions and threats and worries and demands. Stu shouts over all of them, stating that the Elders will deliver their decision at noon. But Mal turns to stare in the opposite direction, where the tall trees mark her Nan's forest.

"We're going to ask the only person around here who was born outside the walls."

She marches off, and we follow her, because we always follow her. Tok and I exchange a glance, and I can't help meeting Candor's green eyes, too, as she perches on his shoulder. Lenna scurries past us to catch up to Mal.

"What do you mean, 'born outside the walls'? That's not possible. All the Founders are dead, and everyone else was born here."

Mal shakes her head. "Not true. Great-great-grandmother Nan was a kid when her parents helped found Cornucopia. She used to tell me the wildest stories. She remembers watching them cut down tall, tall trees, taller than anything in our forest. My dad says none of it's true, but Nan sure thinks it is."

The shouts of the crowd fade away as we walk. Mal steps under the first trees of the forest, and I shiver a little at the chill in the shadows.

"But what's outside the walls? Did she ever tell you?"

We wend between all the torches, placed at perfect distances between the trees. No place in Cornucopia is ever dark for more than seven blocks. Mal's uncle Hugo keeps the torches lit here, and other families have their own torch-tenders. Every family has a responsibility, every person has a job.

"She never told me what was outside the walls," Mal says, all thoughtful. "But then again, I've never asked her before."

4.

TOK

Here's what you need to know:

No, wait.

Here's what *I* need to know: Everything.

How do chickens fly? What is Candor saying when she meows at me? Why are some kinds of stone useful for some kinds of building and not others? Why does bonemeal make plants grow? How far away is the sun? What happens if you start digging in Lenna's mine and dig down forever? What is that odd, musical box we found in the barn, and where'd it come from? What's outside the wall? Why don't my inventions work when they very definitely should?

And, currently, most important, why are all the plants dying, and how can we stop it?

Normally I like a problem that demands my scrutiny, but not when my town and friendships are on the line.

As we walk under the forest canopy, my senses go on alert. The trees provide cool shade, and the sunlight filters through and mixes with the bright torches to create an ever-shifting world of dappled shadow. Everything smells crisp and clear, which is a vast improvement over the burned fish odor of the ruined crops. This forest is an odd part of our town—it's planted within the walls, the trees in orderly rows of exact heights that show how recently they were harvested and replanted. It's huge and vast, and even though it's always been very enticing, children are strictly forbidden from playing here. The forest is too valuable. All our wood comes from these trees. I just hope—

My hopes are dashed as we see a bright spot ahead and smell that now familiar funk. The trees nearest the wall have fallen, their beautiful brown-and-white bark turning sick and gray and wet, just like everything else.

"Nan!" Mal shouts as she breaks into a run.

We follow her when we see what she sees: a fallen tree that has barely missed crushing a tidy little wooden cottage that backs right up against the wall.

All the flowers around the cottage are black sludge, even the ones in the window boxes. Mal scrambles under the fallen tree and knocks on the door, calling her great-great-grandmother's name. No noises come from within the cottage, and I'm calculating how old Nan must be and the likelihood that something terrible has happened to her.

An odd sound comes from around the side of the cottage, and we hurry over there to see what's happening. Somewhere along the way, Chug has picked up a hefty stick, and he edges his way in front of us. There's nothing dangerous within Cornucopia's walls—that we know of. But whatever is killing the plants came from somewhere, so I'm glad that my brother's first instinct was to pick up something he could use to defend us.

The noise comes again, and it sounds like wood being chopped. Much to our surprise, a hole opens in the side of the cottage, a perfect block. An ancient face peeks out, bright blue eyes twinkling.

"Hm. Children," she says. "Hold on. Darned tree blocked the front door."

I see a flash of crystal inside, and another block of the house disappears. Now there's a hole in the wood exactly the size of a door, and the oldest person I've ever seen is standing in it holding an axe that isn't made of iron, like our axes at home.

It looks like it's made of . . . *diamond*?

"A whole passel of you kids, eh? How many am I related to?"

Mal raises her hand.

"Good. Then I don't have to kiss the rest of 'em."

Mal steps forward, just as bewildered as the rest of us, and the old woman dutifully kisses her on the cheek. "Let me think. Mara's daughter, is that right?"

"Yes, Great-great-grandmother Nan. And these are my friends, Chug—"

"Doesn't matter. Won't remember. And call me Nan. All those "greats" grate on my nerves. Did your folks send you out here to chop up that nasty tree for me? You can borrow my axe, seeing as how you apparently forgot yours." She holds out the axe and Mal takes it, gazing in awe at the head, which is so bright it's almost glowing.

Mal, for once, seems lost for words, but she knows what must be done. Hefting the axe, she walks back around to the front of the cottage and starts chopping at the dead tree. Nan stares at us for a moment before shaking her head and walking around the corner, so we follow around to awkwardly watch Mal. As for me, I just want to get my hands on that axe and figure out how it was made.

"Nan, this axe is incredible!" Mal says. She's chopping the tree down three times faster than should be possible.

Nan nods. "It should be. Diamond makes the best axes. It belonged to my mother—she made it herself. Very handy woman with an axe. She cleared most of the ground for the town, all by herself."

In between chops and empowered grins, Mal says, "Do you know what happened to these trees? This blight is all over Cornucopia, and no one knows what it is."

Nan picks up one of her dead flowers, sniffs it, and tosses it away in disgust. "Potions. Must be a witch nearby. Has anyone seen a witch? Or heard cackling?"

We all look at one another in complete astonishment. Behind Nan's back, Chug puts a finger to his temple and twirls it around while crossing his eyes to indicate, rudely, and standing where she can't see it, that the old woman might be off her rocker.

"Witches aren't real, Nan," Mal says gently. "Do you think it might be—"

"Witches aren't real? Ha!" Nan throws her head back and cackles in a way that could definitely be called witchy. "What are they teaching you children these days? Of course witches are real. Witches, zombies, endermen, ghasts, vexes. They're all *real*."

Mal stops chopping and looks up. "Wait. Did you say 'vexes'?"

Nan nudges a log with her toe to see if it's more mushy or solid and then sits on it and resettles her shawl. "I did."

"What are they?"

"Vexes are little gray things with wings that fly around and do the bidding of evokers. They can carry swords and cause a body all sorts of trouble."

Although Lenna is usually wary of strangers, she steps forward excitedly. "These vexes—can they fly through walls?"

Nan nods her approval. "That's right. They certainly can. Glad at least one of you is still learning something useful." The old woman taps her foot, tilts her head back, and sings.

> If you do not wish to sob
> Beware, my child, the hostile mob.
> Avoid the zombie with his moans
> The skeleton, all bow and bones.
> The drowned with trident in the sea
> The enderman, don't look at me.
> The creeper who explodes on sight
> The spider jockey with his bite.
> Evoker, witch, and silverfish
> Avoid them is my only wish.
> Vindicator, ghast, and slime
> Learn it, child, this teaching rhyme.
> Evade the vex, all gray with wings
> Beware the dark and what it brings.

I pull out my notebook and pencil, too late. There were so many things I've never heard of, and I have so many questions. "Could you sing that again, please?"

Nan shakes her head. "Too much trouble to explain. I'll just give you the book." She peers at me from over her glasses. "You can read, right? They *are* still teaching that sort of thing, even if they're neglecting the really important bits?"

"Yes, ma'am, I can read." I can't stop grinning. "I'd love to see this book."

Mal finishes up with the last of the tree and holds the axe out to Nan, who shakes her head. "Stack up the wood, first—only the useful logs, if you please. Put those on the woodpile, and drag the mushy parts up against the wall."

I'm so excited now that I hurry to help the others divide up what's left of the once massive tree, and soon Nan's front door is revealed. She opens it as if this is totally normal and walks into her cottage, and since the door is still open, Mal walks in, with us right behind her.

"May my cat come in, too, ma'am?" I ask, as I've definitely gotten in trouble for bringing Candor into places where she's not welcome.

Nan looks almost affronted. "Of course! Cats are lucky. No creeper will ever come near you, if you've a cat handy."

I step inside, Candor on my shoulder and pencil in hand. "And what's a creeper?"

"Imagine a sort of reverse pig, tall, green, and black, and they can pop up anywhere, aboveground or below. Make a horrible hissing noise. If they get within a block of you, you have a second and a half before they explode. And if you can't get at least four blocks away . . . boom!" She mimics an explosion with her hands. "Even full diamond armor can't save you, if you don't skedaddle. Odd things, creepers."

I'm scribbling down everything she says and trying to figure out how to draw a reverse pig when I don't know what a pig is. Nan shuffles off into another room, leaving us kids alone. All the while, she's humming that song about all the things we should be scared of.

Mal reverently places the diamond pickaxe on a fascinating sort of table unlike anything I've seen before. "She's making this up, right? A creature like that makes no sense. Why would something explode on purpose?"

"It seems awfully detailed for something she's making up," Lenna says, wandering around the cottage to investigate all the interesting objects on display. I don't know what half of them are, and apparently neither does Lenna. She touches a long piece of curved wood hanging on the wall, a bit of cobweb strung between its tips. "Everything here seems like something she made up, but it all looks so old and sturdy and . . . real. Like it has a purpose. So mysterious."

Chug is being oddly silent, which isn't a good sign. I glance around and spot him in the corner, holding the biggest knife I've ever seen, the blade longer than his arm. It has a sort of handle, and he waves it around a little, grinning that dangerous grin of his that suggests someone who deserves it—usually Jarro and his gang—is about to get punished.

I can't help wincing. "Careful, bro. That looks sharp."

"Here we go!" Nan sings, carrying an ancient-looking book into the room. Its leather cover is worn, the words long ago smudged away. "Gather 'round, my innocent little mooshrooms, and try to learn something."

Chug puts down the stabby knife, Lenna abandons the twangy stick, and we all gather around Nan's kitchen table. She sits in the most worn chair and opens the book. The first few pages—the title, the table of contents—have been torn out.

"Had to light a fire," she murmurs. "Those were the least useful bits."

The first page with words says "Passive Mobs" in an old-timey script and features a realistic drawing of two sheep and a lamb.

"Oh, a magical new creature!" Chug squeals. "I've never heard of a sheep before."

Mal nudges his shoulder in annoyance, and Nan harrumphs.

"Okay, smarty, tell me about this one, then." She flips through the book too quickly for me to see any of the pages until she holds it open to an image that my brain can't make sense of. There's a thing—kind of like a skinny cow made of bone—and on its back rides a person made of bone wearing a metal hat and carrying a bendy-stick thing like the one Lenna is obsessed with. "Skeleton Horseman," it reads.

We are all completely silent. Of all of those words, the only one we understand is "man," and there is nothing manlike in the image.

"Ha!" Nan chortles. "Not so mouthy now, eh? When lightning strikes a horse, it becomes a skeleton horse, and if you venture near, a second strike will turn that beast into four of these monstrosities. Nasty creatures! Not afraid of the sun thanks to their enchanted helmets, clever, and a good shot, especially with four working together. Best you can do is find a wall, take aim with your bow and arrows, and hope to knock off the skeleton and keep the horse." Her eyes go misty. "I had the loveliest skeleton horse once. Her name was Helga."

"What's a bow and arrows?" Lenna asks.

"What's a helmet?" Chug asks

"What's a horse?" Mal asks.

"What else is in the book?" I ask, hungry to learn everything within, cover to cover.

5.

MAL

I can't decide if Great-great-grandmother Nan is a genius or a stark raving lunatic, but either way, I want in.

The diamond axe is real, and just a few hours ago, I would've sworn it was an impossible sort of thing. The book is very real, and clearly not something she just made up on her own. It's printed, not handwritten, although there are scribbled notes in the margins. I could spend hours in her house, asking her to explain things to me—and so would my friends, who have all found items that call to them. I can't decide if giving Chug a giant knife would be the best decision in the world or the worst.

I guess it would depend on what he was up against, because if it was anything from Nan's song, I would definitely want him to have the knife—I mean, sword.

"Let's see here," Nan says, flipping through to a different part of the book. She points to a beautiful animal that looks like . . . well, if the bone creature from the last picture was covered in skin and fur. "This is a horse. We had them when we came to Cornucopia, but over time, they dwindled away and we didn't breed more. Horses need room to run, and we don't have a lot of that here." She raises a sparse white eyebrow at me. "And if you want folks to stay inside a wall, you never tell them about swift creatures you can ride, out in the bigger world."

"A horse," Lenna says, all dreamy. "Are they nice?"

Nan shrugs. "They're like any beast. They have personalities. Important thing is that you can tame one and ride it. Now, what was the next question? Ah. A bow and arrows. You seemed particularly taken with my old bow."

Nan gets up and walks over to the bent piece of wood Lenna touched earlier. She takes it off its hook and picks a pointed stick out of a chest and then, much to our surprise, puts them together and shoots the piece of wood into her wall, where it lodges in the planks with a twangy noise.

"Bow and arrow. Excellent weapon for ranged fighting. Simple to make. Just got to practice up a bit."

We are speechless as she rummages in a cabinet and pulls out a metal hat like the one in the book. "And here's a helmet. Protects your head from bows and arrows, swords, you name it. You can make one easily with a crafting table."

Chug takes the helmet from her and puts it on his head, repeatedly knocking his fist against it before shouting, "It doesn't hurt! Quick, somebody get a hammer!"

But Tok edges in close to Nan and prompts, "A crafting table?"

Nan puts a hand on a sturdy square box with a grid on top and various tools hung on its sides. "You can craft anything in the world with a crafting table. Young Stu has the only other one in the town, as far as I know."

"Do you mean Old Stu?" I ask.

"Well, I suppose he's old to you," she concedes. "What other questions do you have?"

Everyone talks at once in an excited gabble, and Nan grimaces. "Thank goodness I'm going deaf. I'm not used to this much noise. That's why I moved out here—it's as close as I can get to the peace of the big, wide Overworld. When you get a taste for it when you're young, it's hard to settle down." A mischievous glint appears in her eyes, and she says, "Do you want to see it?"

"See what, Nan?"

Giggling to herself in a way that makes me reconsider if she's bonkers, my ancestress opens a door to the back room of her cottage and motions for us to follow. It's dark in here and smells musty, and I can sense that something is very wrong.

"Uh, Nan? What are we doing?" Lenna asks.

Chug edges in front of me, likewise sensing some sort of danger, and Tok and Lenna cluster together. Candor's fur is on end, and she looks like a big orange puffball.

"Are you ready?" Nan teases.

"For what? Nan, this is a little—"

Before I can finish, she throws a lever and blocks move aside to reveal a nearly blinding square of light.

A window.

Mesmerized, enraptured, slightly freaking out but thrilled to my bones, I'm the first one to step up to it.

This window—it doesn't look back into the forest toward the town and it doesn't look out on a brick wall or a shoddy old shed or even a neat vegetable patch.

It looks outside the wall.

My Nan . . . has a window to the world.

My friends step up around me, and we are utterly silent as we gaze out at a place we've never seen before, that we never thought we'd see.

Beyond the wall, I see ridges of stone poking up with white stuff on their triangular tips. I see a wide, flat pasture of grass and flowers that seems to go on forever until it kisses the feet of those giant rocks. To the left, there are trees, but so much bigger and wilder than the carefully manicured birches and pines within our town's walls. There's the sky and the sun and some white, puffy clouds—all pleasantly familiar—but they're shining down on a world so different from the orderly wedges of Cornucopia that it's hard to take it all in at once.

And I love it.

"Wow," Lenna breathes. "It's beautiful."

"I know, right?" Nan sticks her head out the impossible, wonderful window and sniffs deeply. "Smells good, too."

And it does. It's somehow fresher than anything in the village, as if our walls block the full glory of grass and flowers and wildness. Candor is purring and sniffing, trying to step down off Tok's shoulder and onto the windowsill. With his usual curiosity, Tok slowly sticks his hand outside and waves it around.

"What, did you think it was going to melt your skin?" Nan says with a laugh. "It's the same as in here, just untamed." She sighs heavily. "Thing is, the Founders wanted to keep their children safe. They'd traveled together a long time, suffered so many losses. So they decided to build the town and make it seem like it was impossible to leave, like the outside is terrifying. They made the walls, put in all the torches, and stopped talking about anything they hadn't brought inside. For generations, everyone has acted like you can never leave Cornucopia, but it's actually quite easy, if you know the trick." She winks at me. "Not that you didn't try to climb the walls a few times as a wee lass."

I don't remember that, and my parents haven't mentioned it. I know I was wilder when I was little, before I really understood responsibility, but I've tried to mend my ways. I step forward, straightening my spine. "Nan, the Elders say we all need to leave. They're having a meeting right now. If we can't stop the plants from dying, we'll have to go." I look around at my friends. "They're going to split us all up, send the families out in different directions. That's why we came here—we're trying to keep that from happening. So this vex thing—how do we stop it?"

Nan leaves the window open as she returns to the table and the book. We reluctantly follow. I am painfully aware, as I'm sure my friends are, that even if we're excited to see the outside world we don't want to see it as our families drag us apart.

Back at the table, Nan flips through the book. Tok's hands twitch; I know how much he wants to hold it and spend all night reading it by torchlight so he can gobble up every ounce of information in it.

"First of all, this is a vex."

As soon as she sees the page, Lenna is bouncing up and down. "That's it! That's the thing I saw! But instead of the long knife—"

"Sword," Nan corrects.

"Instead of the sword," Lenna continues, "it had a magenta potion that it poured on the plants. And then it flew back through the wall."

Honestly, I'm dumbfounded. I've known Lenna since we were babies, and I'm certainly accustomed to how dreamy she is; we all are. We can usually tell her truths from daydreams, but we don't hold it against her. Her version of the world is unique and interesting, and her dreams are a riot. But I never in a thousand years thought that the gray flying thing she described might actually exist, much less that I might see it drawn in a book that my great-great-grandmother has apparently been sitting on for years without telling anyone.

Nan turns to another page, which shows an odd sort of person with big eyebrows and a large nose, its arms raised and surrounded by swirls just like the ones that hovered above the most recently ruined plants. "Vexes come from evokers, which are a type of illager. Nasty fellows. They're not like people—not planful and curious and thoughtful. All they want to do is cause harm. They fight by sending out ghostly fangs that will snap at you from the ground, then conjuring vexes to harry you with swords so you forget about the fangs. Evokers mostly come from woodland mansions."

Tok's mouth opens, and Nan holds up a finger. "I see you starting to ask more questions, Mr. Always-Got-a-Question, but let me finish, by gum! Woodland mansions are . . . well, like the biggest houses you've ever seen, bigger than anything in town and always found in a dark forest. Three stories and chock-full of dangerous things—and their loot, all for the taking. So if you find the woodland mansion, you find the evoker. Kill the evoker, he can't summon vexes. Easy, right?"

"Y-yes?" Lenna ventures.

Nan snaps the book shut, making Lenna jump. "Wrong! None of it's easy! That's why the Founders built Cornucopia. After a while, they just got sick of fighting, and they loved their kids enough to want them to live lives that weren't dominated by violence." She leans in, squinting. "But here's the truth, children: You are descended from grand adventurers, and the world is made for exploring."

Lenna looks stunned by this information. Tok's head is cocking this way and that like he's asking his heart questions and listening for the answers. Chug is so busy playing with the helmet that I'm not even sure he's been paying attention. And me? I keep glancing past Nan, through the door, and toward that open window.

Something out there calls to me, begging to be discovered. Like there's a golden rope tied to my heart, and whatever's on the other end is tugging me onward.

But we're not here for fun stories; we're here to save the town.

"So if we wait in the gardens and kill this vex thing, will that save the town and keep the Elders from moving us away?" I ask. "Because I know that would get us out of the walls like you're saying, but what we really want is to stay together."

Chug turns the helmet around so we can see his face. "Yeah, I'm down for smashing a vex. If I have this helmet, and you let me borrow a sword—"

"Still think it's that easy? Tsk tsk tsk." Nan shakes her head at him. "Kill one vex and the evoker can summon four more. It can do that all day. Can you?"

"So we kill the evoker," I say.

Nan snorts. "And how will you find it? This wall is miles and miles long. You won't want to split up, and not all of you are cut out to be fighters. And children, of course, never go outside the wall."

My eyes are still pinned to the window. Something moves outside, maybe a bird, and the shadow flashes across my eyes.

"So we go to the woodland mansion, find the evoker, and kill it," Tok says, logical as always. "I mean, not us, obviously. We'll tell the Elders, and they'll send the adults. If we take them this book and tell them what you told us, they'll have to agree that it's the only way to save the town."

"No," I say.

He looks at me in surprise. "Why not?"

I tear my eyes away from the window and pick up the diamond axe. It feels sturdy and reliable and right. It makes me feel stronger.

"Because they'll never believe us."

"But that book—" Tok starts.

I shake my head. "You know what our parents will say. *Leave it to the adults. Stop daydreaming. Stop scheming. Don't lie. This is dangerous.*" I turn to look each of my friends in the eye. "They'll just call us 'bad apples' and find endless excuses for how we can't possibly be right. So I say we do it ourselves."

"I'm in," Chug says from under his helmet, because that's the kind of friend Chug is.

But his brother is, as usual, not so easily convinced.

"Do it ourselves?" Tok looks utterly shocked. "You think we— the four of us . . . and a cat—are going to be the first people outside of that wall in a hundred years, and we're just going to randomly find some, some . . . hidden forest fortress? And then find a murderous magic thing and manage to kill it while it attacks us with fangs and yet more vexes, and that will just solve the problem?"

I sling the axe over my shoulder. "Sure. Why not?"

"Because it's crazy! Because it's impossible! Because—"

"Isn't that what your parents tell you about your inventions, Tok?"

"Yes, Mal, and my inventions don't work!"

"Never used a crafting table, have you?" Nan interrupts. She walks over to the odd table and slaps it with a hand. "Can't make anything good without one of these babies. And I just so happen to have an extra one. And a recipe book—for tools, gadgets, and so much more."

Tok's eyes shine like the moon. "Please," he nearly moans. "Give me that book."

Nan rummages in a drawer, pulls out a book, and hands it to him. He opens it to a random page, and without looking up says, "I'm in, too."

We all look at Lenna. She's turned the book of monsters back to the image of the vex and is tracing it with a finger. "I know what it's like when no one believes you," she starts. "It doesn't feel good. And Mal's right—nothing in the world will convince the adults to do what really needs to be done. They just want to run away, not fight, and I'm pretty sure they'll be running right toward the next set of walls they can find. I'm not the strongest or the bravest or the cleverest. I don't know what I can do to help, but I'm willing to try."

Nan slides the bow and arrows across the table to her. "You've got two eyes and two hands, dearie. That and some practice are all you need."

I look at Nan in surprise. I was so certain she was going to beg us not to go, or maybe forbid us, or possibly scold us and send us home to our parents to be punished for suggesting something that goes against every rule in the town.

But instead, she's grinning, her eyes alight. She looks . . . pleased. Proud, even.

"Great-great-grandmother Nan, you're okay with this plan?" I ask, incredulous.

She nods. "I've been waiting for you to suggest it. Convincing people is exhausting. Now, if you're all ready, let's get started."

" 'Let's get started'? Nan, are you coming with us?"

Chug stifles a laugh, and Nan raises an eyebrow at him and smacks his helmet, making it spin on his head.

"Of course not; I'd only slow you down. But I've got a lot to teach you if you're going to set out today. How to build a structure to survive the night, how to use a crafting table, how to make torches—and how to hold a sword, because that lad in the helmet looks like he might grab the wrong end."

She stands and puts her hands on her hips. "C'mon, kids. Let's get you all geared up and ready to go. You've got a woodland mansion to raid."

6.

LENNA

Mal's great-great-grandmother is not at all like my oldest living relative, Great-grandmother Lizbet, a fussy old biddy wrapped in shawls who hasn't left her attic in years and maintains that she would be happier living in the mine because the sun is simply *too much*.

For the next few hours, Nan teaches us more than we've learned in our entire lives before now. Soon Tok has his own crafting table and recipe book and is working on crafting a hoe; Chug is in full armor and learning to wield a sword against Nan's least favorite scarecrow; and Mal is packing our bags and poring over Nan's books to learn how to tame and ride horses to make our journey quicker. I'm out in the forest, aiming for a bull's-eye Nan painted on a not-blighted tree and, much to my surprise, hitting it more than missing it. I'm amazed that I could be useful—my family's been telling me for years that I'm not.

When Nan calls us in for cookies and milk, we all race in, exhausted and hungry. We arrived here pretty early in the morning, and Mal suggests she run into town to see what the Elders have decided about leaving.

Nan snorts. But then again, Nan snorts a lot. "You know what they decided—the safe thing. Running away. Your families are probably busy packing all their prized possessions and paying Stu inflated prices for wagons and wheelbarrows. That's why you've got to get going now. They won't leave without you, but that doesn't mean your time is endless. The vexes could destroy more fields, and someone will come out to talk to me soon. If they see you, they'll stop you." She looks out the window, where the sun is just starting to think about setting. "And like I said, the most important thing about adventuring—"

"Is building a solid structure before nightfall," Mal finishes.

Nan nods and grins, pleased. "Glad at least one of my descendants has sense. Now listen. You could spend your whole life looking for a woodland mansion and maybe never find one, and it's an awfully big world out there. Your best bet is to go to the nearest village, find the cartographer—he might look a bit fancier than the other villagers, and he'll have a cartography table—and trade him a bag of emeralds for a map."

"Oh!" I say, deflating. "Emeralds are very rare in the mines. My family finds maybe one a year. I know they won't give any to me. Or, us."

With that careless, amused flair I'm coming to expect, Nan reaches into her pocket and pulls out a soft leather bag, upending over a dozen large emeralds onto the table. Chug's fingers naturally shoot out to grab one, and Nan smacks his hand.

"No. Don't get 'em all sticky. If it's not enough, you can trade something of yours to another villager and see if he'll give you an emerald. That's where most of them come from—trading with villagers." Her grin grows fiendish. "Or killing certain illagers, but I'm sure you'll get to that part." She tucks all the emeralds back in their bag and hands it to me. "You seem like the underdog here, but I reckon your family knows stones. Keep them safe. Don't let him stick one up his nose."

"I would never!" Chug gasps. "Not after that incident with the carrot."

I stare at the heavy bag in my palm, wondering how much it's worth. Once I might've thought about buying a sled or a nice little cow I could raise as a pet. This bag could buy an entire house! But now all I can hope is that it's enough for a map.

"Wait. How do we find a village?" I ask.

Nan nods. "Good question, quiet kid. The Founders left a beacon outside the nearest village. If it's still there, you'll head directly for a great bright light, shining straight up into the heavens."

All of us kids exchange glances. "And how do we find the beacon?" Mal finally asks.

Nan raises an eyebrow. "You just look for it and start walking. I don't remember how long it took, but then again, we were on horses back then."

Just a few hours ago, I would've asked what a horse is, but now I know.

And I want one with every fiber of my being.

We finish our snack and sort of mill about. Even Mal, ever the bravest of us, doesn't seem quite ready to take the next step. She keeps shoving her hands into her pockets, checking that she still has all the supplies we've been told we need. Nan taught us a neat trick for carrying lots of stuff in our pockets, something they don't know about in town anymore, and we're all loaded up. It's almost magical, how much we can carry now, and I wonder why we don't use this trick all the time.

"I guess we're ready, then?" Mal says. Although it could be a statement, this time it's definitely a question.

Nan nods and puts a hand on Mal's shoulder. "Remember: Adventuring is in your bones. When in doubt, trust your gut."

"My gut mostly whines and grumbles," Chug says, trying to lighten the mood.

"Well, so do you, sounds like, but I'm sure you have your uses. Your gut is mighty, children. It's connected to your brain, and between them, everything you've ever known or learned or felt mixes with what's been passed down to you. Always, always trust your gut. And stay inside at night." She walks over to the window and gazes outside. "Oh, and speaking of guts: Don't eat rotten meat. You'll regret it."

Mal takes a deep breath, putting a hand on the windowsill.

As she lifts her foot to climb out, Nan dashes into the other room as fast as a great-great-grandmother can dash, while calling out, "Silly creature, you forgot something."

When Nan returns with a diamond pickaxe, Mal's eyes go as big as pumpkins.

"Nan, I can't—"

"What, you think I need to mine things? Much like my axe, this pickaxe served my mother when she built this town, and now it'll serve you. Use it well." She puts the pickaxe into Mal's hands, and tears spring to Mal's eyes, making me tear up a little, too. They hug, the pickaxe between them, and then Mal sticks the pickaxe in her pocket and shimmies out the window.

Chug goes next, although he has to take off his armor and throw it out with a mighty clank so he can fit through. Tok carefully clambers out the window and waits for me to hand him Candor. Once Tok is outside, I'm the only one that's left.

And I'm scared.

The world is so very big, and I've been taught my whole life to fear it. I never really understood why until today, and now, if I'm honest, I'm more frightened than ever before. The vex was bad enough, but zombies? The undead, intent on eating me, moaning in the dark? I shiver and take a step back from that bright square of light and what lies beyond it.

"Worried, huh?" Nan says. I'm surprised when her arm snakes around me and she squeezes me to her side. She's warm and compact and feels much sturdier than she has any right to be. "That's good. You shouldn't be too confident. Even with armor, you're never completely safe unless you're tucked up in a solid structure with plenty of torches."

"If you're trying to make me feel better, it's not helping," I say quietly.

Nan takes both of my shoulders and looks into my eyes. "Look . . . Well, I don't know what your name is, but look, kid. Adventuring is in your blood, too. Your great-great-great-grandparents were Founders. They dug the first mine. They built the Hub out of stone they cut and shaped. And before that, they rode horses out there in the wide yonder and fought the mobs just like you're going to. You're good with that bow already. They'd be proud of you. I know I am."

Against my wishes, my eyes well up and dump a billion tears down my face. No one has ever told me they were proud of me before.

Tutting, Nan mops me off and shoves her hanky in my hand. "Go on now. Your friends are waiting. They can't do this without you."

I nod. She's right. At least about how they're waiting; I'm not so sure about the second part. And even if I'm scared, I know that I'm going to do this anyway.

I hand my bow and arrows to Mal and climb out the window, and then I'm standing outside of the wall for the first time.

"Whoa," is all I can say.

It's just so . . . big.

The grass is as high as it wants to be, and the flowers grow here and there, dotting the pastures with red and white and yellow in a way that's patternless and yet more beautiful for its lack of planning. The sky is so much wider here, so much bluer, as if it's happy to finally be free of the constraints of the wall. Everything in Cornucopia is perfectly planned, but everything out here is so random that it makes me feel giddy, like anything is possible.

I slowly smile as I realize that . . . *it is*. Anything really is possible.

No walls, no rules, no adults, no orderly paths.

Before I know what I'm doing, I yell an experimental "Whoop!"

Chug screeches behind me, leaping in the air and waving his sword with a "Yeehaw!"

Tok, eyes wide, lets out a "Woohoo!" that makes Candor jump straight up in the air. Her tail is at half puff, and she's doing a weird half growl, half purr, like she wants to like the world but can't quite trust it.

Mal throws her head back, cups her hands to her mouth, and shouts, "Hello, Overworld!"

Nan's face appears in the open window, brows drawn down. "Dunderheads! They can still hear you. The wall doesn't stop sound. Now shoo, before someone comes to investigate why children would be making happy noises outside my cottage." She flaps her hands at us and mutters, "And then all sorts of nasty children will start visiting. Can't have that. Next batch might be less clever."

We all wave, and she waves back, and then the window disappears, replaced by regular blocks. It's as if her house has turned its back on us, although really it's just a closed secret window in a tall wall stretching on in either direction to what I once thought were the ends of the world . . . but that I now see as utterly normal corners.

Mal shields her eyes with her hand and squints at the sky. "There! That must be the beacon."

I see it, too, and it's impressive. It's the brightest thing I've ever seen, and I can't believe people made it, and that it's lasted all these years.

"I dunno," Chug says. "Wouldn't want to confuse it with any other 'great bright lights shining straight up into the heavens.'" Mal smacks his shoulder and starts walking, and Chug immediately follows her. The armor suits him—it's like he's wearing clothes made out of shiny metal. He already wields the sword like he was born with it in his fist, and just seeing him there, our same old Chug but more lethal, makes me feel a little better about our first day beyond the wall.

Tok follows his brother, with Candor darting here and there, pouncing on flowers like she's never seen one before; the wild ones must smell better. I come last, as usual, but . . . well, this time it's not because I think I'm somehow less than my friends. I have a purpose now. I have great hearing and good eyesight, and I'm the one with the bow. If something should attack us from the back, I'll be ready.

I think.

I keep glancing nervously over my shoulder.

There's nothing there but the wall and the field, and I constantly feel like someone is watching me, but I'm probably just being paranoid.

Mal leads us up a little hill—a hill! Big enough that we can't see what's on the other side of it!—and my legs start to burn. Sure, you can walk all over Cornucopia, but it's mostly just flat paths, and then there are benches or fences to sit on if you get tired. Out here, we could walk forever.

Nan said she wasn't sure how far it would be to the village, so we have no idea if it will be hours or days or weeks. My thoughts rumble around to my family and how they'll react when I'm not in my seat at dinner tonight. They'll roll their eyes and snicker about Loony Lenna, and then they'll send Lugh out to find me, since he's the next youngest. He'll go to Chug and Tok's farm first, and maybe find out that they're missing their kids, too. Then they'll all go to Mal's farm, and that's when they'll know something serious has happened.

No one has ever disappeared from Cornucopia before. I guess they'll probably have another town meeting, tell everyone to check their closets and barns and pastures for the bad apples making a new kind of trouble. My family will descend into the mine, thinking maybe I accidentally fell down a hole while not paying attention.

No one will look outside the wall because no one knows how to get outside the wall.

Come to think of it, how would the Elders get everyone outside, if we abandon the town? They can't all squeeze through Great-great-grandmother Nan's window, especially not the old folks. Do they even know she has the window? I'm guessing not, or they'd be lined up to look outside.

Being outside the wall is nice. Nothing is rushing in to kill us, no adults are yelling at us, no one is making fun of me. But as we walk—and walk, and walk—two things begin to worry me.

We can't reach the beacon by nightfall.

And when it's dark, the hostile mobs will come out.

7.

CHUG

 So it turns out that walking for hours while wearing a bunch of heavy metal armor is actually pretty tiring. Nan gave me an iron helmet, chest plate, and boots. There were leggings, but they didn't fit because my legs are pretty much tree trunks as compared to her chicken legs, so she just told me not to take any hits from the waist down. Should be easy enough. She also mentioned that once Tok is more familiar with his crafting table, he can make a pair of leggings for me out of almost anything—if that anything is leather, iron, gold, or diamond.

Because apparently, those items can be found all over out here, beyond the wall. Back in Cornucopia, where each family has complete control of one resource, you have to trade carefully to get what you need. But out here, any ol' person can just start digging a hole and keep whatever they find, no questions asked and no busybodies fussing. Part of me just wants to borrow Mal's pickaxe and go crazy, but the smarter part of me was listening to

Nan—most of the time, anyway—and I know that what we have to do now is create a shelter before the sun sets and the creepy-crawlies come out.

"I know it's early, but let's stop here," Mal says.

We've been in fields all along, although we can see mountains and forests in the distance. But Mal has found a little hill, which is exactly what Nan told us to look for.

The spot she's picked isn't any different from any other spot, but I guess that makes it just as good as any other spot. The ground gently slopes up like a person sleeping under a blanket, the tall, rippling grass peppered with flowers. When no one objects, Mal pulls out her pickaxe and hacks directly into the hill. Tok sets up his crafting table and starts making torches with the items Nan supplied him, and I watch for a moment, mesmerized. It's cool to see my brother so happy. He's always felt like there was some se-cret ingredient missing from his inventions, and there actually was! Apparently what was missing was a simple crafting table, plus the book of recipes. He's entirely focused and seems to know ex-actly what he's doing.

Unlike me.

I look over at Lenna, who's scanning the horizon in every di-rection, bow in one fist and arrow in the other. She looks so com-petent and cool that it's almost like a different Lenna, but maybe one that was waiting underneath.

"See anything that needs walloping?" I ask, waving my sword.

Her lips twitch. "Nothing. For miles. It's so quiet. It seems like we would hear or see something coming long before it got here. But . . . I still can't relax. Do you feel like we're being watched?"

"Oh, we are being watched," I say darkly. When Lenna looks at me in alarm, I point at Candor, who is napping by Tok's table with her eyes half closed. "By the mighty hunter."

"Torches are ready," Tok calls.

Lenna and I look at each other. Normally, I would send her to do the boring task while I bravely stood watch, ready with fists and words, but she's the one with a ranged weapon—and she's actually good with it. If any of the hostile mobs from Nan's book show up, I'd much rather they face her arrows than get close enough to clash with my sword.

It feels weird to not be the muscle, the protector. Then again, I can't fight until there's something to fight, and Lenna definitely sees better than I do. Looks like I have to swallow my pride.

"You keep watch, I'll set the torches," I say, giving her a nod that makes her puff up proudly—a look I've never seen on her before. "Just don't mistake me for a bad guy and shoot me. My tender rump is unprotected." Lenna laughs, and I salute her and run off.

A big stack of torches waits by the crafting table as Tok works on what looks like a door. I pick up an armload and head over to where Mal is burrowing into the hill.

Now, here's the great thing about Mal: She has this uncanny way of sensing what you need without your having to ask, especially when it's embarrassing. Like right now, when I'm not quite sure what to do with the torches because I'm not that good at math and forgot what Nan said about light, but I don't want to ask anyone what to do because it'll make me feel stupid.

"Nan said mobs can't spawn within seven blocks of a torch, so put one on either side of the tunnel and then all around the hill, maybe every six blocks just in case," she tells me. I look down at the number of torches I'm holding, knowing there are many more than this placement will require. Mal smiles. "And several inside. Nobody wants to spend a night in the darkness."

I nod. She's right. There are so many torches in Cornucopia that I'm not even sure I know what complete darkness would look like. Now we know why: So hostile mobs can never spawn any-where within the town's walls. Even our bedrooms have torches constantly burning. I start placing the torches where she's indi-cated and lighting them, and even if the sun is barely going down, it feels a little like home.

I'm kind of zoning out, lulled by the constant clatter of Mal's pickaxe and Tok's crafting, when Lenna shouts, "Hey, Chug! What's that?"

I drop the unlit torches and run, drawing my sword. Lenna's on the other side of the hill, and I race up to meet her. She has an arrow drawn, her bow arm tense, and she's staring down into the tall grass.

Where something is definitely moving.

Toward us.

I stand beside her, bouncing on my tippy-toes, blood singing.

I try to recall all the different mobs and their rules, but there's no way I could remember them all. It's not a zombie, I know that much; the sun sets them on fire. But that's no comfort.

"Who's there?" I bark in my meanest voice.

The only answer is a deep grunt as whatever it is continues to move steadily toward us.

"Should I just shoot it?" Lenna asks, voice quavering.

And I'm not so sure. It's shorter than the tall grass, but that doesn't mean it's safe. Nan showed us a drawing of a thing called a chicken jockey that I definitely don't want to meet.

It grunts again.

It's heading straight for us.

"Should I?" she asks again.

"I don't know," I admit. "Let it get a little closer. We both have weapons. Maybe it's . . . something nice?"

"Nan didn't show us many pictures of nice things."

"True."

The grass near us quivers, and the thing grunts again.

Lenna draws back her arrow, and I raise my sword. My heart is hammering like crazy, my fingers going numb around the sword hilt, my arm shaking more than I'd like it to. I feel like I swallowed a rotten pumpkin, just like the first time I punched Jarro.

The grass parts.

And the weirdest thing I've ever seen walks toward us. It's pink and chubby with a squashy nose and the appropriate number of eyes and feet, and it grunts and ambles forward like it's glad to see us.

We are both frozen.

"What is it?" Lenna whispers.

"I don't know. It doesn't look mean."

"That would be a beneficial feature for a predator."

"Maybe it's a horse?"

"Definitely not a horse."

"It's . . ." I exhale and deflate. "It's too cute, Lenna. I don't want to hurt it."

I reach into my pocket and pull out a carrot from the stash Nan gave me. There are only vegetables in my pockets—almost like she knew if she gave me anything good, I would eat it.

"Here . . . thingy. Do you like carrots?"

The creature runs up to me and gobbles the carrot, licking my hand clean. It has teeth, but they're not pointy, and its feet are pointy, but not in a dangerous way, more like sheep hooves. And—I gotta be honest—it's hard to be scared of chubby pink things.

"Maybe it's in the book," Lenna says. "You okay alone?"

I look at her bow and then at the pink thing and nod. She jogs back to where Mal and Tok are, and I scratch the thing behind its flappy ears, which it seems to like. It nuzzles at my pocket for more food, but we might actually need those carrots, and I'm sure this thing knows how to find its own snacks.

Lenna soon returns with Mal, who has Nan's book in hand. When she sees us, Mal starts laughing.

"It's funny, right?" I say, my arm around its neck. "Its name is Thingy."

Mal flips through the book and triumphantly shows us a picture of this exact creature, labeled with the word "pig." "It's a food animal," she says wonderingly. "Like a sheep, I guess, although it obviously doesn't have wool. They roam wild, but they're not dangerous."

"Why didn't we have them back home, then?" Lenna asks.

But I think I know. "Because they reek," I say simply, having spent several moments up close and personal with it. I decide to call Thingy a "him" for simplicity's sake. "If you're going to be crammed inside walls, you want to go with the least stinky animals that will benefit you the most, and he is definitely the stinkiest thing around." Also, I think he's way too cute to eat, but I don't mention that part.

"Well, the structure is almost ready, but we don't have room for him," Mal says, nose twitching. "I . . . don't think pigs are good animals for underground living."

"Maybe we could dig a hole in the regular ground and surround it with a fence," Lenna offers. "Then he couldn't escape, but the mobs couldn't eat him."

Mal looks from Lenna to me, trying not to laugh. "So are we . . . adopting this pig? Instead of eating it?"

Much to my relief, Lenna nods along with me. Mal sighs.

"Good thing we have extra torches, I guess. See if you can get it closer to the shelter, and I'll get my pickaxe."

I lure Thingy toward the hill using another carrot, and Lenna comes with us.

"I guess now you know who was watching us," I say.

"I wanted a horse, but he's still pretty neat," she agrees.

Mal shows us what she's accomplished, and it's impressive. The narrow hole in the hill leads down a brief tunnel before widening out to three blocks wide by seven blocks long. There are already two beds in here, and Tok is working on two more. It's snug, but not too snug. There are torches on all the walls, and it feels like home. Well, except for one thing.

"Let me get Thingy out of here," I say, pushing him toward the door. I bet he'd be fun to snuggle with at night, but he smells worse than my armpits under all this armor, which is saying a lot.

Outside, Mal digs a small pit and I toss the carrot into it so that Thingy will jump in and we can surround the hole with a flimsy fence. We help Tok carry in the other beds, and Mal adds old, cozy blankets from Nan's stash. With everything ready, we all stand outside, quiet, watching something we've never seen before because our parents make us go inside every evening: night falling. The sun sinks down with a rainbow of colors, and the whole world feels eerie as the sky turns purple. Tok packs up his crafting table, and we stand around by the shelter's entrance, eating the cold chicken Nan gave us and just . . . taking it all in. The birds are settling down, and an odd quiet descends. Without talking about it at all, we're edging backward, closer and closer to the safe place where we'll spend the night.

"Good night, Thingy," I call, and the pig grunts back, which is a nice feeling.

The sun drops, and everything goes completely black like nothing I've ever seen before—or not seen, as there's nothing to see. Our torches burn, little pops of orange in the dark, and that's it. Far away, something moans, and it is definitely not a pig.

"I think it's time to go inside," Mal says.

Lenna goes in first, then Tok and me and Mal. Mal shuts the door Tok made, and we head down the tunnel and sit on our beds. It's cheerful and cozy, if a little cold.

"Smells like home," Lenna says, and then, oddly, checks under her bed.

"It'll be weird waking up without a rooster." Mal settles back, elbows out and feet crossed. "No rooster. No mooing cows."

"No chores," Tok says. "No Jarro. Nobody yelling at us."

"No apples and bread and honey." My stomach grumbles; that chicken wasn't enough for me, so I pull out a potato from my stash.

"Do you think our parents are mad?" Lenna asks.

Mal frowns. "More worried, probably." That's easy for her to say—she's an only child, and her parents approve of most of what she does. Or most of what they know she does.

I finish my potato and burp into my fist. "I'm guessing ours are mad. They already thought we did something to hurt the fields. Disappearing probably only made it worse. Makes us look guilty."

"But we're trying to save the fields," Tok says angrily. "Parents just don't understand."

"Hopefully one day they *will* understand. And forgive us," Mal says.

I snort. "If they don't kill us first. You know, the way Nan's book made it sound, being outside the walls was scary and terrifying, and everything was going to try to eat us. But it's actually really chill out here. Beautiful views, and we discovered a pig. It was a good day."

"Not a single hostile mob." Lenna sighs. "Maybe they're all gone. Maybe since that book was written, they all just disappeared."

"Except the vex," Mal reminds her.

"And the evoker that sent it," Tok adds. "But it's nice to dream."

For a moment, no one speaks, and we're all content and tired as we settle down into our beds munching on Nan's food—but then we hear the worst sound in the entire world.

Hissing. And it's coming from outside.

"Candor!" Tok says, bolting out of bed. "I forgot to bring her inside!"

8.

TOK

 The moment I throw open the door, I have a crushing realization: I don't have a weapon. Nan didn't give me one, and I didn't think to make one. Too late; Candor is out there, and my friends have weapons. I don't have time to brainstorm solutions or draw up plans—I just have to save my cat.

I stop just beyond the torches Chug placed on either side of the door. My eyes adjust, and I see it—Candor is flat on the ground, at full puff, tail twitching, as four gooey, green people shamble toward us. One of them has a sword and helmet, and I have never before wished to have brawn instead of brains. I want to pound that thing to pulp.

"I got this," Chug says. His hand lands briefly on my shoulder as he charges out, sword at the ready. I give a little sigh of relief, but . . . Chug against four monsters? He's only fought a scarecrow before, and he can't use fists with these . . . things.

I'm frozen in place, but Lenna appears, arrow ready to fly. "Chug, move!"

He's hacking at one monster, but it hits him back, and he grunts in surprise, a soft sound against the background of the creatures' awful groaning and moaning. My heart clenches; I don't want to lose my brother trying to save my cat.

If only he was wearing his armor.

If only I had a weapon.

If only I knew how to use one.

In this kind of emergency, complicated schematics won't save the day.

"Zombies," Mal says, appearing beside me, book open. "I don't think we can beat all four, but maybe . . ."

One of the zombies makes a splattery hiss and flops over dead. Or lifeless, whatever the word is. Candor, clever thing that she is, sees an opening and looks to me.

"Come on, Candor! Here, kitty kitty!" I call, and she darts toward me faster than I've ever seen her move. She tears up my body like I'm a tree, and I feel every claw, but I don't care. I smooth down her fur and whisper lovingly, so glad that she's okay. Guilt washes over me for leaving her outside. She was just enjoying a nap in the sun, and then I forgot about her, just assumed she'd be beside me, as always.

I put Candor on my bed, give her a soothing pat, and slam the door closed on my way back out. Lenna and Chug have figured out a better way to fight, and Mal's helping with her pickaxe. Lenna aims for the two zombies on the left with her arrows, one after the other, while Chug and Mal hack away at the one with the sword and helmet on the right. This one isn't dying as easily as the first, and Chug's left arm looks pretty beat up, since he didn't have time to put on his armor, but he's holding his own, especially now with Mal there to distract the zombie.

"Candor's safe," I shout. "When I open the door, just run inside. They can't follow."

I fling the door wide, but . . . no one is running.

"Guys?"

"I want to finish this," Chug says, nearly out of breath. "I'm not backing down!"

"But it could kill you!"

Chug manages a massive slash, and the zombie gurgles a goopy hiss. "Yeah, well, I'm going to kill it instead."

One of Lenna's zombies falls over, finally beaten. She's graceful and quick as she pivots toward her remaining foe. With one more arrow, it falls. Where it stood, there's another chunk of rotting meat, and, oddly, a potato.

The zombie with the helmet and sword is the last one standing, and it's almost down. Chug and Mal have always worked well together, like they can read each other's minds, and it's almost like they're dancing with the gooey green fiend. Mal swipes at its legs with her diamond pickaxe, and the moment it turns to groan angrily at her, Chug deals a massive blow against its back with his sword, and the zombie finally falls over.

The night is quiet again. On the ground are four chunks of rotten meat, a potato, a helmet, and a sword. The air smells of rot. And pig.

"Yes!" I shout.

And then Chug sways and collapses into the dirt.

Before, every time Chug has fallen, he's bounced right back up.

He usually laughs as he throws himself back into a fight, even if he just got bopped in the nose by Jarro's fist.

But now he's lying still, barely breathing.

This isn't good.

I run to his side and kneel, turning him over gently. He groans and murmurs, "Just let me sleep a few more minutes, Mom." I can't see where he's hurt, but I know that it's bad.

Seeing my brother this way is terrifying, and for all my cleverness, I don't know what to do. Back in Cornucopia, there's a healer, but as with all the families and their areas of expertise, she closely guards her secrets and trades shrewdly to her own advantage.

I have no idea how to help him.

"Chug, can you hear me?" I ask, cradling him.

His eyes blink open. He looks sleepy. "Am I dead? It smells like I'm dead."

I can't help but laugh. Of course he would make jokes while he's gravely injured. "You're not dead, you just insisted on bringing home a really stinky pig and then fighting undead horrors. We're going to get you into the shelter, okay?"

"As long as it doesn't hurt. I'm really, really not into pain."

Mal shakes her head at him, tears in the corners of her eyes. "If Chug's snarking, he's still barking. Let's pick him up."

I get under one of his arms and Mal takes the other while Lenna wisely keeps an arrow ready should anything else appear out of the darkness. We manage to drag Chug back into the shelter, and he tries to help, but he can barely stumble. We put him in his bed and pull the blanket up to his chin.

Mal paws through her pockets, mumbling, "Surely Nan left us a healing potion or something."

"Meat," Chug moans. "I'm just . . . so hungry."

"That's exactly what a zombie would say," Mal replies.

In response, he does a credible impression of a zombie groan, and she lightly slaps his shoulder, which makes him moan for real. Although she doesn't find any potions, she does find some wrapped mutton and a pie, and Chug sits up, suddenly far more awake, to stuff his face. The relief is palpable. He's snarking, he's eating—he's going to be okay. The thing about my brother is that he's loud most of the time—brash, proud, mouthy, quick to anger. That's how I know when to worry about him—when he gets quiet.

I sit on my bed and stroke Candor, so grateful that she'll still purr after what I put her through.

"So, lesson learned," I say. "All the shelters and torches in the world won't keep you safe if you manage to leave one of your party outside."

"It's our first night." Mal hands me a cookie from the bag. "It could've gone worse."

I look at Chug, who winces and rubs his sword arm. "I don't see how." Now I feel guilty about forgetting Candor *and* guilty about my brother getting hurt while fixing my mistake.

"We could be dead," Lenna says simply from where she's tucked up in a ball against her pillow, her knees under her chin. "That's never really been an option before, has it? No one in our town dies of anything but old age. That must be why they kept us inside."

"But if we hadn't come here, outside the walls, we never would've seen how big and blue the sky is. Or watched the sun set. Or smelled the flowers," Mal reminds her.

"Or smelled the pig," Chug adds, cheeks stuffed with mutton.

"I'm not arguing that." It's odd, hearing Lenna argue at all. "I like it out here. It's exciting and pretty, and there are so many possibilities. I'm just trying to . . . understand. Why the Founders did what they did, you know? Why our ancestors and parents followed the rules without questioning anything."

"Didn't know any better." Chug burps. "It's easier to do what you're told."

We all digest that for a minute as he continues digesting his mutton. Mal hands him another wrapped haunch, and he bites into it with gusto, already regaining some of his color.

"I made things today," I say softly. "It never worked at home, but now it does. If someone had just given me a crafting table— maybe apprenticed me to Elder Stu instead of insisting I should weed the pumpkin fields—my inventions might've worked all along. I could've made a hundred hoes! I could've been so useful."

"And if someone had given me a bow and arrows, I could've . . . Well, I'm not sure how that would be useful at home." Lenna's forehead rumples up. "It's like my one skill isn't valuable there. But it is out here, maybe."

" 'Maybe'?" Mal splutters. "You took down two zombies all by yourself without taking a single wound! It's incredible. Maybe you could teach me."

"I, uh." Lenna's face is red. "Sure, maybe."

Mal's pickaxe sits on the foot of her bed. Lenna's bow and the arrows she has left lean against the wall. Chug's sword is outside, along with all the stuff the zombies dropped. I'm full of nervous energy and anxious to feel even slightly less guilty for everything, so I dart outside and, keeping an ear out for any more moans, grab it all: two swords, a fistful of arrows, a helmet, and a potato. I almost grab the rotten meat, but I can't imagine anything that smells like that being good for us in any way, and Nan told us not to eat it. The potato smells fine, though. Back inside, I place

Chug's sword reverently against the wall, well aware of what I owe this weapon—and the hand that wielded it.

"Thanks, bro," I say.

"You're welcome, bro," he replies.

And that's as sappy as we can get, even if we both have tears in our eyes and one of us is covered in zombie wounds.

"Say, he won't turn into a zombie, will he?" I ask.

Mal grimaces and dives for her book. After a few moments of frantic page turning, she sighs in relief. "No. But he'll need to eat a lot of meat to heal, since we don't have a healing potion."

"Oh no," Chug says between chews, his mouth stuffed. "Oh, woe is me. Whatever will I do?"

I smile.

The high-meat diet is already working.

Now that everyone is certain Chug isn't on the verge of death or zombification, we settle down in bed. We're all accustomed to sleeping by torchlight, so it feels very much like home. I'm too emotional to sleep, though, my heart and mind a frantic mess of excitement that just won't dissipate no matter how much I toss and turn. Even Candor gets disgusted with my constant movement and chooses to sleep under the bed instead, which is saying a lot.

I get up and shove my hands deep into my pockets, hoping there's something useful in there I missed while I was completely absorbed by my newfound ability to create almost anything. Nan and Mal were divvying up supplies all afternoon, but I was so busy crafting that I don't really know what might be in everyone else's pockets, much less my own. I have my crafting table and supplies and books, I know Chug has a bunch of food—mostly vegetables— while Mal has the especially tasty things, plus the rest of Nan's books. Who knows what Lenna's got. I rustle around a bit, hoping the noise will wake someone, but everyone is out cold.

"Mal, can I look through your coat pockets?" I whisper.

"You can do whatever you want if you promise not to wake me up again," she murmurs.

I feel a little guilty as I pull her coat off the foot of her bed, but I already felt terrible, so it's not that much of a burden. There's all the meat, plus loads of cookies, pies, and cakes—which I won't be telling Chug about, because he'll eat them all. There are several books—which I want to read cover to cover—and more tools. Finally I find what I'm looking for and pull it out. It's an odd sort of thing that I've never seen before—not until Nan's books and explanations. But I have an idea, and I think it'll make life a lot easier for my wounded brother—and everyone who has to live with him while he's in pain. I long to go outside and give it a try, but those zombies convinced me that I never need to go outside at night ever again. Once was enough.

I make a small pile of my findings by the door and settle back into bed, certain that this invention will work, crafting table or no. Candor crawls up onto my chest and makes biscuits, purring happily.

"Do you forgive me, Canny?" I ask.

In response, she boops me on the nose, and even if I know she doesn't understand language, I'm still pretty sure we understand each other.

"You don't need forgiveness," Chug mumbles from beside me, where he looks like he's deeply asleep—and drooling a little. "Bad stuff just happens sometimes. We all made mistakes, too. I chose not to wear my armor, so this is as much my fault as anyone else's. Let it go, bro."

I choke up a little, hearing my rough, brash older brother say something so deep.

"I love you, bro," I say.

"I love you, too. Now shut up and let me sleep. I'm wounded, for goodness' sake."

"Chug—"

Sweetly, lovingly, he reaches over and puts a finger to my lips.

"Shut your piehole."

"But—"

"Say one more thing, and I'll throw you outside to the zombies."

I smile and go silent.

Chug's going to be okay.

And when he finds out what I've got in store for him tomorrow, he's going to laugh until he breaks a rib.

And then thank me.

9.

MAL

 When I first wake up, I think I'm in my own bed at home. There are the stone walls, the torches, the soft wool blanket. But then I realize that instead of plaintive mooing, I hear Chug snoring, and it all comes back to me.

We're still outside.

We spent the night *outside the wall*.

And I fought a zombie using my great-great-great-grandmother's diamond pickaxe.

My stomach growls, and in the small stone chamber, it echoes.

"Is that another zombie?" Chug asks, and relief yet again floods me to know that he's not in grave danger.

"It's the ghost of uneaten breakfast," I reply, stretching and sitting up. The tiniest bit of light shines around the door Tok made, and I realize that I'm looking forward to another day of adventuring.

Up until now, pretty much every day of my life has been exactly the same. Wake up, eat breakfast, do cow chores, eat lunch, do cow chores, play with friends, do cow chores, eat dinner, go to sleep. But today will be different. Every day beyond the wall will be different in its own unique way. For one thing, there will be considerably fewer cows.

I hunt around in my pockets for bread and more mutton, noting what Tok took from my coat last night. I know Tok, so I know I can trust him not to take too much food or anything, but I'm a bit curious about the items he selected. Lenna and Chug are waking up now, too, but Tok's not in his bed, although Candor is there, curled in a neat orange ball. When I go outside, I find the strangest thing ever.

Tok has put Nan's old saddle on the pig.

And he—the boy, not the pig—looks . . . really proud of his accomplishment.

Before I can find words, Chug follows me out and says, "Bro, are you sure you didn't get your skull cracked last night? That's not a horse."

"No, it's not. We don't have a horse, but we do have a pig. And I've figured out how you can ride him so you won't get tired too quickly or hurt yourself," Tok says, beaming.

He helps Chug get into the saddle, and Chug does it, even though he seems very doubtful, because he'll do anything his brother asks of him and he never wants to show any fear, even if it means he's putting himself in the way of danger. He looks ridiculous perched up there on his pudgy pink steed.

"Uh, so now what do I do?" he asks.

Tok hands him a stick with a carrot on a string tied to the end, and the pig oinks excitedly.

"Just hold out the carrot in whatever direction you want to go, and he'll try to grab it, which means his feet will move. He's very food-motivated."

"We have that in common," Chug says, accepting the stick.

Sure enough, as soon as the pig sees the carrot, his eyes light up, and he walks toward it. Of course, since Chug is holding the stick, the pig can never quite reach the carrot.

"So what do you think?" Tok asks, looking a little uncertain. And I can see why—a big, tough guy like Chug wouldn't be caught dead back in the village riding a ridiculous animal like a pig.

But Chug just laughs delightedly and shouts, "I think you're a genius! Who needs a horse when I've got Thingy?"

As Chug practices steering his pig, we pack up our beds and prepare to head out. We'll leave the shelter here as it is—maybe it will help some future traveler, or maybe we'll need it on the way home. With Candor safely on Tok's shoulder, we walk toward the beacon in the distance. We can see now that these small hills slope up into what Nan's book calls "mountains," with the beacon in the rolling hills halfway between.

After last night, we're all on the lookout for threats. I have the extra helmet on and carry the sword the zombie dropped, which was pretty nice under the slime. It feels heavy and dangerous in my hand, whereas the pickaxe feels very natural. Still, I noticed that Chug could swing his sword much quicker and with more agility than I could swing my pickaxe, so I'll just have to get used to the blade. Tok reads a crafting book while he walks with Candor on his shoulder; I'm pretty sure he'll never let her leave his sight again. Lenna comes last, constantly walking backward to scan the grass behind us for mobs. It suits her, being out here—the bow seems like it was made for her, and she's calmer and more content than I've ever seen her. I'm not sure if that's because she's away from her dismissive family or because she just needed to find a job. Maybe it's both.

I feel a little homesick and worry about how my parents are reacting to our disappearance. The town may think of us as bad apples, but I try to be a good daughter and pull my weight. My parents will have to work harder without me around, and the cows might miss me, but hopefully it won't mess up their milk. It's easy to fall into a loop of guilt and worry, so instead I focus on what's ahead, the beacon calling me forth. My friends follow me, as they always do. Without them, being outside the wall would be scary, but with them, it's an adventure. And more than that, it's our best chance of staying together—and saving Cornucopia.

My legs burn as the hills get bigger. It's past lunch, but I want to get as far as we can before dark. We're huffing and puffing as we crest the biggest hill yet, and I call a time-out and distribute food. Chug swings the carrot out of Thingy's view, and the pig stops in place and nuzzles the nearest flowers in a hopeful sort of way. Tok collapses onto his back as Candor rushes off into the high grass on important cat business, and Lenna joins us, scanning the path we've made up the hill with her hand shielding her eyes against the sun.

"Nothing," she says. Her lips twitch as she scratches Thingy's rump. "Nobody watching us today."

But I see movement on the outcrop up above, some kind of creature leaping up and down the little ledges. At first I think it's a horse, and my spirits lift, but then I realize it doesn't quite match the pictures in Nan's books. It's like someone pulled a horse's neck too long.

"You see those, too?" I ask Lenna.

She squints. "If those are horses, they're really goofy-looking horses."

I fish out the book and flip through it until I find a picture that matches what I'm seeing. Llamas. We apparently can't ride them, but that doesn't mean they're not useful. While everyone else eats, I poke through the bag until I find one of the leads Nan gave us.

"I'm going to go catch a llama," I tell Lenna, and the words sound ridiculous coming out of my mouth. "Can you keep watch?"

Lenna's face screws up. "I don't know if that's a good idea. They're up high. If you fell . . ."

"I'll be fine." I give her my brightest grin. "I know what I'm doing."

"Do you, though? You've never been up a mountain. The highest thing you've ever climbed was a barn."

"And it was easy, and I had no problems, so I'm sure the same will be true here."

"But Mal—"

"I've got this, Lenna. Trust me."

She frowns, brushes the crumbs off her shirt, and silently collects her bow. I can tell she doesn't agree with me and is actually pretty annoyed, but I know she'll do her part because that's the kind of friend Lenna is. With Chug not at his best, it's nice to know we've got someone else who's good with weapons while I'm off on a wild llama chase.

It's a challenging climb, but like I told Lenna, I'm nimble on my feet and not at all scared of heights. The llamas seem to enjoy bouncing around, and when one spots me, it makes an awful noise halfway between Thingy's grunt and a scream. It doesn't seem scared, though, which is good. The closest one is whitish gray with crooked bottom teeth, so I sidle up with a handful of wheat. I swear, Great-great-grandmother Nan really gave us everything but the kitchen sink, and even if she didn't tell me what half the stuff in our pockets is for, I'm glad we're able to figure it out on the fly.

The llama bleats at me in surprise and reaches out its long neck to take the wheat. As soon as it's chewing, I grab a wad of the wool on its back and swing up to sitting, my arms wrapped around the long neck. The llama seems as confused by this event as I am, but this is what the book said to do, and the book has been right so far, so I just hang on for dear life as my steed bleats and honks and jumps around, knocking me loose.

I land in the grass and roll. A lifetime of trying to ride cows has prepared me for this eventuality, so I pull some more wheat from my pocket, hold it out, and repeat the process. On the fourth try, the llama finally settles down and snakes its head around to nuzzle me, and I hop off and hook the lead around its neck.

An irrational amount of pride swells inside me—I've tamed a llama! And even if it's not an animal that can be ridden after taming, it can carry supplies, freeing us up to fight or forage as Tok learns how to craft more equipment; even pockets have their limits. As I lead my new llama friend back down the slope, two more llamas fall in line behind us, one brown with a golden face and one the exact color of a pumpkin pie.

"Okay, now I'm the one who must've gotten bonked in the noggin," Chug says, watching me walk up leading my caravan. "Because those are seriously ugly horses."

The lead llama, who I've decided to call Sugar, raises an eyebrow at him, but at least she doesn't spit, which the book says llamas can do. "Be nice to Sugar," I tell him. "She can kill you with her loogies."

Everyone else is done with lunch, so Tok uses his crafting table to make some chests. We fill them with the goodies in our pockets and load them up onto the llamas so we can start our trek up the mountain. I eat on the way, the llama lead tight in my other fist. If we succeed, I can only imagine what it will be like to return triumphantly to Cornucopia with two new species of animals and the news that the outside isn't as terrifying as we were taught. If four kids can survive there, why should everyone have to hide behind a giant wall all the time? Maybe they'll put in a door—or a few windows like the one at Nan's house. Everyone should be able to see how beautiful the world is outside, even if they're not ready to be in the middle of it.

Nothing goes wrong, and as the sun just begins to set, I find a nice hill and call a halt. Everyone is all too happy to stop. Even for active kids like us, this is the most exercise we've ever gotten, and my entire body aches. I dig pens into the ground for the llamas and Thingy, and Tok surrounds them with simple fences so they'll be safe, keeping Candor on his shoulder the whole time. With the animals taken care of, I select my spot and start hacking into the hill.

It feels good, watching the grass and dirt and stone dissolve under my pickaxe. Even though it's tiring, I feel like I could do this all day. Every now and then, I uncover a block of some new kind of stone or coal, which I leave for Lenna to sort. Last night, I went pretty slowly, but today, I know better how to approach our shelter.

After the opening of the tunnel, I fan out to make the shelter three blocks wide again. Tok sneaks in and places torches along the walls, and I nod my thanks. My arms are warming up, and I'm in the zone now, plowing through the hill, but then I strike the stone and reveal . . .

A hole in the ground.

I stumble back before I fall in—thank goodness Tok brought those torches, or I might've stepped forward and fallen straight down. Lenna told me from the beginning that the three biggest rules of mines are don't dig straight up, don't dig straight down, and don't dig alone, but she never mentioned that I could be following all the rules and still nearly fall down a random chasm.

At least there isn't lava down there.

I think.

It's pitch-dark down below, and the air is still and cold.

I run out of the tunnel and call, "Guys, come check this out!"

Lenna arrives first, and Chug and Tok follow. Chug seems to be moving a lot better, although he's not all the way back to full health.

I point at the hole. "I didn't do that. I dug straight across, and there was already a hole there."

Lenna cocks her head. "Huh. I know there are plenty of natural caverns, but I don't seem to recall this being something I've heard about at the dinner table. I think you can just fit another block of stone in the gap and it'll make the floor solid. We definitely don't want to fall down there."

"But . . ." I pause. I know my friends see me as their leader, and I know they can get really excited over dangerous ideas, so I always carefully measure any suggestions I make—even when I'm pretty excited myself. "Aren't you curious about what's down there?"

"Definitely not." Tok shakes his head and steps back. "What have we learned on this trip? Where there's no light, there are hostile mobs. Anything could be down there."

"My family keeps our mine lined with torches, but we can't

even see if this particular hole ends in a short drop or falls forever," Lenna adds.

"Well, we've got plenty of torches," Chug says. Before anyone can stop him—and we try—he snatches one of Tok's torches, lights it, and drops it into the hole.

I'm waiting for the torch to tumble into eternity, but it falls only a few meters before it lands on stone, a little orange light in the infinite dark.

"That was anticlimactic," Tok says.

And then something entirely unexpected happens.

We hear a voice from somewhere down there in the underground.

"Hello?" someone calls—a guy, I think. "Is someone up there?"

I shoot Chug a quelling look before he can answer sarcastically and call, "Yes."

"Thank goodness," the voice calls back. "Help!"

10.

LENNA

My parents tell me I was born in the mine and cooing, but I apparently caused so much trouble down there as a toddler that they quit taking me with them. I liked to wander, they say, and I didn't take their safety precautions to heart. I seem to recall the cozy flicker of torchlight and the echo of my bare baby feet on stone, but the memories are hazy because I was so young. Apparently I saw the cave as fun instead of work, and in my family, that's a big no-no. I didn't think I missed it—being underground—but looking down into that big, black, empty space, I don't feel scared at all. I'm excited.

Tok's right—there are definitely mobs down there. Not only zombies like the ones we fought yesterday, but also skeletons, spiders, and slimes. Not to mention lava. Oh, and vast, bottomless lakes filled with who-knows-what. After reading Nan's book, I can't help but shiver when I think about how my family's mine stretches so far and deep underground. It must've once contained such horrors, and as my parents and siblings work to expand it, they face new dangers each time they strike an innocent-looking bit of stone.

These two sides of me are at war with each other—the need to explore, and the need to stay safe. But once I hear that desperate voice call to us beseechingly from down below, I know that we can't just fill in the hole and go to sleep in our comfortable beds. We have to help whoever is down there.

"What do we do?" Mal asks, and it takes me a minute to realize that she's looking to me.

Right. Because I know more about being underground than anyone else.

Still, no one has ever asked me for advice or next steps before, so it takes my mouth a moment to catch up with my racing heart and mind.

"What's your situation?" I call down. Because maybe this person needs water, or maybe they just need a ladder, or maybe their leg is caught in a chasm as spider jockeys approach. The complete lack of light suggests that any torches they've brought with them have burned out. I do not envy their position.

"There was a rockslide. I lost my torch. Now I'm trapped by a skeleton—maybe more than one. Arrows keep clattering off the rock. I'm not hurt but . . ." He trails off. "I thought I was going to perish down here."

Judging by his voice, he's not miles and miles below, but it's not like we could reach him in one tidy leap, either. I look around at my friends. I don't have to ask if they're willing to help—they share my determination. We are not the kind of people who could just walk away from this. And they're still looking to me for aid.

I take a deep breath.

"Tok, get all your torches. Mal, look in the chests and see if we have a ladder. Chug, get your sword—and bring me my bow and arrows." They get moving, and soon Mal holds out a ladder. I take it and, hands shaking, reach my arms into the darkness below. Luckily, it touches down on a rock shelf.

Mal hands me her pickaxe, several torches, and my bow and arrows, which I slip into my pockets. "Hold the ladder. I'll get down to the first shelf and place some torches so we can see what we're dealing with."

I can't describe the feeling of descending into that hole in the ground, hands tight around the ladder rungs, willing myself to step down into nothing. It's the scariest thing I've ever done, but the people holding the top of the ladder are the three people I trust most in the whole world.

"I can do this," I murmur.

"You totally can," Chug says, and he's Chug, so I know it's the truth.

I take one step and then another, clinging tightly to the wood. The lower I get, the colder the air grows. It's not long before I'm standing on a solid rock shelf. I pull out a torch and hold it far away from the ladder. The cavern is much larger than I thought it would be, taller than the wall back home.

Zip.

I feel air whoosh by my face and look down to where my torch reveals a skeleton pulling its next arrow. On instinct, I throw the torch at the skeleton and use its moment of distraction to reach into my pocket and prepare my own weapon. I fire off two shots before it returns an arrow, which, again, barely misses me. How do these things aim so well without eyes?

"What do you see?" Mal asks from overhead.

"I'm trying to hit a skeleton!" I squawk, loosing my next arrow, which slams right into the skeleton's spine, causing it to collapse. I feel momentary relief until something groans from the cave's darkness, beyond where my torch burns on the ground below. "Let go of the ladder—I need to go down another level!"

I pull the ladder down and feel around for a flatter bit of cave floor. I wish my friends were here to hold the ladder this time, but I have a new kind of confidence—I know I can do it. The wood wobbles more than I'd like as I climb down until my feet touch stone. I immediately pull out a torch and place it on the wall. Another skeleton lurches out of the darkness, and I fire four arrows in rapid succession before it gets off one shot.

Thud.

I look down. An arrow is sticking out of my leg. It feels hot and dull, and I yank it out and shoot it right back at the skeleton, destroying it.

"That was two skeletons," I say to whoever is trapped down here. "Do you think there might be more?"

When no one answers, I get a little worried.

"Hello? Where are you?"

The only answer is a weird, squeaky, flying animal that explodes out of the darkness. Red eyes come right for me, and I dance around and swat it away. I wasn't scared before, but now I'm starting to get a little freaked out.

"Hello?"

I pull out more torches and place them around the cavern. Over near where the first skeleton's bones lie, I find a place where two rocks have fallen, forming a little space that could fit a person. I'm pretty sure this is where the voice came from, but whoever it was is gone. There's nothing left but some broken glass and a puddle of magenta liquid. I stick my finger in it, wondering if it is sweet berry jam, but when I touch it to my tongue, it tastes very strange, like soap mixed with melon. I instantly feel stupid—who tastes liquids they find on the ground?

Then I realize my leg no longer hurts where the arrow pierced it. It wasn't a big wound, but it felt hot and pulsed with my heartbeats, and now my skin is smoothed over with a pink scar.

"You okay down there?" Mal calls.

I . . . do not know how to answer that.

"Maybe," I say. "I know this sounds weird, but could you toss me down a piece of bread?"

Moments later, a heel of bread bounces on the stone, and I carefully sop up as much of the liquid as I can. Sure, it's probably got rock dust and cobwebs attached to it, but if it can help Chug like it helped me, I'm willing to risk it.

Whoever was here—and someone definitely was here—they had a healing potion, and they dropped it when they ran away.

With the pink-stained bread in one hand and a torch in the other, I walk around the cavern, and I find the oddest thing.

Metal tracks.

The kind my parents use for mine carts.

There is no cart, of course, and it seems like a very strange thing to randomly find underground. This isn't a mine. I don't see any useful ores or the evidence of a miner's pickaxe marking the cave walls. There's just the tracks, disappearing into the darkness. I don't find any more dropped items, and I don't find the guy who asked for help and then ran away after I got rid of the skeletons.

"Lenna, are you okay?" Mal calls, more urgently this time.

"Yeah, I'm fine. Coming up now." I walk back to where the ladder waits, put everything in my pockets, and start climbing.

When I reach the rock shelf, I pull the ladder up and resettle it. My friends hold the top again and help me climb out onto the stone floor. After I've wriggled up to standing, the first thing I do is pull out the soppy bread.

"Chug, eat this. I'm pretty sure—"

And since it's Chug, he doesn't wait for me to explain why he should eat a wad of wet pink bread that was recently on a cave floor. He just says, "Okay," and stuffs it in his mouth.

"Chug, no!" Mal says, but it's too late.

"Chug, yes." He touches his lips gently. "Uh, what was that? It tastes like a furry melon with rock sauce."

I point to my healed leg. "I got shot in the leg with an arrow, but when I licked a drop of that liquid, it healed me. So I think whoever was down there dropped a Potion of Regeneration."

"That doesn't make sense—" Tok starts.

Before he can finish, Chug starts jumping up and down, careful not to fall through the hole in the floor. "This is great! I don't hurt anymore! My ribs, and my leg, and my arm! They're all fine!" He clears his throat. "But I still call riding Thingy. It's much more fun than walking."

As he jumps from bed to bed, whooping his enthusiasm, Mal stares down into the hole, thinking. "So you went down there, killed two skeletons, and found a potion, but no person?"

"I think he ran away while I was dealing with the skeletons. I know he was there. I found the broken potion bottle where he'd been hiding. But I didn't see him. There was this flappy flying thing—"

"A bat," she fills in.

"Sure. And then he was gone. But something isn't right down there. I found tracks, like for a mine cart. But with no cart. We could follow the tracks to see where they go and maybe find the guy and see why he ran away."

But Mal shakes her head. "No way. The only thing he's proven, whoever he is, is that he can't be trusted. Nan spent so much time telling us about the mobs and animals outside of the wall that she never really mentioned what the people were like. You saved that guy's life, and he didn't thank you. He just ran away. Whoever he is, I don't want to be trapped in the dark with him."

A little shiver runs through me. "Me neither."

We all share a look, the kind that suggests we'd best remember that the world is not necessarily all llamas and pigs and flowers. Tok heads to his crafting table and builds a trapdoor to fit over the hole, and once it's sealed, we head to our beds. Mal passes out food, and we eat in silence. As snug as it is to be safely enclosed in a shelter where none of the scary mobs can reach us, there's still something discomfiting now that we know there's a cavern beneath us, dark and echoing and filled with strange things and possibly stranger people.

We know everyone in our town. Everyone, down to the oldest person and the youngest baby.

Today we met our first stranger—or almost met him. And now I begin to see why our Founders built walls. Hostile mobs are clearly dangerous, but it's harder to know with people. I saved someone's life, and now I'm wondering if I did a good thing or a bad thing.

"I wonder who he was," Chug says, tearing into a chicken leg. "His voice sounded like an adult."

"Well, you can't imagine children just roaming around out here all alone." Tok strokes Candor and shakes his head. "Even if most people don't have high walls, I'm sure they gather in groups. I definitely wouldn't want to be on my own."

"Me neither." My fingertips play over the scar on my leg.

That's another new thing—I got shot. By a skeleton.

Before today, my worst wound was a broken arm when I fell out of a tree. I went to the town's healer, Tini, and she put my arm in a splint and made me drink a spoonful of potion that tasted a lot like the potion on the cave floor, and my arm stopped hurting so much. In return, my parents paid her a diamond, and then my family pretty much shunned me for a couple of weeks for causing a problem and costing them resources.

Being shot in the leg wasn't so bad—even without the potion, it probably would've healed on its own in a day or two, if I ate a lot of meat. But now I can't stop thinking about how the skeleton could've shot me in a more dangerous place, like my chest or my head.

"Do we know how to make armor yet?" I ask, as it seems no one else can sleep, either.

"Knowing and doing aren't the same thing." Tok yawns. "I can make armor, though, I think. I would just need a lot of supplies. Lots of leather, iron, gold—that sort of thing."

"Or we can just kill more zombies and hope they drop some," Chug says, in high spirits now that he's not in pain anymore. "Thingy would look fabulous in a helmet."

Mal sits up straight. "No one goes outside at night. It's not worth the danger. If we're smart and safe, we shouldn't need armor at all. We travel during the day, we go to the village, we get what we need."

"But then we still have to get to the woodland mansion and kill the evoker," Chug reminds her. "So armor would be pretty helpful for that, probably."

Mal flings herself back into her pillow. "Our parents left us so unprepared. Sure, I can milk a cow, and you can weed around a pumpkin. But outside the walls, we're having to learn as we go. Nothing strange happened at home, but something strange seems to happen out here every day."

"That's what makes it fun!" Chug says.

She rolls her eyes at him. "You can only say that with enthusiasm because Lenna accidentally licked a random potion off a cave floor. Two hours ago, you could barely move."

"Yes, and you have to admit that in this case, something strange, like licking random potions, turned out to be fun."

"But it could've gone badly," she reminds him. "If there are good potions, there have to be bad potions, right?"

That makes Chug and me both shudder.

My family calls me Loony Lenna, and if they knew I'd tasted a random potion I found on the ground, they'd laugh at me forever. It turned out well this time—we got lucky. But Mal's right. Just like the skeleton and the zombie, it could've gone very badly.

If there are bad mobs and bad potions, there must be bad people, too.

Who was that man under the rocks?

11.

CHUG

I am a huge fan of floor potion, let me tell you. The taste is weird and maybe a little gritty with actual grit, but the effect is immediate and intense. I no longer feel every rib when I breathe. I can do cartwheels again. I am one hundred percent Team Floor Potion.

And I don't know what everyone else is so weirded out about. There have always been good and bad things in our world. There are delicious cakes—but then again, there's beetroot, which I hate. There are cute, sweet cows—and awful ones that kick you when you're just trying to enjoy a pleasant ride around Mal's pastures. There are nice neighbors, like Inka with her melons, and there are bad neighbors, like Jarro's family or Krog. It shouldn't be surprising that everything beyond the wall isn't rainbows and pumpkin pies, and also that just when you need it most, you might find a potion that fixes your ills.

If we weren't all so exhausted, I'm sure we'd stay up all night, staring at the door in the floor and wondering what sorts of creepy-crawlies might come knocking. Mal and Lenna are right—there was a man down there, and he needed our help, and then he disappeared, which is not how normal people act. I quietly ask Tok if the door can be opened from down below, and when he shakes his head no, we move my bed over it anyway. I sleep with my sword under my pillow.

It would make sense if I didn't sleep well, but I totally do. Must have something to do with that potion. When I wake up, Mal is sitting in her bed, reading through a book, looking like she never even closed her eyes. Lenna and Tok are still asleep, and I smile when I see Candor curled up against my brother's side. I'm so glad we managed to defeat those zombies, because if anything had happened to that cat, Tok would never forgive himself. And I would never forgive *myself*. And Mal wouldn't forgive herself, and the vicious loop would just go on and on.

Seeing that I'm awake, Mal tilts her head toward the door, and I slide out of bed to follow her outside. I almost forget my sword, but I doubt I'll ever forget my sword again.

The morning is gray and dreary, and I dread the rain that's coming. I've never particularly liked baths, and rain just feels like constantly having a bath against your will. It might make Thingy smell better, though, which would be nice.

Mal walks over to the llamas and gets them back up to the grass safely, and I fetch Thingy. He follows me everywhere now, even when I'm not holding the carrot on the stick.

"I think we'll reach the beacon today," Mal begins. We both stare at that solid beam of light blue. "Do you think the village will be anything like Cornucopia?"

"High walls, no one in and out? Now that we're out here, it

sounds a bit barmy. Like, why not have a door? Why not let peo-ple go out to look for interesting new animals or dig for new ores?"

"Nan said she visited the village, so hopefully it will be more . . . open."

"And maybe we'll find out about that weird guy from the cav-ern."

Mal scratches a llama around the ears, and it makes a blarting noise. "Hopefully these villagers won't run away. Everything out here is so strange."

"Or maybe everything back home is strange, and everything out here is normal."

When she looks at me with surprise, I grin. "That's right. Sometimes I say smart things."

"You say what now?" Tok asks, rubbing his eyes as he emerges from the shelter. Candor bounds past him and into the grass to do her business.

"I said something smart."

My brother looks at me like I'm an idiot. "You say smart things all the time. Don't act like you're stupid."

It makes me so uncomfortable when he talks that way. We know our roles—he's the smart brother, I'm the dumb one. Dad calls us the Brains and the Brawn.

"I'm so good I don't have to act," I say.

Mal covers up the weird vibe by handing out food, and Lenna appears to collect her breakfast. It's gray and cool outside, but it's gray and cool inside the shelter, too. We don't talk much as we eat. I think we're all probably a little worried about arriving in the village. What if there's a wall with no door? What if we can't find the villager with the maps? What if we don't have enough emer-alds?

These are not issues we've ever dealt with before in our simple, predictable town.

We pack up the beds and our equipment even faster than we did yesterday. I'm the last one out, and I stand in the doorway to the shelter, looking inside at that sinister door in the floor. Part of me, the part that doesn't like leaving things undone, wishes we had the time and resources to find out where Lenna's mine cart rails go. But the biggest part of me, the part that doesn't really like dark, creepy caves very much, especially when they're full of skeletons, would rather take its chances up here, where at least some of the creatures we encounter are cute and useful.

I ride Thingy as we head for the beacon. Truth be told, the carrot on the end of my string is looking pretty gross after a pig's been licking it for a day, so maybe they'll have fresh carrots at the village. I wonder about the people there and whether any adults will try to stop us. We're just a bunch of kids, after all, and we're about to roll up into a village on a mission that we don't necessarily want to explain. What if we told the villagers our problem, and they decided to escort us right back home to our parents?

I shake my head. Too much thinking makes Chug a dull boy.

We eat bread and chicken on the road and press on. The llamas follow happily behind Mal, honking at one another, and then I ride Thingy behind them, where they can't spit on either of us. Tok and Candor are next, my brother's nose in a book, as always, and Lenna comes last, her bow and arrow always ready as she scans the path behind us for danger. I miss the plains, where everything was mostly flat and we could see forever. Now the mountains are looming close, and the trees are all of one sort and seem heavier than our orderly little trees back home in Nan's forest. I get the feeling we're being watched again, but this time, I don't think it's by a pig.

It's late afternoon when we spot the village. My eyes aren't the best, but it looks like a loose cluster of buildings and little plots of farmland, arranged all willy-nilly at the foot of a mountain. There is no wall, no orderly plan. It's like people just randomly decided to build whatever they wanted, however they wanted, wherever they wanted. It's as weird to me as someone wearing pants as a hat and socks as gloves, but then again, wearing pants as a hat sounds pretty fun.

Before the village, however, is the beacon. All along, it's been a curious and tantalizing sight, but as we get closer, it's like the moon and fire had a glittery baby. I run up to it, and as I get closer, it feels like I'm getting faster and stronger somehow.

"Don't lick that, bro," Tok warns, and I grin at how well my brother knows me.

"I'm not gonna lick it, but I'll hang out around it. It feels great!"

My friends join me, and now I can see it—they're moving faster, too. We're zipping around, laughing, and for just a moment, it's like I'm able to forget the weight bearing down on my shoulders—the blight, the thought of leaving town, the zombies. Even Lenna is laughing, and Thingy's little tail is wiggling like crazy.

"This beacon—it's affecting everything around it." Tok is doing some kind of experiment, moving toward the beacon and then farther away. He's clearly fast when he's close to it and almost in slow motion when he's out of range. "Maybe Nan has a book on stuff like this? I need to study it."

"I need to hug it," Lenna says. "It's like the world's biggest sunbeam."

Mal walks away from the beacon, toward the town, and I can tell that she's worried. When she motions to us, we reluctantly leave the beacon's glow to join her.

"I'd love to play with the beacon all day, but we need to focus. It's getting late. I don't think we can trade with the villagers and still have enough time to make a proper shelter." She looks up at where the sun hides behind the clouds. "So either we try the village now or make a shelter and check out the village in the morning."

Nothing moves in the village, which is . . . weird. Sure, people head inside when it's about to storm back home, but it's never this still.

"Let's build the shelter now," Lenna says. "Just to be on the safe side."

"That's probably wise," Tok allows. "Once the rain starts, our vision will be limited, and we don't know how the water will impact our weapons."

"If we made shelter, we could eat. And eating is always good," I add.

Mal shakes her head. "No. We need to forge ahead. We can't lose half a day. Every moment we spend out here is another moment our families are closer to leaving Cornucopia forever. We need to be bold."

"But what if they're not friendly?" Lenna counters. "I'd rather show up on a stranger's doorstep on a nice day than surprise them in the middle of a squall."

"You've never even met a stranger before," Mal starts, and right on cue, the clouds dump rain on us. I'm soaked immediately, and miserable. I doubt Nan packed towels for us, and I don't want to sleep in a wet blanket. Digging a shelter right now would stink for Mal, and it wouldn't be a ton of fun to wait outside for her to finish, either. Only the beacon is unaffected by the storm.

"We're trying the village," Mal says, giving me a look.

She needs me to agree with her, so I nod. "My sword will work fine in the rain." I don't mention it, but I'm pretty sure I can smell meat roasting somewhere up ahead, which definitely entices me.

"And Nan wouldn't have sent us here unless it was safe," Mal adds. Lenna rolls her eyes, and she amends it to, "Safe-*ish*."

"If you say so." This is the first time I've ever seen Lenna fight back like this, which means it's the first time I've seen Mal pull rank. Lenna looks back the way we've come, wary. "I think someone is following us."

"Then the village will obviously be safer." Mal grins through the rain and leads her llamas onward. I look behind us, but if someone was following us, they could easily hide, thanks to all the trees and hills and bushes. Now that it's raining, I can barely see a block in front of my face. I hop off Thingy, put away the carrot, put on my helmet, and hold up my sword. I hope things won't go badly in the village, but I'm going to be ready either way.

Since there's no wall or door or sign reading "Welcome, Travelers," Mal just walks toward the first building she sees. There are no people around outside, but why would anyone be out in this weather? We're almost to the building when a huge shape steps out from around it and blocks our path.

It's a—

I don't even know.

Like if a block of iron got really ugly and learned how to walk. It's big and lumpy like a boulder with a nose, and it just stands in front of us, blinking down at us with eyes that remind me of chocolate chips in a cookie. I stride forward to get in front of Mal and the llamas. Thingy oinks in terror and hides behind me, trembling, and I raise my sword. My knees are knocking together, but the rain hides that. I don't care if this thing is made out of diamond, it's not going to hurt my friends.

"We're looking to trade," Mal shouts over the rain.

Water courses down the iron thing. It shows no sign of understanding.

"So either trade or get out of the way, Rusty," I shout menacingly.

Its head turns toward me, one arm extending like it's thinking about pounding me into the ground.

Mal steps in front of me, which I'm not a fan of in dangerous situations. "Let me handle this," she says. "I don't think it likes threats." In a louder voice, the same one she uses when the cows won't go through the fence, she yells, "You have a very nice village. Can you please take us to a cartographer? We don't want to cause trouble."

The iron thing cocks its head at her before just walking away like we don't even exist. It disappears in the rain, and now I'm looking around for the next one, imagining an entire village of them. It wasn't human, it wasn't an animal, and yet it didn't quite seem like a machine that Tok might make.

"That was incredible!" my brother shouts. "Iron, but sentient. Not programmed for immediate violence. Almost as if it were patrolling. So cool!"

He looks like he wants to chase it down in the rain and ask it for a stool sample, so I say, "And you can ask the villagers all about it once we find them, bro." He's carrying Candor under his shirt, as she hates the wet.

With the iron creature gone, Mal knocks on the door of the nearest building. No one answers, so she peeks through the glass panes in the door.

"I think it's a business," she shouts over the rain. "There are lights on inside, and a counter. Tok and Lenna, wait out here."

With the sort of bravery only Mal has and that the rest of us can only follow, she ties up her llamas to a nearby post, pushes open the door, and enters the building. It's not huge inside, and pigs are probably not welcome, so I hand Thingy's carrot to Tok before following her.

My first reaction is that it's marvelous to be slightly less cold and wet.

My second reaction is that this building is nothing like any of our buildings at home. It's built strangely, shaped strangely. It even smells different.

But the weirdest part is this: When the person behind the counter turns around, it's clear that they aren't even the same species as us. And when they speak, all they say is "Hmn."

"Hello, we're looking for a cartographer," Mal says.

"Hmn," they say again, hands clasped firmly in the deep sleeves of their robe.

"A map," she tries.

"Hmn."

"We'd like to buy four hundred chickens and form them into some sort of super chicken so they can fight your iron man," I say.

"Hmn."

"I don't think they speak our language, Mal."

She sighs and reaches into her sack, pulling out the bag of emeralds.

At that, the villager finally lights up. They produce a stack of books, but none of them appear to be in our language.

"Map," Mal says, slowly and clearly.

"Hmn," the villager responds, shortly and annoyingly.

She mimes unrolling a piece of paper, pointing at it, and then shielding her eyes as if looking off into the distance. The villager points at the shelf of books. Mal walks her fingers across the table, and the villager points at the books, harder. Finally, after they've said "Hmn" so many times that I never want to hear the sound again, Mal pulls out a bundle of wheat.

Much to our surprise, the villager produces an emerald. Mal and I look at each other. Is this too good to be true? She hands over the wheat, and the villager gives her the emerald before saying, with blissful revery, "Hmn."

"I don't think this weirdo has any maps, Mal."

"Me neither. Let's try something else."

"Goodbye. We're leaving," Mal says, waving. The villager doesn't wave or say thank you or do anything except mutter, "Hmn."

"I hereby name this village Hmn," I say as we close the door behind us and are immediately soaked to the skin with rain.

"Hmn," Mal responds, and I have to laugh.

"Did you get the map?" Tok asks.

"No, but we traded some wheat for an emerald. They don't look like us or speak our language, but at least this one seemed really happy to do business."

We try two more buildings and find a villager making arrows and another one brewing potions, and I'm pretty glad Tok is staying outside for this part because I can only imagine the way he'd moan if he saw the weird contraption that makes potions. We trade one emerald for a Potion of Regeneration, only because we know how much we need it—and because we just got that emerald today, it's like an extra bonus emerald, so it doesn't count.

The next building we find is, weirdly, empty. No counter, no barrels, no furniture, no nothing. Mal's eyes meet mine, and we both nod. We set up our four beds, open the door, and rush Tok, Candor, and Lenna inside, leaving the llamas and pig tied up outside and bringing in our chests—and beds.

"Whose house is this?" Lenna asks.

"For right now, ours," Mal says.

Lenna sits on her bed, looking doubtful. And, hey, there are a lot of reasons to be doubtful. This village is nothing like our town. I think we were all hoping for the comforts of home, for friendly people and a warm meal, and instead we've got cold rain, strangers with a communication issue, and bread that's honestly getting kind of stale. In our town, where everybody knows everybody, people seeking succor from a hard rain would be welcome in any home they passed. They'd be sat down and fed something warm and offered comfortable and noticeably unsoggy beds.

We have to hope that the customs in this village are similar and that someone isn't going to suddenly bust in and shout at us—not that we're not used to being shouted at.

The sun is just about to go down, so Mal and I run back out into the rain. She uses her pickaxe to hack a small paddock out of the dirt for our animals, and I surround it with fences. We're a well-oiled machine now—or at least a well-rained-upon machine. Mal and I skid inside the door right as night falls. I'm so glad my strength is back so that Tok and Lenna can be spared this sort of stress.

Even with plenty of torches around the building's honey-gold walls, it doesn't feel homey. The wood is different, the roof is different. We eat our dinner in silence before huddling in our beds, cold and wet. It's funny how after all we've been through, the zombies and skeletons and cave and everything else, this is what makes me want to cry: a house that doesn't feel like a home.

"Do you think we'll be able to find a map tomorrow?" Lenna asks.

"Graaaarh," someone says.

But that someone isn't any of us.

That someone is outside.

12.

TOK

 I know that sound now.

It's a zombie.

Candor knows it, too. She puffs up, hisses, and darts under my bed, and I don't blame her. I'd like to join her. It would be great if we could go a single day without having to fight something.

"It can't get through, right?" Lenna asks. "Because there's the door and the—"

"The torches," Mal groans. "But they only keep the mobs from spawning, not from attacking. And this village is wide open."

As if in agreement, two green, gooey arms reach in through the decorative holes in the door, black-rimmed fingernails twitching toward us. Chug grabs his sword and stabs at the zombie through the door until it leaves, but there's another one right behind it. He stabs away at that one, too, and even though we're all tense, this feels more like an annoyance than a life-or-death situation. The zombies can get their arms through the door, but that's it. I hope?

"I don't get it," I say, because thinking out loud with my friends helps me figure things out faster. "This village is permanent, but they don't have protective walls. Zombies and other hostile mobs must spawn here all the time. So how come the villagers aren't—"

The zombie reaching for us disappears with a surprised, "Grunh!"

Chug, who's nearest to the door, squints out through the panes. "It's the iron blocky guy. He's beating up the zombie. Go, Rusty!"

The rain is tapering off, and we can hear the sound of a zombie getting the compost kicked out of it by the iron monster we saw earlier. I wish there was more light so we could see what's happening, but the end result is the zombie hitting the ground, a sound I'm beginning to love.

"Tok, torches," Chug says, and I hand him two torches. I already know what he's going to do. He opens the door, hangs the torches on either side, and then stands there for a moment, staring out into the dark. "There're two of them. The iron monsters. Rusty and, uh, Clank. They see another zombie, and they're gonna go smash it!"

"Let's stay inside and let the nice monsters do their jobs," Mal says, tugging him in. She turns to me, but I'm already getting my crafting table set up to make a door without any of those pesky holes. Whoever owns this place can thank me later when they aren't suddenly being awakened by reaching green arms.

Once I've got the new door traded out, we all settle back down. Mal has a book from Nan's bags, so Lenna and I each reach for another one. We all want to know more about what we're seeing— this strange village, the patrolling metal monsters, the fact that walls are relatively easy to build yet these people choose to live without one surrounding their homes. They clearly understand how to build sturdy edifices, and yet they choose not to protect themselves. While we read, Chug sits with his back against the door, his sword over his knees. That's my brother—keeping us safe no matter what. I toss him one of Nan's carpets for warmth, and he winks at me and keeps chewing on the apple he pulled out of his pocket while the rest of us were getting books.

I fall asleep reading and wake up with Candor on my chest. I bolt upright and am glad to see that Chug is sleeping on his nest on the floor and that everything is totally fine. Two windows let light into our borrowed house, and Lenna and Mal wake up and rub their eyes. We're not used to seeing sunlight in the morning, out here beyond the wall. We pack up quickly, but Mal digs through her pockets and frowns.

"We're going to need more food. We have more wheat to trade, but we need to get that map and then think about replenishing our stores."

Chug sniffs the air, grinning, and I smell it, too—pies baking. "Just give them all the emeralds for those pies. Emeralds are no good for breakfast. Too crunchy."

When we're all packed up, the little house doesn't even look like we spent the night here—except for my new door, which is much sturdier than the old one. Outside, the day is that gorgeous, sunny blue that happens only after heavy rains, and the village is lively with folks going about their daily business. Most of them seem intent and focused, but a couple seem like complete nitwits, just wandering around and doing nothing. The iron monster walks past us without pausing, and I'm consumed with curiosity— and grateful for whatever it is. I find a single potato where one of the zombies fell and give it to Mal to put in her sack.

"Tok, why don't you come with me. Chug and Lenna, can you stay here with the animals? And not get in trouble?"

Chug looks offended. "Get in trouble? Me? Us? Why, I never!"

Lenna twirls an arrow; she still looks a little annoyed. "I'll keep him in line, Mal."

Mal nods, and when she walks away, I leave Candor with Chug and Lenna and follow. I'm slightly confused, though—Chug is her best friend, and they usually do this sort of thing together, like they did yesterday.

"So what's the plan?" I ask when we're out of hearing range. "I mean—I don't usually—maybe Chug is better suited for—um—"

"I don't understand these villagers," she says. "They don't speak our language. It's clear when they want to trade, but I'm not sure how to find who we're looking for. It's just . . . not obvious. So how do we find the one with the map?"

She's walked us to a small rise, and the village spreads out below us. My mind kicks into gear, and I can identify a few of the buildings by their output. The one with tons of black smoke has got to be a smith or a forge, the one that reeks is a leatherworker, the one that reeks in an entirely different way is selling fish. I can identify bakers and shepherds and farmers, and the sound of a tool hitting stone must indicate a mason.

"We're looking for a business—not a home—that's quiet," I say. I point at the three buildings I've identified as possibilities. "So, no smokestack, no side garden, no children. It's got to be one of those three."

Mal nods and grins. "I knew you'd have a strategy." In classic Mal style, she aims for the nearest one, and I follow behind her. It makes me a little uncomfortable when she doesn't knock on the door first, but once it's open, it's clear that it's a business.

The villager behind the counter is . . . well, clearly a villager, but very clearly nothing like us. They're inquisitive, hands clasped, standing before a wide variety of tools. It would almost look like Stu's storefront, except Stu would be chasing us out instead of looking at us like prospective clients.

"Hmn?" they say.

"Uh, no thanks. We don't need tools today. Bye." Mal waves as we beat a hasty retreat.

The next building is a fletcher, and Lenna would drool over the variety of arrows, feathers, and bows. We finally find what we're looking for in the third building, which is also the most elaborate. Mal opens the door, and the loveliest smell rolls out. Not the baked pies my brother is drooling over, but the kind of odors I crave: old leather, crisp paper, new ink. The scents of knowledge. There are shelves full of books and scrolls, painted banners hanging from the walls, and a villager with a fancy gold monocle.

"This is it!" Mal whispers.

"Hmn," the villager confirms.

Mal walks up to the cartographer's table and reaches into her bag. I can see her thinking hard. Instead of pulling out the entire bag, she holds up a single emerald. The villager shakes their head. She holds out two emeralds, and they shake their head again. This goes on so long that I'm worried we're going to get kicked out before we can trade, but when she offers seven emeralds, the cartographer finally nods and holds out a worn leather scroll.

After they trade, the villager settles back, says "Uh-huh!" and radiates satisfaction.

Mal stares down at the rolled-up map. "Is it rude to look?" she whispers.

"Of course not. If it's wrong, we'll ask for another one."

She unrolls the scroll, and at first, it makes no sense. Then I realize that while I carry an idea of our town in my mind, I've never seen land actually laid out like this. It takes a moment to orient myself, but I locate our wall, the mountains, this village, and on the other side of the mountains, a dark forest and exactly the place we're trying to find: a woodland mansion. That's got to be the big building surrounded by sinister trees.

"Thank you," Mal says.

"Hmn," the villager says, somehow managing to cram a lot of happiness into that single syllable.

Back outside, we find the rest of our crew exactly where we left them. Chug and Thingy are both straining toward the baker's building, where several golden pies steam gently on a windowsill.

"Did you get the map?" Lenna asks.

Mal holds it up and nods. "And we still have a few emeralds left, so we can replenish supplies."

"Can we—" Chug starts.

"Buy plenty of beetroot? Absolutely we can," Mal finishes.

Chug's immediate response is absolute horror, but then he grins back at her. "Oh, well, I already sold one of your llamas in exchange for some salmon. I know how much you love burned salmon."

"I could make a beetroot and salmon casserole," Lenna offers. "I'm an excellent cook."

We all double over in laughter. Lenna couldn't cook a piece of toast. For the first time since we started this journey, it feels like we know what we're doing and nothing can stop us.

Our next destination is the baker, of course, where Mal trades more wheat for pies. We get Lenna some arrows from the fletcher and pick up some meat from the butcher. These villagers are just crazy for emeralds, and it's funny to think that in Cornucopia, everyone acts like they're the rarest thing in existence. And yet these simple villagers must have hundreds, as they pass hands all the time with little flashes of green and happy "Uh-huh!" sounds. It makes me wonder if the gems really are rare at all, or if the various families of our town must each find ways to wield their unique powers and resources to get what they want.

We could shop all day, but the truth is that every moment we're away from home, our families are one step closer to giving up on us and abandoning our town—and leaving without us. Maybe every day, more fields are ruined. Maybe the livestock are running out of fodder. I know our mom has a pantry full of food, but I also know that Chug can eat two pies by himself at one meal and that other families aren't as well-provisioned. As much fun as it is to buy new things and eat something that isn't stale bread, we've got to get back to our task. Judging by the map and according to my calculations, the woodland mansion is probably two days away.

Since the village doesn't have a wall, we're not entirely sure when we've officially left it, but we wave goodbye to an iron monster and begin the steeper climb into the mountains. The llamas are carrying our chests, and Chug is in full armor, sword in hand, a wonderful change after how weak he looked when he was riding Thingy. Lenna is, as always now, behind us, still in view but making sure that nothing follows us. She's dropped back a bit and is spending more time staring out into the wilds. Something feels off to me, but I don't know what. Candor can feel it, too, and she's settled up on my shoulder, her claws dug in a little more than I find comfortable.

Mal must sense our unease, as she gives Chug the llamas' leads and walks back to chat with Lenna. I may look like I'm reading a book, but really, I'm listening in as I walk. That's the thing about being the cerebral one — everyone else just assumes I'm lost in my own thoughts, but half the time, I'm managing my own anxieties by paying attention to what they're saying and doing, especially when they think I'm ignoring them.

"What is it?" Mal asks Lenna.

"I'm not sure. Something is following us. It was following us before the village, and now it's out there again. Not directly behind us, like Thingy. Whatever this is, it's clever. It's hiding. And I still haven't seen it. Just . . . the crack of a branch, the rustle of some leaves."

"What do you think it is?"

Lenna shakes her head. "I don't know. According to the books, it could be plenty of things, or it could even be a person who intends us harm. It could be that guy from the cave. I hate not knowing. Back home, we knew everything. But here?" She shrugs. "At least we know it's not a zombie or drowned."

Mal stares where Lenna is staring. There are rocks and trees and bushes, all sorts of places for something or someone to hide. But unlike Lenna, she's not cautious at all. "Come on out!" she calls. "We know you're there."

Lenna shakes her head in annoyance at Mal's brashness and raises her bow, scanning the horizon, but nothing so much as twitches. I'm not breathing, and I doubt they are, either.

A bush shivers, and something begins to step out, something big and gray. It growls.

And Lenna releases an arrow.

13.

LENNA

 My arrow goes wide, and I'm forced to stare at the creature I've almost hit. It's a gray, furry thing with a long nose. Its big, black eyes roll up to stare at me like it's not sure what to think, either.

"What is it?" I ask Mal, nocking another arrow but pretty sure I don't want to hurt this animal unless it tries to hurt me first.

"A wolf," she says wonderingly. "I read about them in Nan's book. Some people keep them as pets. They're like . . . maybe a bigger cat who really likes people and wants to help them."

Tok wanders up with no Candor in sight. "So not a cat then. They're nothing if not aloof." When I raise my eyebrows, he adds, "As soon as Candor smelled that thing, she went full puff and ran ahead to hide behind the llamas."

"So it won't hurt us?" I ask Mal.

She's got the book out now, and she shows me a page with a picture of a wolf very like the one in front of me. The one in the book looks nice and is wearing a collar. "If you give it bones, it should begin to see you as a friend."

Mal smiles as she hunts through her pockets and hands me . . .
Some bones?

"They're from Nan," she explains. "I didn't kill anyone."

"I would hope not." I laugh, although my eyes don't leave
the wolf—in case it attacks. Tok thinks of Candor as a girl, and
Chug thinks of Thingy as a boy, and I decide I'll consider this
wolf a girl, too.

I offer the wolf a bone, and she takes it gently, crunching it
open with huge teeth that look a lot friendlier now that I know
we're not necessarily mortal enemies. When she's done with that
one, she perks up a little more and her tongue rolls out, making
me laugh again. I offer her another bone, which she eats with
more relish. By the fourth bone, she's sitting up, her eyes round
and friendly, her tongue goofy. When the bone is done, she licks
my face, leaving a slimy trail across my cheek. That's wolfish forgiveness for nearly hitting her with an arrow, I guess. I reach out
to pet her and find an old red collar under the fur around her
neck.

"The llamas are kind of freaking out and Candor won't let go
of my leg," Chug calls from a bit away. "Can someone come help
me get . . . untangled?"

We look up, and he's a complete mess. Candor the cat is indeed using his leg like a tree—thank goodness for the leather
armor Tok made for him—and the llamas are all clotted up and
staring in our direction like old biddies suspicious of a neighbor.
Tok pats the wolf on the head, which goes over well, and then
runs back to help his brother.

"So I guess now we know who was following us." Mal stands
and puts Nan's book back in her pocket. "It doesn't look like it was
starving and desperate."

"I think she was just curious. Or maybe she used to have a human, and something bad happened. She seems much happier now." I've been stroking the wolf's back, and it's nice, the way it makes her tail wag and her eyes smile.

Mal holds up a hand and pulls me to standing. I was annoyed with her decision to just barge into the village in the rain, but I can't stay mad at her for very long. I scan the area behind us, wondering if there are more wolves out there, but that feeling that's been bothering me, that sense that we're being followed and watched, has dissipated. It was the wolf, and now she's not hiding. There shouldn't be anything else to worry about or keep us from going on our way. I feel a little bad for holding us up for nothing— well, except that Nan told us to trust our guts, and my gut told me that I needed to address whatever was following us. The wolf apparently isn't dangerous, but the book says that sometimes they can be, and that they often hunt in packs of four or more. I don't think there are any more wolves nearby, though. This wolf—my wolf—must've been all alone.

Mal and I start walking, and I look back over my shoulder to see what the wolf will do. The book said feeding her bones would tame her, probably, but I don't really know what "taming" entails. I wouldn't say the cats I know are tame, just that they mostly abide the people they live near. Mal's cows aren't tame, even if they have personalities and some of them seem glad to see me when I stop by to feed them wheat.

But the wolf, much to my surprise, pops up and follows us. She's almost jaunty, bouncing a little, her tail wagging and her mouth open in a jolly grin, tongue swinging. I stop, and she stops and sits beside me, looking up adoringly like I didn't recently accidentally, ignorantly, foolishly almost hit her with an arrow.

"Wow, she's really focused on you," Mal says. "If the book is right, which it always is, she's just going to keep following you like that. And if we get in a fight, she'll help us."

"I don't want her to get hurt on my behalf," I say quickly.

"She's an animal. She'll do what's in her nature, whether you like it or not. But I think as long as you feed her little bits of meat and give her a bone every now and then, she'll stick around."

"I don't know. What if . . ."

Mal stops and puts a hand on my shoulder. She does this sometimes when I get too wrapped up in worries, when my brain gets caught in vicious loops. "You almost shot a wild animal. You were just trying to keep us safe. The wolf doesn't hold it against you. So forgive yourself and let's go. She'll decide on her own whether she wants to follow." Mal smiles and nods. "And maybe, before we get to Chug, give her a name that's better than Thingy Two. It definitely doesn't roll off the tongue."

We walk again, and the wolf paces easily by my side. I've never named a living thing before. My family doesn't keep any animals—there's dust from the mine everywhere, and it's not good for them. We do well enough to trade for whatever we need, eggs and meat and crops. The enormity of giving a creature a name feels a little overwhelming, but it's not like there's a deadline or an audience. I plan to give it a lot of thought.

Well, right up until we reach Chug, who looks utterly delighted despite the fact that Candor's claws are sunk into his leg.

"Hey, you tamed a big, fuzzy cat-pig. We can name it—"

"Her name is Poppy." I don't know I'm going to say it until the second it comes out of my mouth, but I know instantly that it's just . . . right. She's happy now, bouncy and cheerful as a poppy bloom, with her red collar and pinkish-red tongue.

"Poppy." Chug considers it. "Not as great as Thingy, so far as names go, but it could be worse."

Poppy is staring hard at Candor, her tail wagging furiously. Tok reaches down to untangle his cat from his brother's leg, and Candor continues glaring, now at half puff, her tail twitching. They sniff each other, and Candor, much to my surprise, rubs up against Poppy's legs. The llamas are grumbling and bumping together nervously, but Poppy is undeterred. She trots over, and the lead llama reaches down her long neck to bump noses with the wolf. Poppy licks her, and the llama snorts and sighs like she's just going to have to get used to traveling with a bunch of goobers. Thingy seems weirdly chill about the whole thing. After five minutes, all of our animals have gotten over their interspecies beefs and are ready to go again.

Mal keeps the map out and constantly checks it against the land ahead. It would be a lot more useful if we could fly, but as it is, we have to look at the mountains and landforms around us and hope they correctly correspond to what we see on the scroll.

"We'll have to cross water soon," Mal warns. She points to a ribbon of blue on the map with green on either side. I've never seen that much water in one place, and I have no idea how she intends to cross it.

She begins discussing it with Tok, and I head to the back of the caravan to take the place that now feels like my own. Poppy remains by my side, mostly. She sometimes roams to investigate a particularly interesting tree or flower, and I relate to that on a deep level. Sometimes she bounds after a bee, and her joy is so infectious that it makes me wonder why our Founders didn't bring any wolves with them inside the walls. With pigs, it's pretty obvious—they're big and stinky and loud, which are not ideal characteristics for living in close quarters. With the llamas, it makes sense, because they're great at carrying stuff but don't seem useful for much else, and it's not like anyone planned to carry things around once the town was settled.

With wolves . . . Well, I just don't know enough about them yet. Maybe they make noise when they're angry or hungry, or maybe they chase chickens. Or maybe they're animals that don't do well behind doors and walls, wild things hardwired to run and explore.

I begin to understand that point of view.

I liked walking back here before, liked having room to think and digest all the new things that I've been seeing. But with Poppy by my side, gamboling around me, I like it even more. I've always felt so crowded at home, but here, I can take a full, deep breath — and not have to smell Lugh's stinky feet.

I'm looking back the way we've come when the strangest thing happens. A person just . . . appears. Out of nowhere. And not a normal person, either, but a very tall person, all black with glowing purple eyes and long arms. I say it's a person, but maybe it's an animal or a mob. It certainly doesn't act like a person. It reaches down and picks up a chunk of grass and flowers. The sunny yellow dandelions are extra bright against its dark skin, and it just walks around carrying them like it knows where it's going and what it's doing despite the fact that it's in the middle of nowhere, randomly holding a block of soil with roots dangling out the bottom.

Poppy doesn't seem to notice this happening, as she's busy digging something up, the dirt exploding out of the ground behind her. Mal and the rest are walking onward, their focus tuned to the mountain pass we'll soon cross and the water waiting beyond it. For now, it's just me and this odd creature carrying its flowers.

I don't even draw my bow.

If there's one thing Poppy taught me, it's that this world is full of scary things, but it's also full of delightful things. This thing isn't attacking me—it doesn't even seem to notice that I exist—so I'm not going to hurt it. I'm just going to watch it, but not too aggressively, not staring it down or anything. I squat in the grass, and the thing puts its block of flowers down like a little table, disappears, and reappears a little distance away, where it picks up another block, this time with poppies. It doesn't eat the flowers or tear them out, it just carries them around like it's on an errand of its own making.

The creature pops out of existence, taking the flowers with it, and Poppy looks up with vague curiosity before returning to her hole. I stand and notice that my friends are farther away than I'd like. I momentarily feel that queasy homesickness, like I'm just too far away from safety and comfort, so I jog ahead. Poppy abandons her hole and lopes at my side, tongue out, and I relax a little and enjoy the sensation of really stretching out in a run and finding my stride.

My stamina is increasing, and I love running like this, flying over the terrain. We're headed uphill toward a pass between two mountains, and I can see that we'll reach it this afternoon. Part of me wonders what it would be like to climb up to one of the mountain peaks and stand high over the world looking down. Could we see Cornucopia from here? I wonder. Would it look small and silly compared to the whole wide grandness of everything outside those walls?

I catch up to my friends, and Poppy stops to shake herself, sending dirt flying. Candor looks offended, Thingy looks curious, and the llamas look like the mean girls downtown who wouldn't talk to me even though one of them was my sister. Mal is studying the map, frowning as she considers the next stage of our journey.

"See anything cool back there?" Chug asks, slinging an arm around my neck—and a heavy arm, because he always wears his armor now.

I think about telling him about the creature I saw, but I'm not sure how I would describe it. A person, but not quite. There, but not there. Moving flowers around playfully, but for no apparent reason.

"Just a lot of butts," I say, trying out the sort of thing Chug would say to me, were our positions switched.

"Ha! Good one! I saw my fair share of llama plops. They remind me of—"

"Guys, come look at this," Mal calls, interrupting at exactly the right time.

Chug and I run to join Mal and Tok where they stand up ahead, framed by the craggy slopes of the mountains.

We're nowhere near their peaks, but we're still high enough up that it makes me a little dizzy, considering the highest I've ever been before now was on the roof of a barn. The land unfolds below us in a way that would be dazzling and striking . . . if our goal didn't lie on the other side of it.

A treacherous path zigs and zags down, down, down from the pass into the darkest forest I've ever seen, the heavy green canopy interrupted here and there by round, red structures—huts, maybe?—and so thick I can't see any of the ground below.

My brain, now constantly scanning for dangers, does the math.

It's unlikely the sun can penetrate those trees, meaning hostile mobs can appear in the constant darkness at any moment. The entire time we travel there, we'll be in danger. The huge square roof of a massive structure is the only thing that can break through the dense blanket of leaves, and a chill goes through me as I realize this must be the woodland mansion.

And then I look down, and what I see there is even worse.

14.

MAL

 On the map, the river is a pretty blue ribbon, swirling between the jagged cliffs that slope down from the mountains on one side and the deeper green of the dark forest on the other. On the map, it's just pigment, sitting there peacefully in a meandering curve, painted by an artist's brush.

But in real life, it's a moving thing, an angry thing, a foaming, fuming, tumbling, crashing thing. Even from all the way up here, I can hear it, more water than I've seen in my whole life combined bashing into the rocks, spraying white foam. A slender line of brown crosses it at a narrow point, a fallen tree providing a way to reach the forest on the other side. I glance back at our group and frown. Although I'm sure Candor and the wolf will find a way across, there's no way the llamas and pig can make it. Everyone is looking to me, waiting for me to provide guidance, but . . . this is a bit more complicated than what I'm used to.

First, of course, we have to get down there, and the path is treacherous. I look to the left and the right, hoping there's a better option, but the well-packed earth shows that years of travelers have sought a pass through the mountain, made this same choice, and forged a trail along the path of least resistance.

This is the only way to reach the woodland mansion, making it the only way to save our town. I'm terrified, but I've been terrified before. I can feel the group beginning to fall apart around me as each of my friends looks down and sees their worst worries realized. It's my job to pull them back together.

"We can do this," I say firmly. "If we can run through the apple orchard without getting caught, walk the spine of Tommi's roof, and jump down the tree beside his barn, we can do this, no problem."

Chug grins, remembering that day—and touching the scar on his forehead. "That was pretty fun," he admits. "Almost as much fun as setting Krog's beetroots on fire. And I've only grown more agile with age."

"There could be interesting creatures in the water," Tok says, warming up to the idea. "Now that we're discovering new animals everywhere, I'm assuming there's more than salmon."

"There's just no other way." Lenna puts a hand on the stone wall of the pass. "Unless we want to start digging, but that could take days." She shivers, and I know she's thinking about her last trip underground. It bothers me, too, how that mysterious stranger ran away after Lenna saved him. If we weren't on the most important errand of our lives, there's no way I would've walked away from that cave.

But here we are, and now our job is to get down there as quickly and safely as possible.

The llamas are agile, and even if they can't cross the bridge, they can carry our chests down the steep path, which will help us conserve energy. We unpack our pockets and put everything that isn't strictly necessary in the chests. After the past few days, Chug is almost unrecognizable without his armor, but he does keep his helmet on—he's more comfortable with it than without it now, I guess.

I take the lead, and the first step sends my foot skidding, sending small stones tumbling over the cliff. Tok darts back among the trees and returns with four long sticks of wood. He hands me one, and I hold it like a torch before realizing it's actually a walking stick to help me pick my path among the scree. He has one for each of us, and I smile my appreciation. One bad move, and anyone could go tumbling over the edge and into the water below.

The first few steps are the scariest, but soon I learn the rhythm of walking on ground that wants to slip right out from under me. The llamas don't even seem to notice the danger, but then again, I found them bounding up the side of a mountain. Our chests sway from their sides, leaving our balance unencumbered and our hands ready to grasp for anything should we fall. Thingy is more nimble than anticipated, and Poppy seems eager to explore but nervous as she constantly sniffs the air. She looks down the path and growls, then looks to Lenna and whines, but none of us know what that means in wolf-speak. Candor clings to Tok's shoulder, and his grimace tells me the cat's claws are sunk in tight.

At the first switchback, I almost fall over the edge—it's a tight little pass.

"Be careful here," I call back, and each person calls it out to the one behind them. I pull the llamas along to a more secure spot and wait until our entire group is safely around the corner and then speed up as soon as it's safe. The less time we spend lingering here, the better.

That's how it goes—hurry along the straightaway, inch around the corner as the water foams and hisses below. With each zig and zag, we're closer to it, and the river's immensity is impossible to ignore. That pretty blue ribbon on the map is not the same as the seething surge we have to cross, and the raging gulf whipping mist into our faces is so intimidating that I stop in the shelter of a scraggly pine and hand out the last of Nan's cookies to give everyone the strength to get down the last steep curve.

Finally I tug the llamas down to the river's bank and consider the bridge while I wait. It's a huge log that's fallen in exactly the right place to make the river passable. I can tell by the way that the top is lighter colored and flat that either tools or feet have shaped that mighty trunk, that other people have crossed here before—lots of other people. That must mean it's relatively safe, or at least not an instant death sentence. The water is perhaps ten feet below it, raging and splashing in a way that suggests anyone unlucky enough to fall off the log would be dashed to bits against the boulders and banks.

On the last curve, Chug's foot slips, and even over the sound of the river, I can hear his gasp. He lurches forward as stones roll under his foot, but Tok grabs the neck of his shirt and yanks him backward with all his strength. Thingy squeals as Chug lands on his butt in the dirt and Tok wobbles for just a moment on the edge, having pulled himself off balance. Candor puffs up and screeches, and Tok's arms pinwheel until he finds his center and collapses to the ground.

I haven't breathed in several moments, unable to get to my

friends in time to save any of them, and I can't inhale again until the brothers are both sitting in the dust, hyperventilating. Behind them, Lenna is on her hands and knees, not yet willing to brave that hairpin corner.

"Careful," I say, knowing full well it's a stupid thing to say to someone who is extremely aware of the stakes but unable to stop it from coming out of my mouth.

"No, I want to go for a swim," Chug says. "Looks real refreshing."

"Not a great time to joke," I snap, immediately regretting it when I see a look of hurt flash across his face.

He stands shakily, and Tok follows suit. They both hang back as close to the wall as they can. Candor has apparently decided that Tok's balance can't be trusted and is on the ground, crouched and miserable and wet with water spray. Lenna crawls around the turn and stands, and one of the llamas grunts impatiently, bored to death with all this petty two-legged drama.

I look to the log bridge, but . . . we need a few minutes. We're all too shaky to cross it now. It's going to be slippery. We need a place to rest, and there's a small clearing on the bank, as if it were made for weary travelers to catch their breath and get up their gumption. There's an unlit campfire with a couple of logs around it, and I exhale and walk toward it, glad I bought those pumpkin pies back in the village, as cold chicken and stale bread aren't going to fortify us to get us across that river.

"So that was fun," I say.

"This is going to be fun, too," says a new voice.

Before I can even process what's happening, people appear from where they've been hiding in the scrub brush and behind boulders around the little clearing. They're adults, and they don't look friendly. The man who's just spoken is in front, grinning, a sword in his hand. His helmet obscures his face, but I catch a glint of teeth and notice that his fingernails are black with dirt. I count five more people, all of them holding weapons that look sturdy and well-used. Swords, an axe, a bow that looks bigger and meaner than Lenna's bow.

Poppy growls, and Lenna murmurs something to her.

"If the wolf attacks, someone dies," the leader warns.

I glance back, nervous. We don't know what wolves do, or how to stop them from attacking, but I don't think he's lying. These people look comfortable with violence, almost hungry for it.

"What do you want?" I ask, my fingers longing for the smooth handle of my diamond pickaxe.

"Nothing much. Just everything you've got." The man points his sword. "Drop your sticks and hand over the llamas. It's all ours. Don't give us trouble, and we'll let you cross the river."

I can see it now, and my naivete makes me bite the inside of my cheek. These men—they're bad people, and they must wait here for innocent travelers to choose the mountain pass and river crossing, then surprise them and steal all their belongings.

The thought of what we're about to lose makes me see red.

Nan's books. Our weapons. Our food. That one Potion of Regeneration. Tok's crafting table. Everything we were given, everything we've made, everything we traded for.

Gone, and why?

Because these meaner, stronger people say so.

"Mal, this is cow patties. We can't—"

"Do what he says, Chug. Everyone. Just . . . drop everything."

Chug can't see what I see, can't see the rusty spots on the leader's sword that might be bloodstains. Can't see the brigands exchange excited glances like they're just begging us to run or attack. Chug has never entered into a fight he couldn't win, but this fight is unwinnable. We're just a bunch of kids. Maybe we can take down a zombie or skeleton, but I'm not willing to stab another human being, even in self-defense. And I'm not willing to let my friends get stabbed, either.

I throw the llamas' lead to the man and step back, my hands in the air. They step obediently past me, and even if Sugar doesn't want to go and swivels her head to honk at me, she allows herself to be led into the clearing, and the others follow her because that's what llamas do.

"That's all I have," I say. I look over my shoulder and see Chug baring his teeth, his hands in fists. "Chug, it's okay. Let it go. Drop the stick."

He doesn't want to, but hopefully he sees the fear and desperation in my eyes. He tosses down his stick. "There. Happy now?"

"Not a chance. Give us that helmet. And I'll take the pig, too." The leader looks back at his band. "Pork chops tonight, eh, lads?"

"Huzzah!" they call.

"Hey, nobody's eating Thingy!" Chug growls.

"Chug." I look him directly in the eyes, pleading. "This isn't Jarro. This isn't Cornucopia. Just do what he says."

Grumbling to himself, Chug yanks off his helmet. He looks like he's about to throw it in the water, but the leader puts his sword against my belly.

"Throw it on the ground, kid. Nothing funny."

I don't want to whimper, but I do. His sword may look rusty, but it's sharp.

Behind me, I hear Chug's helmet thump in the dust.

"Now the skinny kid and the girl. Lose the sticks."

I can't turn away from the sword, but I hear things hitting the ground. I can't imagine what it must cost Tok to know every-thing he's losing—his crafting table and books, the missing element of his inventions that he's spent his entire life searching for. If Lenna is less affected by losing her stuff, I can only hope they don't take Poppy, because that's what would really break her heart.

"Go on and cross the bridge," the leader says. "If you're scared, do it sitting down. It can be a little intimidating the first time." There's a weird kindness in his voice, and I wish I could see Chug punch him in the gut, but I know that my job here is to keep my friends together and safe, not fight an impossible battle that could get them killed.

I nod and turn to the log. It's bigger than it looked from the mountain pass, but that doesn't mean I trust myself to balance my way across it. I look at each of my friends, directly in the eye, and give a reassuring smile before focusing on the bridge. I straddle it, legs hanging down, and start scooting across. I want to watch my friends, watch the thieves, but it takes every ounce of attention I have just to get across the log. Even sitting down, it's slippery, and my pants catch on the bark. I don't let myself look down at the water; it'll only make me panic.

"Please let me go last. I need to make sure my little brother and friend get across safely," Chug says, and I can only hope he's not going to make the leader mad.

Chug is not generally one for manners and diplomacy, but I can appreciate what he's doing. He wants to make sure neither Tok nor Lenna are left alone over here with these violent people who don't even pretend to have morals or empathy. This courageous nobility is one of the many things I appreciate about my best friend. He's willing to face a bad man's sword rather than let his brother do this alone.

"No funny business," the leader says warningly. "Keep your hands up."

I give a little sigh of relief as I keep scooting, and I feel the log shudder as Tok adds his weight to the bridge. I finally reach the other end and drag myself onto solid ground. I want to hug the earth and kiss the dirt, but I need to watch my friends, as if just my attention can keep them from harm. Tok is scooting along the log just like I did. Candor is on his shoulder, but she must reach her limit of tolerating human frailty, because she skulks down his arm, skitters down the log, and hops onto the ground, where she washes her face like everything is totally normal. Then it's Lenna's turn, her hands shaking and her eyes scrunched shut as she scoots. I can see her lips moving, and I know that she's murmuring to Poppy, encouraging the wolf as she daintily tiptoes behind her mistress with more grace than I assumed a wolf would possess.

Only Chug is left, watching us carefully, Thingy pressed up against the backs of his legs.

"Go on, kid," the thief says. "We got what we needed."

"I have to make sure Lenna gets across," I hear over the water. "She's scared."

I help Lenna up onto the ground, and Poppy lightly leaps to join us.

The leader shoves Chug toward the bridge. "Good. You kids need to be more careful. There's worse stuff than us in the dark forest."

"There's nothing over there that *smells* worse," Chug says, and I groan as he picks up his pig in both arms and . . .

Oh no.

Tries to run across the bridge.

The leader shouts "Hey, that's our pig!" as if that's going to make Chug turn around and bring Thingy back, but Chug is running across the log like it's Tommi's roof and his butt's on fire. I'm not even sure he can see over Thingy, who's squealing his head off but at least not flailing too much. The thieves fire a few arrows, but they don't make it across the river, and then Chug jumps off the log and sets Thingy on the ground.

"He's his own pig!" Chug bellows back. "And you can't eat him!"

The leader leaps up onto the log bridge with far more agility and confidence than any of us showed—except perhaps Chug, and I realize that he's about to cross the bridge with all of his friends and punish us.

And we don't have any weapons.

"Chug, are you feeling strong today?" I ask.

He grins. "Oh, I always feel strong."

With a snort and a head shake, he squats down and wraps his arms around the bridge. The faintest crease of fear crosses the leader's face, but Chug can barely nudge the massive log. I step up and grab my own section of log, and Tok gets the very end.

"Don't you dare!" the leader shouts, backing away until he's safe on the ground.

But it's too late. All together, the three of us topple the log bridge right into the river, stranding him and his band of villains on the other side.

With all our stuff.

And our only way back.

"Uh, how are we going to get back home?" Tok asks in a small voice.

"We'll cross that bridge when we come to it," Chug answers.

Despite the fact that we've lost everything and possibly destroyed our only route home, we all sit down in the dirt and laugh until we cry. What else is there to do?

We'll just have to find a way.

15.

TOK

My brother is the world's biggest idiot, but he's definitely got the biggest heart—and a dancer's grace, apparently. I'm still completely gob-smacked that he can carry a pig, much less while running over a slippery log over a raging river. Between the two of them, I'd take the brother over the pig, but I wish he didn't take such stupid risks. It just goes to show that when Chug wants something badly enough, he can do the impossible.

Not that there's much he can do now.

Because we have nothing left.

I'm still sitting in the dirt, and Candor is winding around me, rubbing her head against my shoulder, purring as if she's trying to coax me out of a bad mood. She always understands, but she's incapable of grasping the magnitude of my current despair. All my life, I've been building things, and they never really worked—until I got my hands on that crafting table and the book of recipes. It was like the entire world opened up to me and everything suddenly made sense. Now that it's gone, I just feel . . . empty.

Chug's stomach growls, drawing my attention away from my own hopelessness.

"What's for—" he starts brightly before dimming considerably. "They got all the food, too, didn't they?"

He turns to look across the river at the brigands, who've given up any hope of punishing us and are settling for sorting through our chests, delighted at how much they've managed to take from a quartet of dumb kids.

"Let's find somewhere more private," Mal says as one of the thieves jeers at us and hefts her great-great-great-grandmother's diamond pickaxe in triumph.

The dark forest isn't far away, and the shade from its canopy is ominous and sinister. We head for a small clearing that's closer to the mountain, a smallish meadow with flowers that's hidden from the thieves' view thanks to boulders and brush. Lenna and I both sit back down, all floppy like we've been completely drained. Chug is still buzzed on the adrenaline that got him over the log, but Mal has that look we know so well, the one that suggests she's ten steps ahead of us and preparing to save our collective rumps.

"We've got to find food," she says. "But I haven't seen anything edible."

Chug pats Thingy on his round pink back. "Darn right you haven't."

"There's nothing." Lenna falls onto her back, and Poppy licks her forehead. "This place is barren. We have no tools. We can't even dig out a shelter. They took everything. Everything."

"Our beds," Chug moans, finally realizing how dire our situation is. "Our weapons. My armor. I feel practically naked. And don't even get me started on the food. I'm already starving to death. I can feel it in my bones."

"No one's starving to death," Mal says firmly. "We just have to think."

Chug snorts. "About what? How to die quicker in the scary forest?"

"How to *survive* in the scary forest," she corrects. "We can do this. We've been doing it. We just have to . . ." She sighs, drained of what little energy she'd mustered to keep us all going. "We have to figure out how to go on."

I look around—grass, dirt, rocks. No crops. No random chickens. No handy chest containing pretty much everything we need. They're right—it's pretty hopeless.

But I can see something they can't.

Possibilities.

"We can fish in the river," I say, watching sleek gray bodies flash in the white foam down below. "All we need is a stick and some cobwebs. There's our protein. And once we get into the forest, I'm pretty sure those big red things are mushrooms."

"Mushroom stew," Chug says, nodding. "I like it."

Mal is starting to smile as she, too, looks around. "There's plenty of wood. Maybe you could build a new crafting table?"

My jaw drops.

I hadn't really thought about it before, but . . . I do know how to make a crafting table now. And with it, I can make new weapons, plus the tools we'll need to dig out a shelter.

"I can try," I say with conviction.

"I can find cobweb for the fishing rod, I think," Lenna says. "Same materials as a bow, really." She scurries into the forest, with Poppy gamboling on her heels.

"And I can pull down branches. I feel strong enough to fight that rusty iron guy! For about thirty seconds!" Chug flexes his muscles, and we all laugh.

I stand and stride toward the trees. I'm not quite ready to tread fully into those soul-sucking shadows, but I can see plenty of sticks and branches just sitting around. "Chug, I'm going to need a lot of logs. As uniform in size as you can get."

He salutes me and marches into the forest, where I hear sounds of splintering and breaking as he shouts at trees. Thingy follows him and squeals his enthusiasm. Soon I have a growing stack of oak logs, and I get busy building my crafting table. It's not perfect, but we don't need perfect.

"Mal, if we had a wooden pickaxe, could you find some iron? You know how to mine stuff, right?"

She cocks her head, a look of charmed wonder crossing her face. "Yeah, I guess so."

I grab several planks and sticks, and soon I'm handing her my first pickaxe. "If you and Lenna can dig a shelter, maybe you can find something harder than wood for a better pickaxe. And Chug will need a sword."

She grins. "And arrows for Lenna! Maybe I'll find some flint, too." Muttering to herself about various ores she's found digging lately, she takes the pickaxe and walks off.

"And don't forget charcoal for the torches!" I call.

Chug delivers a steady stream of wood, and I focus on turning it into the things we need to survive the night. I'm so tired and drained that I'd love to make beds, but without wool, there's not much I can do there. I focus on what I can create with just wood: a sword and more pickaxes for when the first one inevitably breaks. Lenna returns with some cobweb, and I make a fishing rod and assign Chug the job of catching fish, now that he's dragged over every log for miles. He soon has a pile of glittering salmon, much fatter and shinier than the ones from back home, plus one super freaky black creature with eight legs that Poppy instantly feasts upon—I have to turn away from that spectacle, although I do collect the odd little bag of ink left behind.

The wooden thud of Mal's mining ceases, and she drags over a couple of lumps of iron and one of coal. She's frazzled and sweating, and she holds up the handle of her wooden pickaxe, now missing its pick. With a feral grin, I snatch up the chunk of iron and get to work. The surprise on her face when I hand her a new iron pickaxe is deeply gratifying, and she goes right back out to work. When I hear the ring of iron on stone, I feel a frisson of absolute pride. All those times I tried to make things and couldn't, all my great dreams that never came to light and just made my parents sigh—it's all justified now, because I can create something out of nothing.

I can save the day—by being a major nerd!

Soon Mal brings me some coal, and I craft a pile of torches. Without being asked, Chug starts a campfire and lays the salmon on logs to cook over the flames. I can tell he'd like to go back to fishing or log-fetching, but with a hungry cat and wolf nosing around our only source of food, my gruff big brother becomes a glorified babysitter, calmly saying, "No, Candor, that's not for you. Please, Poppy, wait your turn," over and over again like he's tending to children.

Lenna returns from the forest with another armful of cobwebs and some feathers. She digs through the pile of stone and ore and dust Mal has left behind and plucks out several smaller pieces of stone. When I'm at a break in my work, she asks to borrow the crafting table for a moment and sets about making arrows with a level of concentration I've never seen out of her before. It's like this is the first thing that's ever interested her enough to engage her full concentration, and she dives into that focus with a single-minded intensity that's laudable.

While she's working, I go check on Mal and find her digging into the side of the mountain. Instead of our usual narrow shelter, which requires the least amount of work possible to house all of us almost comfortably, this shelter starts with the usual narrow opening but then widens to also serve as a mine, and I can see where she's followed a vein of iron to produce the metal I'll need for weapons. I fetch a few more torches for her and place them around the mine, and she grins her thanks.

"Lenna said to follow the veins," she says between strikes. "Do we have what we need?"

"It seems foolish to compare what we have now with what we lost," I answer honestly. "But I've got one sword ready, and we should have enough materials for some armor for Chug, a sword for you, plenty of torches. And Lenna is making her own bow and arrows. If we had some wool, I could make beds, but . . . well, here we are." I shrug. "The fish should be done cooking soon. We have enough room in here. I think you can stop, if you're ready."

Mal leans against her pickaxe to catch her breath. "Mining is not for the faint of heart, but I think I might like it better than cows. They're always the same, but this . . ." She looks around the cavern she's created with a proud smile. "Something exciting could happen at any moment. The first time I found iron, it was like waking up on your birthday, you know?"

I nod eagerly. "That's how I felt making a crafting table. Like I'm doing exactly what I was supposed to be doing all along."

"Fish is ready!" Chug calls from outside. "Come and get it before the animals do! Or don't! They won't complain! And I think we all know I already helped myself! Burp!" I can tell he's in a great mood by the way he practically sings the word "burp."

We all meet at the campfire he's created, and I have to admit that the salmon smells delicious. I was never that big into the farmed salmon back in Cornucopia, but this fish tastes meaty and fresh, or maybe I'm just so exhausted that anything would taste good. We eat and toss pieces of fish to Poppy and Candor and exclaim over what everyone has accomplished. Lenna has a nice new bow and a bunch of arrows that will save us when the mobs come; Mal has created a shelter for us and produced piles of raw materials for me to craft with; and after fetching all the wood, Chug provided the fish and cooked it to perfection, a skill I would never have guessed he might possess.

And even I contributed. I made the tools that dug the mine and shelter, crafted the torches that give us light, and gave Chug his fishing rod. For the first time in my life, I feel like I might almost be a hero.

The sun is going down faster than it seemed to back when we were on the plains and could see forever. The dark forest looms, full of new sounds. When we hear the first groan, we collect our leftover fish and weapons and tools and run for the shelter.

"Oh no. I forgot to make a door!" I cry, smacking my forehead.

I put Candor into Mal's arms and run back out to my crafting table. Without being asked, Lenna and Chug run out, too. He stands beside me, sword drawn, and she stands a little off, her bow and arrow ready as I sort through the remaining wood.

When the first skeleton appears, she takes it down before it can get anywhere close to us. Sweat beads my brow, dripping down my nose, and I work faster. Another moan comes, and a baby zombie appears, toddling out of the forest and toward us, and Chug almost lets it get close enough to bite him—because he thinks it's cute, I'm sure, and feels guilty about dispatching it. I work frantically, knowing that I have to hurry but that if I'm not careful, the door won't be strong enough to keep us safe.

"Done!" I finally shout, running for the shelter.

Chug jumps over the baby zombie and follows. Lenna is last, covering our retreat. I hear her arrow thunk into something but I don't look back. As I attach the door, the groans and moans persist and grow.

"Hurry, bro," Chug murmurs.

Lenna says nothing, but her bow sings and her arrows hit home, her face a mask of grim concentration.

The moment the door is firmly secured, I shout "Now!" and we all pile into the shelter. I slam the door shut behind us, and something claws at it, making the hair on the back of my neck rise up.

But it's a good, sturdy door, and I know that we're going to be fine, even if we're sleeping on hard, cold stone with no beds and no nighttime supply of cookies.

For now, we're together and we're safe.

Tomorrow, when we venture into the dark forest . . . Who knows?

16.

CHUG

 Lying on my back on cold, hard stone is not a great way to end the day, but neither was having some jerk steal all our stuff and threaten to eat my pig. Thingy is curled up against me, a little stinky but much safer than he would be left alone outside. I wasn't scared for him before, but now I am.

There have been lots of new feelings lately. Seeing the world beyond the wall, leaving home, fighting something besides a human bully, nearly dying multiple times—even one of those events feels like it's ten thousand times more intense than the most exciting thing that ever happened at home. I'm beginning to realize we've been living a sweet, soft life.

In the past few hours, my friends and I did the impossible. Tok made tools out of trees, Mal dug this shelter out of stone, Lenna took down a freaky little zombie with a weapon she made by hand. And I caught fish—lots of fish. And cooked them. And it was maybe the most fun thing I've ever done. Back home, Edd's family ran the salmon farm, and he said it was awful, and it smelled much, much worse than awful—as did he. Sometimes when the pumpkins weren't growing like they should, Mom traded for scrawny little salmon, a few days past their prime, to make the protein stretch out. I never thought fish could taste good. I never thought that I could *make* fish taste good.

I've never been particularly fond of pumpkins. Pumpkin pies, yes, but I didn't feel like I was put on the world to farm gourds. Still, that was my family, that was my future. Tok and I would inherit the farm, or maybe split it between us—the farms are all split up among kids and cousins these days, but we rarely see Aunt Becca and her family where they grow their own gourds on the other side of the cobblestone wall dividing our farms. Tok doesn't like pumpkins either, I don't think. We've never talked about it— why talk about something that's going to happen no matter what we really, truly want? But now I'm starting to think the world is a very big place with lots of jobs, lots of paths. Maybe I'm not doomed to pumpkins after all.

Or maybe it's the salmon talking. I ate a lot, and I'm very sleepy. Stone floor or not, I fall asleep counting shiny salmon as they leap over a log across a river.

The next morning, we're all cold and achy and missing our beds. Fish doesn't taste nearly as nice when it's cold and it's breakfast, but it's better than starving. Tok whips up a sword for Mal while we pack up what little we have now, but we're unfortunately out of iron, so no armor for me. It's rather sad, not being greeted by the llamas honking at us from their pen. Tok's door is covered in scratches, and we leave the shelter and door behind for the next batch of weary travelers who get fleeced by the thieves—if they can make it across the river. I string the remaining fish on the line of my fishing rod and make a loop so I can carry it over my shoulder.

It's a sunny day, and we mill around just outside of the sharp line where the dark forest looms. These trees are somehow scarier than normal trees, bigger and . . . yes, darker. Which I'm sure is why they call it a "dark forest," but that doesn't make me want to go in there. We're all holding torches, but we know that won't stop the mobs from attacking us. Still, heading into that thick, sinister shadow with a jolly orange light in one hand and my new iron sword in the other feels a little better than going in empty-handed.

Mal finally nods and says, "Okay, here we go," psyching herself up.

I move closer and give her my most confident smile. "Pfft, dark forest. What's so dark about it?"

"Right?" Tok steps closer to me. "It's barely crepuscular."

"Ew."

He snorts at me. "'Crepuscular' means 'resembling twilight.'"

I didn't know that, and he knows that I didn't know that. "Just sounds like pus to me, bro. Creepy pus."

Lenna giggles, and Poppy pants like she's laughing. It's nice that we can still be ourselves, those same old bad apples, even when we're scared out of our minds and headed directly into the most dangerous place we're ever been, which is currently saying a lot. When Mal finally walks under the trees, sword and pickaxe in hand, I give Tok my usual "it's going to be okay" smile and follow her, with Thingy by my side, snorting cautiously.

The moment I'm under the canopy, everything just . . . changes.

The air goes cold and almost wet, like the forest is breathing. The ground feels softer, like it never quite dries out. The noises change completely, from the rushing of the river and the call of birds to just . . . this eerie silence.

"I vote we rename it the Yark Forest," I say. "Because it makes me want to yark."

"It can hear you," Lenna replies, almost a whisper. "Let's not make it mad."

Mal is jumpy, walking slowly with her new iron sword at the ready, scanning the forest for movement or sound. Behind me, Tok holds Candor to his chest, her orange-striped tail lashing and her ears flat. Even Poppy looks suspicious, hunched down and teeth bared as she trots by Lenna's side. Now that we're within the actual forest, we can't see the woodland mansion peeking up—or rather, looming over us—but Mal has a good sense of direction and it seems to me like we're headed the way we should be.

"The map shows a little clearing right before it," Mal tells us. "Although I remember that it was a different green from everything else." She's nervous about reaching our goal, but I'm looking forward to it. I miss the sun and all the normal things that grow when they're not blocked by brooding trees.

At first, it feels like the dark forest is just a regular forest, for all that it's, well, darker. But then we hear groans, and four zombies lurch out of the shadows. One of them has a helmet, sword, and chest plate, and Lenna and I share a strategic glance before focusing on that one first. I drop my fish and strike out with my sword. I'm not as scared this time—I guess because I know what to expect, and because the zombies aren't actually that smart. They don't plan, they aren't creative. They just groan and shamble mindlessly, so I distract the helmeted zombie with my sword while Lenna shoots it full of arrows. The moment it drops, I slap on its helmet and chest plate and hand its sword to Tok.

He takes it like it's an angry bee, staring at the slime on the hilt. "Fight or get gnawed on," I say, and he nods and does his best.

Mal takes down a zombie with her sword, Lenna gets another one, and I focus on the fourth. Tok even gets in a few good jabs, and soon all four zombies are nothing but rotten meat, a potato, and a carrot. Poppy lunges for the meat and wolfs it down, Thingy attacks the carrot, and then we're alone in the dark again, but at least now I have armor. And a potato.

Except . . .

"Tok, you should put on the armor," I say, taking off the helmet.

He shakes his head. "No way. If you're the one fighting, you're the one who needs the protection. We need you healthy. There's no potion to scrape off the floor out here."

"But there might be in the woodland mansion," Mal reminds us. "There should actually be plenty of loot in there, according to Nan's book."

"We've got to get there first." Lenna pats her wolf on the head and stares into the trees with this faraway, determined look she never had back home.

I don't like it—I've proven I can take care of myself, while Tok's scrawny arms can barely hold a sword, much less swing one. He should wear the armor. I'll fight better if I know that he's safe. But nobody listens to me when I'm the only one who disagrees. It's that old brawn-versus-brains thing. I'm going to lose either way, so I just plop the helmet back on my head and don't bother.

We walk for a while without hearing any more groans, but we're all on high alert. A familiar smell assaults my nostrils, and after a moment, I recognize it: mushroom! It's bigger than a house, and we gladly attack it with our tools and weapons, whittling off big chunks. There's no good way to carry it all and no good way to cook it, so we just stuff our pockets and hope it doesn't melt into goo. I can't believe how much I miss Mal's llamas, who could carry tons of stuff and look hilarious doing it.

Since we know better than to eat raw mushroom, we snack on the leftover salmon, which has somehow grown even colder and stinkier with time. At least Candor is happy about it.

The trees block the sun, but it's just starting to feel like afternoon when I smell something completely new—and not good. It smells kind of rotten and thick, but not meaty like a zombie. I adjust my armor and ready my sword, because so far, most new things out here are dangerous. As we move forward, sunbeams pierce the trees, and something shimmers brightly up ahead. Mal meets my eye, and I give her a nod. She speeds up, and I follow. Whatever's coming, we need to face it before night falls. We still have to build a shelter, and with no convenient hills or mountains, it's going to be tricky.

We reach the edge of the trees and stop.

This place is—well, I've never seen anything like it, and now I know why that clearing on Mal's stolen map was a weird shade of green.

It's water.

Not pretty, blue, moving water. Not a fountain. But a big patch of still water gone mossy green in the sun. I guess that's where the smell comes from—the water is basically just cooking itself and rotting.

"A swamp," Tok says, voice full of wonder because he loves nature and understanding how things work. "I read about it in one of Nan's books. It's a biome—like, its own sort of place, with its own animals and plants and rules. I hoped we'd see one."

"Too much water," Lenna says, finally catching up with us. She shivers. "Way too much water."

"But water means fish," I argue.

Mal points at something partially hidden by trees and vines. "And a structure. Someone lives here. Maybe they'll help us."

Lenna and I exchange glances. Mal always looks at the bright side, but "help" isn't something we've received a lot of since leaving Nan's cottage. "Maybe," I say.

Mal is undeterred. "We have to try. It'll be sunset soon, and the land here is too wet to dig in."

I feel cold down to my boots when I realize what she's saying.

She can't build a shelter before nightfall.

When she splashes into the goopy water, I follow. My boots and socks are immediately soaked, which is not my favorite thing in the world. I turn back to where Tok and Lenna stand. "Stay here while we check it out. Lenna, have your bow ready. Tok, maybe start getting some planks ready in case we have to build a little shelter." Tok nods and turns to the trees behind us, and Lenna and I share a meaningful glance. She gives me a small nod, and I know she'll keep Tok safe.

I hurry to meet Mal, and she's striding in knee-deep water to get to the structure, which I can now see is a small house of birch and spruce, up on stilts to keep it out of the water. There are no steps up to it, which is going to be a challenge.

"Hello?" Mal calls. "Is anyone home?"

The only answer is the meow of a curious black cat that peeks down through an open window beside a bouquet of red mushrooms in a clay pot. It doesn't sound distressed, though, which means someone must live there and feed it, right? Maybe they keep a secret ladder up there so random people like us can't just show up and annoy them. Maybe it's a nice old lady like Nan who will give us pies and cookies.

"I don't think there's anyone in there." Mal looks back to the shore, if you can call it that, and shouts. "Hey, Tok, can you whip up some quick stairs?"

I'm about to ask why a ladder wouldn't be easier when I notice Lenna stroking Poppy's head. Of course she could never be comfortable with her wolf on the ground.

Soon I'm helping my brother set up a staircase that will allow us to climb to the open platform of the structure. It's not super sturdy, but it should work.

"Who goes first?" Lenna asks as she scans the swamp for danger—or the shelter's owner, coming home to shout at us.

I step forward. "I will. I'm wearing armor. If the cat attacks, I'm ready."

Mal grins and nods her agreement, and I silently tell myself I'm an idiot before putting my soggy boot on the first rickety step.

Thingy squeals at me from the ground, but Mal rubs his back to quiet him. Step by step I climb toward the shelter, unsure of what I'll find. Anything could be in there. A skeleton, a zombie, an angry old man with a beetroot obsession. I don't hear movement, though, outside of that cat.

I hope it's just a cat.

I clamber up onto the platform, hating how awkward it is. Sword out, I call, "Hello? Anybody? Anybody who's not currently a cat?"

Of course the only answer is from the cat, which meows at me from a few feet away like we're having a perfectly normal conversation. Shaking a little, sword out, I step into the shelter.

And it's completely empty.

Seriously, it's just me, the cat, a crafting table with a potion bottle sitting on it, a cauldron, and that weird bouquet of mushrooms.

I don't see anyplace a person could be hiding. There's no bed, no furniture, no back door, no trapdoor in the floor or ceiling.

This is great news.

"It's empty!" I call down. "Come on up!

Mal joins me next, then Tok and Lenna. Thingy absolutely refuses to try the stairs, so he just stands belly-deep in the swamp and oinks his concern. The black cat and Candor sniff each other at half puff but don't try to get in a fight, which is good, because this structure is pretty small, maybe the size of our usual night-time shelters.

"Well, that makes things easier," Mal says. "I just wish they had a bed."

"Not a lot of furniture stores in the swamp. Who knew?" I go to pick up the potion, but Tok smacks my hand away and picks it up himself, giving it a cautious sniff.

"Don't lick this until we know what it is," he chides me, and I'd smack him back, playfully of course, except that he's right. That potion could be anything. We just got lucky last time.

Lenna stands at the window, looking out. The black cat leans up and rubs against her, purring, but all of her focus is outside. "Something isn't right. This is just . . . too good to be true."

"It's not *that* good," I say. "Again: no beds."

"And it kinda makes sense, finding a structure out here," Mal argues. "Every place we've stopped for a night, we've left the shelter ready for the next travelers. Except in the village, where we took advantage of an empty house. Maybe this is just how people do things out here: You're having a hard enough time getting by, so you make it a little easier for whoever shows up next."

"I wish that were true," Lenna says. She turns and looks Mal in the eye. "But after those thieves by the river, I just don't know."

For a moment, I'm speechless—me! Because before this trip, I don't think Lenna had ever argued with Mal or defended a point, and now this is the second time it's happened. Being out here has given her a strength she's never had. I bet even Jarro wouldn't mess with her now.

"Well, we can stay here for the night," I say, trying to break the tension. "Poppy will let us know if anything bad is coming. Thingy will have to stay down there, I guess." I frown, considering what it would take to heft a pig into a swamp house. "We have weapons. We have the element of surprise. So let me whip up some mushroom stew, and let's take advantage of what feels like a win."

Tok sets Candor on the floor so she can play with the black cat. He stands beside Lenna at the window. She looks suspicious and tough, but he looks curious and like there's nowhere else he'd rather be, which is something new for him, too. My brother usually looks like he has no idea how he's got to where he is and isn't sure where he should be instead.

Tok is thinking hard. "The sun is going down, so I think the decision is made for us. I vote for mushroom stew and caution. If someone really does live here, I think they'll understand why some kids might seek shelter for the night."

No one asks for my thoughts, but I still want to be heard. "I mean, hey, mushroom stew!" I say, and that's three against one.

Decision made, we get to work. I focus on my stew while Tok

investigates the potion. Lenna keeps watch from the platform, bow and arrow ready, while Mal ties up Thingy. I hear a ruckus outside, and soon Mal comes in with two plucked chickens to eat alongside the stew.

"They were just wandering around the swamp," she says, delighted, and I'm glad to have any protein of the nonfish variety.

We're not entirely at ease, but maybe at 80 percent for me. I like the coziness of a windowless shelter at night, but there's something to be said for being up high and hearing the subtle splashes of the swamp. I toss down bits of food for Thingy, and the cats companionably eat the last of the leftover fish, and Tok is fairly certain that the potion we found is for slowing, which isn't quite as useful as healing but certainly smells a lot worse.

With full bellies, we each curl up in a corner and fall asleep. All this walking has me more tired than I've ever been before. In my dream, I'm at Mal's cow farm, but all the cows have long, goofy llama necks and goofy llama teeth, and they honk instead of mooing, which is hilarious.

But there's this one llama that keeps saying hee hee hee hee in the most demented sort of voice, and it's making me very uncomfortable.

I open my eyes in the darkness, an eerie blue glow from the moon filtering through the window.

My blood runs cold when I hear that sound again.

Hee hee hee hee.

It's not a llama-cow.

It's coming from below us, down in the swamp.

17.

MAL

A hand lands over my mouth, and I wake up trying to scream.

"It's me, Mal," Chug whispers. "Please don't scream. Or bite me."

I should've known. His fingers smell like old fish and mushroom stew.

I nod, and he cautiously removes his hand.

"There's something in the swamp."

I sit up and see the sword in his hand, moonlight glinting off the blade. I'm about to ask him what's out there, and then I hear it.

Hee hee hee hee.

It's a terrible noise, and the splashing that accompanies it is getting closer.

Back home, when I was very little, Nan told me that if I wasn't good, a witch would get me. And she would cackle like that, almost. Hee hee hee hee, she'd say, waggling her hands as she chased me to bed at sunset. My parents told her to stop, but she thought it was hilarious, and so did I. I thought it was our special game. It always made me laugh.

Now, hearing that same noise coming from the darkness outside at midnight, I realize how very well Nan replicated the sound.

"It's a witch," I whisper back. "We need Lenna to get her bow ready." Chug nods and turns to her, but I shake my head. I'll wake her and save her the terror. And the fishy residue. "Lenna," I whisper from very close.

"Leave me alone, Letti," she grumbles. "I'll sleep on the floor if I please."

I give her shoulder a shake, and she wakes up, mouth open in protest. When she sees me, finger to my lips, she remains silent.

"There's a witch outside."

When she hears the hee hee hee hee, she creeps to the window, bow and arrows ready.

The black cat leaps up onto the windowsill, meowing, and I snatch it away. I don't know much about witches and how they feel about cats—I didn't read that page of the book, as witches are rare and I was focusing on more common dangers—but I don't want the cat to get hurt.

The old Lenna might have waited or asked me what to do, but this new version of Lenna knows exactly what we need. She starts shooting arrows at the witch, one after the other. Chug tugs on his armor and looks at the stairs, but I put a hand on his shoulder and shake my head. This isn't something we should be fighting close up. I seem to remember witches can—

Crash. Splash!

Lenna ducks as a potion bottle flies through the window and breaks on the floor, sizzling as it dissolves a section of the wood planks. Tok wakes up flailing, and Chug drags him away from the widening hole in the boards.

"What?!" Tok screeches.

"Witch," Chug answers.

"Not 'which.' What?"

"The what is a witch. Don't ask how or why. Just keep your cat out of the way in case it throws another potion."

Confused, Tok clutches Candor to his chest and crawls backward into a corner.

I know Lenna's arrows have landed multiple hits on the witch, but another potion splatters against the side of the window, splashing Lenna's arm. I rush to her side, unsure what to do, certain that the potion is going to burn through her skin like it did the wooden boards, but nothing really happens.

"Are you okay?" I ask.

"Iiiiiiiiiiii thiiiiiiiiiiink soooooooooooooooooooooooooo," she says, super slowly. She nods her head, and it feels like it takes a full minute. When she goes to draw back her next arrow, it takes so long that another potion zips through the window and crashes against the wall.

"Slowness," Tok fills in for me from his corner. "It was a Potion of Slowness, like the one I found by the cauldron. It'll wear off in a while—"

"But we don't have a while. Sorry, Lenna." I gently take the bow and arrow from her, and I can see her opening her mouth to object, but it's going to take an hour for her to just say my name. I'm not sure exactly how this works, so I just start shooting at the witch, doing the best I can.

"Sheeeeeeeeeeee's aaaaaaaaaalllllllmoooooooooooooost—"

I land a lucky hit, and the witch grunts but doesn't go down.

My next three arrows miss. I'm running out of arrows, and I know that I can't finish off the witch with the arrows I have left; I just don't have Lenna's skill or practice. But there has to be another way. There always is. The witch is weak—probably just needs one more shot, but I've got only one arrow left.

I . . . don't trust myself to make it count.

"Chug, let Poppy loose. She'll distract the witch, and you can hit her. She only needs one more solid hit."

Chug—good old Chug—still on the first stair, just nods once, snaps Poppy's lead, and charges down the rickety stairs, screaming bloody murder with a wild wolf on his heels. I fire off my last arrow before he gets in the way, but it goes wide, which smarts. I'm so used to being good at everything and being able to take care of everything myself that it's hard to admit that I couldn't end this fight on my own. If we get through this, I'll ask Lenna to teach me archery, because I know she could've already taken this witch down, if not for that sneaky potion.

Chug splashes through the muck to bash the witch with his sword as Poppy harries it from the back, tugging on its cloak and growling.

"Poooooooooopppppyyyyyyyyy, nooooooooooooooooooooooo!" Lenna cries in agonizing slow motion.

Hee hee hee hee hee, the witch crows, whipping out a potion to drink, and then with one mighty swing, Chug takes our enemy down. The witch falls into the swamp, dropping all sorts of strange items—the potion it was about to drink, several bags of powder and stone, and a bag of what look suspiciously like tiny red berries. Chug collects it all and stands there, ankle-deep in the swamp, patting Poppy on the head. The moon hangs overhead, icy white and cool, lighting the whole world in silver.

"Good job!" I call.

"Iiiiis Pooooooppy oookaaaay?" Lenna asks, and she seems to be talking a lot faster than she did a moment ago, which is a relief.

"She's fine. I'm going down there to see."

"Take a weapon," Tok reminds me, standing up to come look out the window, probably to make sure his brother doesn't do anything stupid. "Witches may be rare, but other mobs aren't, and it's still night."

I pick up my iron sword and head down the stairs. The black cat meows at me from the window but doesn't seem interested in braving the swamp. I wonder if it was attached to the witch or if it just took shelter here, like we did. It doesn't seem upset, in any case. When I reach the ground—well, water—and glance up, the black cat is on the sill and rubbing against Tok as he pets it.

"What do you think these are?" Chug asks, holding up a bag.

I slosh over and look inside. "Berries, maybe?" I poke the mound of bright red spheres with a finger, and one rolls over to reveal . . . "Ew. Nope. Eyes. But what has red eyes?"

Chug closes the bag tightly. "I don't think I want to know. The other stuff is weird, too—powders and a rock. But maybe the potion will be useful."

"Chug! Mal!" Tok calls.

We look up. "What?" Chug calls back.

"There's a . . ."

"A what?"

"A thing."

Puzzled, Chug looks to where his pig is tied to the hut's post. "Yeah, Thingy is fine."

"No, a different thing. Look. Over there!"

We look to where Tok is pointing, and he's right. It's definitely a . . . thing.

A green, transparent block is hopping toward us. It has no legs or hands, no wings, no tail. It's just a cube. It has something that's almost a face, but it doesn't seem expressive or like the eyes can see anything. As it bounces, little splurts of green goo splatter around.

"It looks slimy," Chug says. "Should I kill it?"

I'm . . . not sure. It doesn't look cute like a llama; its color—green—is honestly a lot closer to zombies. I seem to remember the word "slime" as part of Nan's song. Still, I don't want to hurt something passive. "Leave us alone!" I shout at it as I wave my arms. "Shoo! Go away!"

The block keeps bouncing toward us, and I see another, smaller one behind it. They're headed right for us, squelching along.

The first one is about to reach us, and it's not stopping. "We have to run," I tell Chug, and we do, back to the hut and up the stairs, with Poppy right behind. Whatever those things are, even the wolf doesn't want to tussle with them.

"What is it?" Tok asks.

I rack my brain. "I think it might be a slime, like from Nan's song. *Vindicator, ghast, and slime*, it went."

"Great. It's a slime. At least it can't get to us." Chug sighs and stretches before leaning his sword against the wall. "Now, are we expecting more witches, or—"

Squelch.

Squelch.

Squelch.

Each squelch is louder than the one before, and we look to the hut's platform.

The slime hops up from our stairs and squelches toward us relentlessly. I still have my sword in hand, so I instinctively strike it.

But the slime doesn't die or make more angry squelching noises.

It . . . divides.

There was a medium-sized slime, and now there are two small ones. They hop toward us, and I lunge forward to slash at them, first one and then the other. They disappear, leaving only little balls of yet more green slime.

I look back at my friends, who are as shocked as I am at this event.

"A door," Tok murmurs. "Let me build a door." He hurries to the witch's crafting table.

"Oh no." Chug runs to the platform, sword back in his hand. "Are they gonna eat Thingy?"

I hurry to his side and we watch a variety of the slimes squelching toward the hut. Some reach deeper water and swim for a few moments before dividing into smaller slimes and then even smaller slimes before sinking. But some of the slimes, seemingly randomly, find enough solid ground to reach our stairs and bounce toward us, thankfully ignoring the pig. Chug waits on the top step, jabbing and slashing at them and sending the little slimes plopping back into the swamp, where they struggle and sink.

"This is kind of fun until—aggh!" He staggers back, reeling, after one of the bigger slimes bashes him in the face. He takes his revenge swiftly, and more little slimes tumble into the water. "Faster would be better, bro," he calls over his shoulder, sword flashing in the moonlight as Tok pulls down ornamental wood from the hut to make a door.

"Wiiiish IIII haaad myyy arrows," Lenna says, sighing in relief as the last word lands in a normal cadence.

"We'll get them in the morning. It seems like the slimes are a nighttime thing." We watch at the window as they bounce toward us, and I wonder what else this world can throw at us tonight. We've encountered witches and slimes and harming potions—things I didn't know existed just last week. I can only hope that Tok's door is strong enough to keep whatever wants to hurt us from getting in.

"Done!" Tok shouts triumphantly. He rushes to fit his door to the open space, his head swiveling toward his brother every time he hears Chug grunt or call a slime a rude name, which is often. "Come on, Chug!"

Chug whirls and dashes for the door as another slime leaps onto the platform behind him. Once he's inside, Tok slams the door shut, and the slime squelches against it indignantly. The black cat hisses and hurries to the corner where Tok is settling down with Candor.

"I don't know if I can sleep," Chug says as he slides down the wall to sit on the floor, legs out straight and head tilted to show a huge bruise on his face where the helmet couldn't protect him. "But I also don't really see the charm in staying awake."

I look around at my friends.

Lenna stands at the window by the stains of the potion that slowed her to a standstill, probably counting the arrows she lost in the swamp. She looks annoyed. Tok leans against the crafting table, nervously murmuring to the cats as he stares worriedly at his brother. Chug looks like he's about to fall over completely.

Whatever they need right now, I don't have it.

I don't have a rousing speech or a great idea.

I don't have cakes and pies.

I don't have answers.

There's a bottle of healing potion, but we all know we need to save it in case someone is in serious danger and not just dazed and slime-bruised.

I settle for digging some stew out of the bowl, scraping up as much meat as I can and taking it over to Chug. "This should help," I tell him.

"But that's for everyone," he protests.

"I didn't really like it anyway," Tok says. Chug's face falls, and his brother's eyes fly wide in shock at what he's just said. "Okay, you know what, Chug? I'm lying. It was delicious. You're a great cook. Really. But I'd rather you eat it right now and start healing than me wait four hours and eat it cold for breakfast."

"You can have mine, too," Lenna says.

"And mine. So there. Now you have to eat it. But you'd better enjoy it, because it was really good."

Half glow, half bruise, Chug practically dumps the stew down his throat. It's pretty amazing how food cures almost everything with him. I meet Tok's eyes and then Lenna's, giving them each a reassuring smile. I know they haven't suffered real damage, but I don't want to underestimate how terrible stress can make a person feel. Healing from a slime bruise or a zombie bite is a straightforward thing—eat food and sleep and you'll feel better soon. But healing from damage to your mind and heart takes a lot more work, I'm learning.

"I'll keep watch. Try to get some sleep," I tell them.

Everyone finds a wall to nestle up against—walls without potion stains or acid burns. The hut feels tiny and not nearly as safe and secure as the shelters I make digging into solid, dependable earth. Chug finishes his stew and burps before rolling over and almost immediately settling into snores.

I sit beside the hole in the floor left by the witch's potion and stare down into the swamp. By the moon's light, I see more slimes squelching around, but I know Tok's door will hold them off. Time goes funny, and it's just me and the sounds coming in through the window. I wonder what's happening back home, if my parents are packing up or too worried about me to bother. I wonder if all the crops have been destroyed. I can't bear to think about the plight of our gentle cows, mooing for their breakfast when there's no breakfast to be had. We have some wheat stored up, but our fodder for next year must be gone by now. Surely before it gets that bad, someone will have the good sense to break down part of the wall and let them out.

The cows need grass more than they need safety, and I hope my family and town understand that. It's different, once you've been outside those walls. You know what's out here, but you also know how far you'll go to take care of the ones you love.

Lenna wakes up at some point in time and tells me I need sleep, and she's right. She still looks annoyed, but I'm too tired to ask why. I settle into the warm spot she's left against the wall. The black cat curls up against my side and starts purring, and I stroke its soft fur and feel my eyes grow heavy. I try to fight it, try to stay awake in case something else happens tonight. I want so badly to keep my friends safe, and I don't want Lenna to feel alone. But sleep is one thing that can't be fought, and I can't hold on anymore. Even I'm not that strong.

18.

LENNA

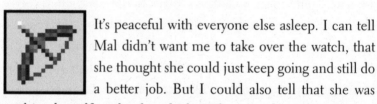 It's peaceful with everyone else asleep. I can tell Mal didn't want me to take over the watch, that she thought she could just keep going and still do a better job. But I could also tell that she was pushing herself too hard, and why? There are four of us. We can all take turns. She doesn't have to do everything herself. I'm not incompetent.

For the first time in my life, I'm mad at her, but I need to sort out my feelings before I bring it up. When that potion hit me, it was like everyone else was moving superfast, and she just snatched the bow out of my hands—and then told Chug to let Poppy loose to fight the witch. I know Mal was trying to make the best decision she could, but that was *my* bow, and that's *my* wolf, and I didn't agree to just be—well, not quite forgotten. And not quite removed. Ignored, maybe.

With the witch attacking us, there wasn't much time to make those decisions, but for me, trapped in my own little bubble and watching the world go on without me, it felt terrible. I hated seeing Poppy charge down the stairs toward danger knowing there was nothing I could do to help keep her safe.

I push those feelings down, just like I do at home. I'm accustomed to having my emotions ignored, and the world is too dangerous for us to fight among ourselves. What's a lifetime of friendship compared to two minutes of bad decisions? And, well, yeah, she did overrule me back at the village, too. It still smarts, but I'm not willing to keep chewing on it like a piece of tasteless, gristly meat. Mal is asleep, and the little hut is quiet.

Back home, I've spent plenty of nights as the only person awake. Sometimes I read books, although there aren't many of them in town and I've read them all. Most of the time I just curl up under my bed and think about things, let my mind wander wherever it wishes without any of my siblings around to complain that I'm daydreaming again.

Can you even daydream at night? Because what I do isn't night dreaming, but it's definitely dreaming, and no one else seems to understand it. Poppy is stretched out beside me, and idly stroking her fur only sends me further into my trance. Soon the sun is coming up, and nothing has happened, and it's as if time leaked out like water in a cracked bowl.

"Think we'll reach the woodland mansion today?" Chug asks as he stretches. His bruises from last night look much better, and even though my stomach grumbles, I'm glad the stew helped him recover.

"Maybe," Mal says. She points out the window toward the canopy of the dark forest. "You can see just a little bit of it peeking up through the trees, the dark brown bit."

We circle around the window and stare at that itty bitty corner of what must be a truly massive structure, much bigger than I'd imagined. Then again, I hadn't imagined the world was this big, much less one building in it. When you grow up behind tall walls, you begin to think you can take up only so much space. But once you're beyond those walls, you begin to see that everything is endless, including yourself.

Chug's stomach grumbles loud enough to startle Poppy. "I'm going to go pick some more mushroom for stew," he says, putting on his helmet. "Back in two twists of a pumpkin vine."

As he bounds out the door, Tok shouts, "Take your sword! It's not safe!"

But Chug just flaps a hand at him. "Nah, I need that hand for mushroom collection. It'll be fine. All the mobs spawn at night, and the mushroom is right here."

And, yes, there is a mushroom so close that I could throw a rock and hit it—or hit Chug, which might actually be a little more entertaining. Mal frowns as she watches him, and when she glances at my bow, I know that she's thinking about how much safer it feels when I have a full complement of arrows in hand.

"I'll see how many arrows I can find," she says, heading down the stairs without meeting my eyes. I'm not sure if she picked up on my mood or just feels guilty, but offering to bring back the arrows she lost is a welcome gesture.

Tok and I are alone, and we stand at the window with the cats on the sill, rubbing against us. He's as tense as I am, but I know he doesn't do well with interrogation, so I just wait to see what he'll say.

"My brother is so stubborn. He knows it's not safe. Why won't he listen?" Down below, Chug has climbed up a giant mushroom stem and is yanking down thick, rubbery chunks of red fungus. It tastes better than it looks, luckily, although I wish we had more meat to eat with it.

"Experience is a bad teacher," I say, echoing something I read in a book once. "And he's also Chug, so he's thinking about zombies, not about humans with bad intentions."

"But some mobs do show up during the day," Tok argues.

I shrug. "He hasn't seen one yet, so for him, maybe that isn't real." Picking up my bow, I head down the stairs, tapping my leg for Poppy to follow.

It's uncomfortable, feeling my boots sink into the mud as water oozes into my socks. At least I know I'm ready to go now that I don't have things to pack. All I need are Poppy and my weapons, and I can be ready the moment breakfast is done.

Mal walks over and hands me a fistful of wet arrows. She's gathered the ones that were sticking straight out of the bog, but we'll have to forage a little farther to collect the ones floating on top of the water.

"About yesterday," she starts.

I look up, curious to hear what she has to say, as Chug saunters away from the mushroom, arms loaded with spongy red and white fungus.

"We should grow these back home," he calls. "Think of it. Mushroom stew, mushroom sandwiches, mushroom salad—"

"Wait, what's that?" Mal asks.

There's movement behind Chug, and a strange creature appears out of the shadows. It's a mottled green with a frowning face, long neck, and short, skittering legs. Utterly silent, it stalks up behind Chug while he stands there, innocently grinning.

"Look out—" Mal calls.

"Run!" I scream, drowning her out.

The green creature stops with a hiss and starts to flash and expand, and I remember Nan showing us the creeper in the book. Chug runs toward us, and Mal has the good sense to point to the right, altering his course. I nock an arrow and fire it, hoping against hope that being wet all night didn't warp it. The arrow thwacks into the creeper, a solid hit, and it stops flashing.

For just a second, I think we're safe, but then it runs toward Mal and me. I hit it with another arrow before we dash for the hut. At least it's not as fast as us. Chug is still on the shore, but Mal scrambles up the steps, growling, "I should've brought my sword."

"Meow?" the witch's cat sits on the lowest step, tail twitching. I nock my third arrow, but much to my surprise, the creeper turns and runs away. I fire the arrow, but it's a miss.

After looking all around to make sure there are no more dangers, Chug hurries to us, having dropped half the mushrooms in the goopy swamp.

"What was that?" he asks.

"A creeper. It was in Nan's song. You know, *The creeper who explodes on sight.* It was a second away from blowing you up." I pet the witch's cat. "Luckily, they hate cats."

"So that's why we haven't seen one before," Mal says as she squats on the steps, watching the creeper disappear into the forest's shadows. "We're always close to Candor."

"I knew I liked that cat." Chug boops noses with the black cat, as his arms are full of mushrooms. "This one, too."

"You complete loon!"

We all look up at Tok, who stands on the hut's platform, furious. "All of you! You can't go running around without weapons. Nothing is safe here! Ever!"

Chug's jaw drops. "I was just picking mushrooms. How was I

supposed to know that a . . . galloping green reverse pig was going to come after me and explode?"

"Because Nan *told* you! She told us how dangerous it was out here. And we haven't even gotten to the illagers yet. Just because we can take on a zombie doesn't mean we're ready for an evoker." Tok exhales, and it reminds me of how my parents look when they're completely fed up with me. "Look. We can't let our guard down. The only time we're safe is when we're behind a locked door in a shelter, surrounded by torches. Every other moment, we have to look out for each other. If Lenna hadn't had her arrows, we'd be picking up chunks of you."

"Chug chunks!" Chug shouts, but Tok shouts back "It's not funny!" before Chug can laugh at his own joke.

What follows may be our first uncomfortable silence as a group. Back in town, it was us against everyone else — against our demanding parents and our fussy neighbors and the kids who excluded or bullied us because we were weird. But out here in the greater world, we're the only people around. The dangers are real, the stakes are higher, and when someone messes up, it could very well get one or all of us killed.

When one of us is sad, everyone else usually rallies to cheer them up.

But now we're just a mess of emotions. I'm a little angry at Mal still, I'm annoyed at Chug for being careless, and I'm uncomfortable with Tok because I've never heard him shout before, never seen him angry at his brother. Normally Chug protects Tok and Tok is grateful, but now Tok is fuming, which makes Chug act like a little kid who dropped a bowl and wants to melt into the floor while also yelling about how unfair it is that bowls are breakable.

Finally, Chug barrels past us up the stairs, muttering, "Stew. We can't keep yelling at each other if we've starved to death." Tok slides over so his brother can pass, but they both look away.

Mal and I go back to collecting arrows, and soon we've got all but one, which the swamp must've claimed. I sit on the porch while Mal runs over with her sword to chase some more of those random swamp chickens. I may be annoyed with her, but I still keep my bow ready, scanning the general area for anything that could hurt her. She takes the meat up to Chug, and I stay outside, as the air in the small hut must be fiercely thick just now.

"Stew's ready," Chug tells me after a while, and I head upstairs to eat.

The size of the hut doesn't give us much room, so we settle into corners, but not with our usual camaraderie. The stew is incredible, and I can tell Chug wants someone to say so, but Tok is as stiff as a board and Mal seems lost.

"It's delicious," I say, and Chug gives me a wobbling smile.

Tok clears his throat. "Not worth dying for, though."

For a long moment, the only sound is stew slurping and Poppy sniffing hopefully. The silence is oppressive and my friends are upset and I can't take it anymore. I feel like I'm going to explode like that creeper, like I should be flashing and hissing.

"We can't be like this."

Everyone looks up at me in surprise, so I go on.

"We can't just be angry and silent."

I look to Mal, expecting her to speak up, but for once, she seems speechless. I go on.

"We knew it was going to be hard outside the wall—Nan made sure of that. She tried to prepare us, but she only had a few hours for what she'd learned in a lifetime. It's scary out here. There are more dangers than we realized, more than we'd ever imagined. And all we have is each other."

I look into Mal's eyes, and Chug's, and Tok's. Do I see a glimmer of hope there?

"It's us against the world. Jarro might not have us cornered in an alley, but we have to accept that every time we step outside that door, any one of us could get injured. Or die. Not taking precautions doesn't just endanger one of us—it endangers all of us. And the pets."

Mal is fighting tears, so I give her a gentle smile.

"But they're in it, too. We all work together. We keep our weapons ready, and we don't take risks unless we have to. We're going to reach the woodland mansion soon, and from what I remember of Nan's books, it's going to be harder than anything we've seen so far."

"Worse than getting exploded by a reverse pig?" Chug says.

"Injured is injured and dying is dying, and we only have one healing potion. You saw what the vex's potions did to the pumpkins." I rub my toe over the hole in the floor. "And what the witch's potions did here. That's what we're facing. Not just stupid zombies, but mobs that attack with cunning. And if we want to save our town, we have to end them before they can end us."

"Yeah!" Chug shouts, loud enough that Thingy squeals in surprise from down below. He stands. "Lenna's right. I messed up, leaving my sword behind, and I'm sorry. I won't do that again. I just don't want to be fighting with my best friends."

Mal stands up beside him, her confident smile back in place. "I messed up, too. I know I can be bossy, but I made decisions without consulting you guys, and we're a group of equals. I can't promise I won't do it again, but I'll listen better."

Tok stands, and since I'm the last one on the floor, I stand, too.

"I'm sorry I'm not a fighter," he says softly. "When I can't contribute, I feel helpless, and when I feel helpless, I get mad. I just want to keep everyone safe, but that's hard to do when you're no good with a sword or a bow."

Chug slings his arm around his brother's neck with a grin. "What you do is plenty helpful. You've saved our rumps again and again. You made a sword out of nothing, bro! You make the doors that keep us safe. I'm so proud of you."

He pulls Tok into a hug, and Tok pretty much disappears. They pound each other on the back in the way that boys do, and when they pull apart to dash at their eyes, there's a new respect and understanding there.

And then my friends look to me.

And I realize that giving a speech to everyone is a lot easier than talking about your own feelings, but since they all did, now I have to, too.

"I'm used to people making decisions for me," I say, choosing my words carefully. "Out here, without my family, it's a relief to just be exactly who I am and not have to change myself so I don't get yelled at. But I'm starting to realize that I like making decisions and you guys can't just automatically guess how I want to be treated. So don't tell my wolf to do things. And don't touch my arrows. Please." My smile wobbles, tears in my eyes.

Mal pulls me and Chug into a hug, and since Tok is still under Chug's arm, he's caught up in it, too. We're all in a tangle, and whooboy, does somebody stink.

"Chug, you've got to wash your hands more," Tok says quietly, and then Chug starts shaking before breaking out in great big guffaws of laughter. I can't help joining him, and neither can anyone else.

We're not bad apples, we're not misfits, we're not living soft lives inside tall walls. We're just four kids standing in a witch's hut in the middle of a swamp, laughing maniacally as we prepare to raid a woodland mansion full of hostile mobs in order to save our town. For just a moment, while we laugh, it feels like we can do anything if we're together, like it might actually be easy.

I know very well it won't be.

I should be scared, but with friends like this by my side, what could stop us?

"We're not the Bad Apples anymore," I say with a grin. "Now we're the Mob Squad."

19

CHUG

Emotions make me hungry, but then again, everything makes me hungry. I've still got bruises from the slime attack, and I stubbed a toe running through the swamp, so I'm extra *extra* hungry. Might as well eat the rest of the stew before we go gallivanting into a big scary mansion, right? Gotta keep that health up.

Once I've licked the bowl clean, we head out. The witch's cat follows along with us, and I can tell that Tok is really happy about that. Candor doesn't officially belong to Tok—she's a barn cat from Krog's farm that somehow ended up in our yard and stayed, yet another reason Krog is always annoyed with us. Now I guess we have two cats. And a pig. Although I don't feel particularly safe in the swamp right now, I'm glad to have Thingy back by my side, and if we hadn't lost all of our loot, I'd probably rig him up to ride again so I wouldn't have to deal with all this moist squelching.

"What are you going to name her?" I ask, falling in step with my brother, who's in a much better mood after Lenna's speech.

"*Him*, I've decided," he corrects. "And his name is Clarity."

I blink at him as Candor and Clarity bound past us, anxious to get out of the swamp and onto dry land. "You name things weird."

"All names are weird. They're just made-up sounds."

And that stuns me into silence. My brother says stuff like that all the time, stuff I've never even thought about thinking about, and it definitely makes me think.

The forest becomes crowded, with trees and hills and outcroppings all jumbled up so closely that we can barely tell where we're going. We definitely can't see any sign of the woodland mansion, but I trust that Mal will get us there. She always knows what to do and where to go. We've never needed a map before, but Mal's already mastered how to follow one—and committed it to memory. That blows my mind, too. Lots of things do.

We're a well-oiled machine now. Mal leads, sword in hand. I follow in my armor, sword also in hand and ready to wield it. Tok follows me, and now that he can't read Nan's books, he has to settle for peering at the wonders of the woods. Every now and then, he murmurs in surprise at something new he's found, some plant or creature he's never seen before. I didn't know there were more than two kinds of trees in the world, but there are apparently many kinds of trees, even if they all look alike to me.

The cats dart in and out of the bushes, always coming back to check in with us. Thingy stays by my side, snuffling hopefully at the pocket that once held little treats. Last of all comes Lenna, a bit behind us, scanning all around with her bow at the ready and her wolf at her side. Lenna looks like she belongs here, like she's part of the forest. It seems very natural, and yet it's very weird. Lenna never really fit in back home.

Thwack.

I look back, and Lenna has just shot a zombie. It falls, dropping a potato and some meat, and Poppy darts over to eat the meat and retrieve the potato. I can't imagine choosing to eat raw, rotten, green-tinged meat when there's a perfectly good potato sitting right there, but I've also never been a wolf.

With no food packed, all our stomachs make a grumbling chorus. A random sheep appears, and soon we're handing out bits of raw mutton. Raw anything is not my favorite food, and I can't help fantasizing about the snacks Nan packed for us, pies and cookies and bread and cooked meat. I like it out here, beyond the wall, but I really miss decent food. I'm bigger than anyone else and I eat more than they do and honestly, it just takes a lot of fuel to keep me going. I briefly wish we were back home, eating Mom's steak and potatoes, but then I remember that we weren't supposed to leave Cornucopia at all, and that it's possibly the biggest rule we've ever broken.

I don't want to think about what's going to happen when we get back home. Maybe they'll treat us like heroes and throw a big feast. Or maybe they'll never really know what we accomplished— if we accomplish it—and they'll just be furious with us for leaving and then make us all abandon the town anyway.

Nope.

Not going to think that way. That's stinkin' thinkin', and I'm all for the sunny side of things. I scratch Thingy's back the way he likes, and he oinks happily. He keeps eating flowers and digging up roots, so he, at least, is content with our progress.

"I think we're getting close," Mal calls, but softly.

I walk faster to keep pace with her. "Are we going to build a shelter?" I look up at the tiny splotches of sky that can be seen through the dark green canopy. I'm pretty sure it's afternoon.

"I'm worried that making all that noise might alert the mobs to our presence. We can find a place in the woodland mansion to hide." No one says anything, and she adds, "But I'm open to feedback!"

We all laugh at that—it's a definite change in our Mal. I kind of want to argue, but I don't. I trust her, and if Tok doesn't have anything to say, that means he agrees. It's nice that she's more willing to consider our thoughts, though. A good leader should always listen, not that my parents listen when I try to tell them that.

Still, how are we just going to hide in someone's house? I get that it's a *big* house, but I can't imagine a random group of kids just deciding to come hide out in my house overnight and expecting that they won't be found. I guess if things get really bad, we can climb up a tree and sleep there, but it certainly doesn't sound comfortable.

"There!" Mal points at a darker brown blotch among the trees up ahead, obscured by branches and leaves. She speeds up, and I match her pace. The mansion comes into focus, and . . .

Whoa.

It really is huge.

Our house has two bedrooms and a kitchen and common area, and it's very comfortable. Compared to some houses in Cornucopia, it's big. But this house, this mansion, is downright enormous. It's not quite as big as our town, but it could barely fit within the walls. No wonder Mal isn't worried about shelter—there's got to be plenty of places to hide in here.

Unless every room is full?

Maybe there are dozens or hundreds of hostile mobs living in there, doing . . . whatever mobs do.

I shiver but hide it by tossing my head, which really just makes my helmet clank. My fingers tense on my sword's hilt. I wasn't prepared for something quite this large, and it's making me break out in goose bumps.

I drop back beside Tok. "Are you seeing this, bro?"

He nods eagerly. "It's fascinating. Who built it? Why? If there are many of them around the world, were they all built by the same person or people or by different groups? Do they share blueprints?" He shakes his head. "I can't wait to see what's inside."

My brow scrunches down. That's so Tok. I get stung by a bee, and he's fascinated by the bee. "Bro, it's basically a monster box. Just a big ol' box full of monsters."

He grins at me. "But possibly other things! I get that you may not be excited about the possibility of books, but there will probably be food."

I nod. He's right. "Good call. You take the books, I'll take the food. Just be careful, okay?"

He cocks his head at me. "I'm always careful."

"Not when you're so focused on something you want to learn about that you put yourself directly in harm's way."

"Good call. But you have to be careful, too."

I hook my arm around his neck and give him a noogie, which I know he doesn't really mind, because I've asked. "Okay. We'll both be careful. No big deal. Kill a couple of hexes—"

"Vexes."

"Yeah, that's what I said. Kill a couple of vexes, take the loot, and head back home."

The weird thing about having your arm around someone is that it can't go on for as long as you might prefer because it just gets weird. I'm scared, but I don't want anyone to know I'm scared, and I know I can't keep walking with my arm around Tok, so I let go and pat his shoulder before dropping back with Lenna.

"You ready?" I ask.

She holds up a stack of arrows. "I wish I had more, but I don't have the raw materials to make them. And I heard Mal say we weren't going to dig today, so I guess I just have to be careful with what I have."

I look down at my armor. It's rough stuff, but it works. "Do you want some of my armor?"

Lenna shakes her head. "No way. If you're running in close, you get the armor. I plan to stay back with my bow. Just make sure you never stand between me and a mob, okay?"

"I mean, I'll try. When I'm in the middle of taking down a zombie, I don't really think about where you are and what you might be doing." Poppy reaches out to lick my hand, and I pat her smooth head. She wags her tail, and I am again dumbfounded that our Founders brought cats into the town but not wolves.

Then again, considering what I've seen of cats so far, they may have left cats out entirely, but the clever things climbed over the wall and just decided to stay.

I give Lenna a fist bump and jog back to my place between Mal and Tok. Swishing my sword through some branches, I'm satisfied to see a clean cut through the leaves. It's funny, how just a few days ago I saw a sword for the first time and thought it was just a really awkward knife. There are so many things in the world that have just gone on existing outside our walls while we've lived our same old lives, unaware of them.

Mal moves a branch aside, and there it is—the woodland mansion. The walls are dark wood, and big glass windows show flashes of stone and red fabric within. We both instinctively duck—if we can see in, then anything inside can see out. We watch for a moment as Tok and Lenna catch up with us, but I don't see any movement.

"Where's the door?" I ask.

"The map didn't say."

I scratch Thingy's head and frown. "We should dig a little pit for him. I'll fight better if he's not trying to get in my pockets."

Mal nods and jogs a bit away, behind a stone outcropping. She quickly makes a little place for Thingy to stay in, and I lure him in and kiss his forehead. "Stay here and be quiet," I say. I used to worry about him, but we've learned that the mobs don't really care about pigs all that much. And Thingy himself is mostly concerned with food, or the current lack thereof. I toss in our last zombie-dropped potato and hope he can live off his fat for a while.

When I rejoin my friends, I can't help wishing the cats would stay put as readily as a pig. They come and go as they please, but I'm not superexcited about them twining around my ankles while I'm fighting a skeleton or meowing loudly and alerting some monster to our presence. Still, they do keep creepers away, so hopefully they'll behave. And I can't ignore the fact that they make Tok feel better, and I want him to have what he needs.

Of course, what I really want is for him to find somewhere safe and hide there while we fight the mobs. He's the only one of us that hasn't naturally discovered a skill for fighting. We need his tools and equipment—I can't ignore the fact that he made this sword out of pretty much nothing—but in the middle of a fight, a crafting table isn't going to save anyone. I just have to keep myself between him and danger. But that's what I've always tried to do.

Mal leads us along the mansion's wall, and we stay low and out of sight of the windows, which are a little higher up. The mansion is three stories tall, and as we pass each window, I hear ominous grunts and groans. The wall seems to go on forever, just like our town's wall, except now we're the ones on the outside trying to get in.

That's kind of funny—we're here because those vexes found a way past our wall, and now we're trying to find a way past theirs.

We don't pass any doors, but we do reach a corner. Mal scouts around it before we continue creeping along the next wall. There are some pretty flowers in the little clearing around the mansion, the only break in the darkness of the forest's heavy canopy. I glance back, and sure enough, Tok is staring at them intently, wishing, I'm sure, for a book to tell him their names and uses. It takes hours for us to hurry along the wall—or, yes, okay, minutes, but they feel like hours—and then we're at another corner. The building begins to feel impossibly huge, and I wonder if maybe it has no door at all and the mobs have sealed themselves within, just like we do in Cornucopia.

But—well, we know at least one evoker left this place. It brought the vexes to our town, which is why we're here.

On the last wall, we finally find stairs up to a grand set of open double doors. There are big windows on either side, and Mal watches them for a long time before determining that it's safe—or safe enough. Not a single shadow has moved beyond the glass, and so we rush up the stairs and through the doorway. A thick red carpet, bigger and brighter than any I've ever seen, leads into the mansion and down two identical halls, one to the left and one to the right. A stone stairwell lies straight ahead. The floors are polished wood, as golden as honey, while the walls are dark and shining, lined with torches and higher than our ceilings back home.

It's impressive—I'll give them that. I've never seen a building so big, so beautiful, so imposing.

And yet is seems so devoid of life. The illagers we've come to exterminate must lurk farther within.

Not a single thing appears. No one greets us—not that we made ourselves known. And I don't hear a single sound.

Mal hurries behind the stone stairs, to a dark and empty alcove.

"Let's sleep here," she says.

"Out in the open?" Lenna asks.

Mal shrugs. "Why would anyone ever go behind the stairs? It's as good a place as any, and it's totally hidden from view."

It's dark back here behind the stairs, but the sun is going down swiftly, and we all know we don't have much time to do anything else—we can't explore this place at night. I pass out my last bits of mutton, and we take turns cooking them over a torch.

"I'll take first watch," I say—because I ate the last of the meat, and now I feel a little bad about it.

Mal nods, and Tok and Lenna curl up in the corners. The cats snuggle with Tok, and Poppy turns three times and settles against Lenna. They're both asleep in moments. Life outside the wall has that effect—all the walking, all the fighting, all the worry. It's better to be dreaming of food than listening to your stomach rumble.

Only Mal and I are left, one torch between us in the darkest part of our nook, directly behind the staircase.

"Think we'll make it tomorrow?" I ask.

Mal stares into the flames, looking as uncertain as I've ever seen her in all our years as friends.

"We have to," she says finally. She sits back against the wall, eyes on the torch.

"You sleep," she says. "I don't think I can."

I would argue with Mal, but I've never won an argument with her, so why start now?

I curl up as much as my armor will allow and go to sleep, my sword tight in my fist.

20.

TOK

When I open my eyes, everything is dark, and I would panic if not for Chug's hand on my shoulder.

"Shh. It's fine, bro," he whispers. And this is so vastly preferable to having his fishy-mushroomy-muttony hand over my mouth that I just nod and sit up. I have no idea what time it is, and I start to freak out, and—

Ah, yes. We're directly behind the stairs of the woodland mansion, meaning that there's no way for any light whatsoever to reach us. But we're all here and safe, and the cats wake and stretch and purr, so all is as well as it can be.

Everyone is awake now, but no one looks well-rested. We're all uneasy and jumpy. It's a funny thing how as you work toward a difficult goal, you tell yourself that once you reach it, everything will be easy. But sometimes—often—you get where you're going and only find a new challenge at the end of that road. We wanted to find the woodland mansion, and we did. But now we have to deal with it.

And whatever lives inside it.

As Chug stands, he knocks over his helmet, and we all wince at the noise. We have no idea what we're going to find here, no idea if the mansion's denizens are listening for interlopers. No one found us last night—that we know of—but who would expect four kids and their pets to sneak into a gigantic house and camp out? And for that matter, who built this place, and why? There was nothing on the topic in Nan's books, and believe me, I looked.

When Mal stands, Lenna and I scramble to our feet. The three of them take up their weapons, and I—well, I don't have a weapon. Mal hands me her pickaxe, and it's funny how I felt competent making it and yet feel completely incompetent holding it with both hands.

"Left or right?" Mal asks, referring to the identical symmetrical halls leading away from the mansion doors, which are still, against all sense, thrown wide open. "Or should we start with the stairs?"

"It doesn't matter," I tell her. "Each option has a fifty percent chance of being wonderful or terrible."

She nods and heads to the right. I keep my usual spot between Chug and Lenna, wishing I could make the cats do anything other than trot along beside me like we're having a perfectly nice time. They're not like Thingy or Poppy or the llamas—I can't change their behavior at all. Which is the nice thing about cats until it isn't.

The hallway turns a corner and continues. We walk down the center of the red carpet, the sunlight shining through big windows, bigger than any windows back home. There's an open room on the right, and Mal holds her sword more aggressively as she steps inside, torch held aloft. Chug follows, and when I don't hear the groans of zombies or the clash of swords, I follow.

Mal and Chug have stopped side by side and are staring, dumbfounded, at a very odd room. It's all stone, and there's a live tree growing out of a basin in one corner and a fountain with flowing water in another corner.

And nothing else.

"Uh, what is this place?" Chug asks.

I stand beside him. "No one knows. We've never been here before. We are literally experiencing the same mystification as you are right now."

"But what—"

I pat him on the back. "Let it go, bro. Some questions can't be answered."

It's definitely peculiar, but at least there's no one in here trying to kill us. And maybe whoever lives here—or whoever built this place—has a love of nature and art, which usually suggests a sense of culture and reason.

Maybe.

Lenna is by the door, glancing up and down the hall, bow at the ready. Poppy sits at her feet, tongue out, waiting. When Mal heads for the next room, we follow. It's ominous, the way we haven't seen a single person here. Doors wide open, no footsteps or voices. Maybe there's no one here? Which would mean the vexes and evokers and vindicators from Nan's books and song are elsewhere.

Like headed right for our town.

I don't voice this concern. Making everyone else worry is pointless. We're only one room in, and there must be dozens of rooms here. Either we'll see someone or we won't, but we have to be ready either way, not philosophizing.

The next room is full of tulips—and nothing else. They're

pretty flowers, but neither they nor their pots are useful to us right now. The third room is a bedroom with one bed, and we all stare at it covetously. The thought of an open, airy room with a cozy bed is a siren song we'd all like to give in to. But I'm aware, as I'm sure the others are, that it's not wise to sleep in someone else's bed, especially when you're expecting hostility.

We move to the next room, and it's the strangest room yet, because it contains only a giant statue of a chicken.

"If only Rex could see this, right?" Chug says with a chuckle. "For a guy whose family has always raised chickens, he kinda seems to hate chickens."

It's funny because it's true. The people in our town are born and bred to continue their family's farms, but Rex is always complaining about chickens. Krog hates his beetroots, too, but that makes a lot more sense. Then again, Chug and I aren't super-excited about pumpkins and Lenna barely has anything to do with her family's mine, so maybe some people are just a bad fit. I know what Chug's thinking about—how much fun it would be to put this statue in Rex's front yard. It really is quite impressive and lifelike. My stomach growls in recognition of the artistry. We haven't had breakfast, after all.

As we head for the next room, I realize that I couldn't begin to guess what we'll find. It's like this place was planned by someone closing their eyes and pointing at a list of oddities. Outside of the bedroom, nothing makes sense. And because it's in the middle of nonsense, the bedroom seems odd, too.

The fifth room is clearly for storage, with fences and torches and a big chest.

We all sort of meet one another's gaze, deciding that whatever is here is free for the taking. If we're going to fight these people, why wouldn't we take what we could from them? Lenna guards the door and Chug stands in the middle of the room, sword ready, while Mal opens the unlocked chest.

"Whoa," she breathes.

I join her, and "whoa" is right. The chest is packed with useful objects, and I'm immediately dreaming of returning for that bed. There's a diamond sword, a healing potion, and a book labeled *Flame Enchantment*. Mal gives the diamond sword to Chug, who hands her his iron sword. She puts both the sword and the healing potion in her pocket, which is much safer than handing it to Chug, who might get thirsty and accidentally gulp it down.

I of course snatch up the book and flip through it quickly, a grin spreading across my face. "Lenna, hand me your bow."

"What? No! Why?"

It's nice to see her so attached to something—and so willing to defend it. Back in Cornucopia, she just seemed to drift, and whenever there was an argument, she gave up to avoid conflict. Now she's staring at me like one of Mal's cows when denied a pumpkin.

I point at the book. "I'm going to enchant your bow. Now every time you shoot an arrow, your target will catch fire."

Lenna grins ferociously, and I realize I always want to be on her side—although, to be honest, I've known that for a long time. She hands me her bow, and I read the incantation in the book, but nothing happens.

"Oh, I forgot. We need an anvil. There's got to be one somewhere around here, right?" I return her bow and tuck the book in my pocket, excited by the prospect of having the power to make someone else more lethal, even if I'm not skilled at wielding weapons myself.

Back in the hall, we find another corner, and Mal scouts around it before leading us down the next hallway. The first room we find is a dining room, and the moment we spot the food sitting on a small serving counter, we drool. For Chug, this means wet spots appear on the red carpet under his boots, but no one chides him because we're all starving. It looks like breakfast was just served, a nice buffet, but then someone ate a bit from each pot and left. A stack of bowls waits beside bottles of water.

"No way that's poisoned, right?" Chug asks.

I poke his chin to make him shut his mouth and stop drooling. "What would be the point? If no one knows we're here, they wouldn't think to poison their own food. Some rich guy probably lives here, and there's no way he could eat all that."

Mal catches my eye, giving me a significant look. "So it's safe?"

I lean in and sniff, which is mostly for show, as I have no idea what poison smells like. It occurs to me that if someone wanted to hurt us, they've had plenty of chances. And yet we've seen no one.

I reach for a piece of bread and take a bite, and I realize this might be the bravest thing I've ever done. It tastes totally normal, and I've barely swallowed before I take another bite.

"My highly specialized opinion is that it's probably reasonably safe," I say.

Chug grabs a bowl and scoops up some potatoes, and we all follow suit. It's weird, eating food that doesn't taste like my mom's food. I've never had anything else, unless you count treats from the Hub in town or Nan's goodies or Chug's grub. I have no idea if dinner at Lenna's house tastes like dinner at my house. All I know is that these potatoes are better than starving, even if they could use a little salt.

We eat quickly, wolfishly—especially Poppy, who receives her own bowl and licks it clean. I give the cats some fish in two separate bowls so they won't fight. Chug glances wistfully out the window, and I know he's thinking that Thingy is probably hungry, too. It's not long before I'm stuffed, although it takes Chug a few minutes more.

"Don't get too full," I warn him.

"Like that's even possible," he shoots back.

We shove cookies in our pockets and head for the next room. I'm fairly certain I've been poisoned and am hallucinating, because this room is a library filled with books. Hundreds of books. Thousands. More books than I've ever seen in my whole life put together. Shelves and shelves and shelves of books, with a few lounge-type places to read them.

"It was nice knowing you guys," I say, wandering over to the nearest row of leather-bound tomes and running my fingertips reverently over their spines. "I'm going to live here forever."

Chug gently tugs the back of my shirt. "Maybe once we've taken down all those vex things and all the zombies and whatever, but if I don't get round two at the buffet, you don't get to sink into a book stupor."

"But there could be knowledge!" I squawk. "More enchantments! Recipes! A book titled *So You Think You Can Storm the Woodland Mansion.*"

"Kill monsters, *then* steal books," Chug croons.

It takes everything I have to leave the library, but he's right. We don't have time for me to immerse myself in delicious books when we have a town to save, and I don't have time to pick just the right ones to carry with me, not when I need that pocket space. I can feel the library pulling me back, but I follow Chug into the hall, where Mal is already standing in the doorway of the next room. This one is full of cobwebs, and we all shudder in harmony.

"No thank you," Mal says, hurrying to the next door.

This space, mercifully and thankfully, is full of wool—just a big pile of luscious wool in a range of blues—and we stuff that gleefully into our pockets, very well aware that now all we need is some spare wood to make the beds that will save us from another night on the cold, hard ground.

"I like stealing wool better than smelling sheep," Chug notes. He's right—Robb from school always reeks of wet sheep, even if his clothes look nice.

The last room on this back hall is another bedroom, very ostentatious, with banners and thick rugs and an enormous bed. We don't take it, as it would be way too big for our shelters, and the carpets are too heavy and ugly to even consider.

In the back of my head, all this time, I'm thinking about how something feels slightly wrong about just taking whatever we find here. Then again, whoever lives here didn't seem to mind sending their vexes to destroy our crops. Is it okay to take from someone who has taken from you? Does that make us bad guys, too?

I'm overthinking it. We need every advantage we can get. In the world outside our town, a helmet or sword is the difference between life and death. A meal is the difference between damage and healing. A bed is the difference between good sleep and waking up without the strength you need to stay alive. We've earned everything in our pockets.

Mal peeks around the hallway and returns looking grim. When I hear a groan, I know why.

"Zombie," she says. "Lenna?"

Lenna barely has to look around the corner before she's taken down the zombie. She grins, cocky, and Chug gives her a high five. We're all feeling confident, right up until someone runs around the corner and hits Mal with an axe.

21.

MAL

I stagger back, seeing stars.

Did I . . . just get struck with an axe?

The monster sprints at me again, axe raised, and my arm feels dead. An arrow lodges in the creature's chest, and then Chug darts forward and gets in a strike with his new diamond sword. This thing is not a person. It looks a little like the villagers we met when we were looking for a map, not like us at all, but it's a strange, dead gray. Its eyes are empty, its mouth set in a frown.

"Hn hmm," it grunts with satisfaction, raising its axe as Chug ducks and gets in under its guard with the sword.

My assailant falls to the ground, and I can only stand there and hold my arm. It hurts, but my brain is the real problem. Thing is, no one has ever hit me before. Jarro has threatened, the brigands prodded, but no one I've encountered thus far has actually *hit* me. And I'm pretty likeable, with a reputation as a good kid, except in the eyes of neighbors who don't like our friend group. I do my chores, treat my parents with respect, show deference to the shopkeepers in the Hub.

But this stranger, this—"monster" is the only word that comes to mind—hit me.

With an axe.

It's a lot to take in.

"Are you okay?" Tok asks, rushing over as Lenna and Chug keep watch for more enemies.

"I—I don't know. It hit me." The words sound empty and hollow and wooden.

Tok inspects my arm, which—I can't look at right now.

"It could be worse, but you should probably eat something." He nods at Lenna, and she runs away, probably to the dining room. She's back in two twitches of a cow tail, and they all cluck around me while I fill up on steak. I do feel better afterward, and I'll admit I thought about using the healing potion before remembering that things could get a lot worse.

"What was that thing?" Chug asks.

"Vindicator," I croak, my brain starting to work again. "We're lucky it wasn't an evoker. Evokers are the ones that command the vexes, like the one Lenna saw in the field. Vindicators just attack you with axes. Evokers attack you with magic." I can see those pages of Nan's books, clear as anything in my memory. As interesting as all the animals and zombies were, it was the witches, vindicators, and evokers that captured my imagination, I guess because . . . well, they look so much like us. And we know that, for whatever reason, they want to actively cause us harm. But we have to remember: They're not people.

According to the books, they don't talk or think or form bonds. They don't have children. They just . . . spawn, fully formed. No one knows how or why, or they didn't when those books were written. And yet, when one attacks you, it definitely feels like you're being attacked by a person, and now I know that for myself.

While I'm recovering, Tok stands nearby, his cats rubbing against me. Chug faces down the new hallway while Lenna stands at the corner, defending us from whatever dangers might still lurk in the previous hall. There's one more hall on this floor, and then the stairs go up to another floor that will probably be just as nonsensical as this one. The loot we found in the chest was superhelpful, but I see now that we've grown complacent.

A zombie here, a skeleton there. Those guys, we know how to handle.

But this woodland mansion is a whole new sort of place where we have no idea what to expect. If there's a vindicator here, there will be evokers, and the evokers may be the reason that we're here, but that doesn't mean vanquishing them will be easy. We have to be ready.

"Let's try the next room," I say as I finish my last chunk of steak and stand, glad to feel my strength returning. Being out here in the hallway makes me feel vulnerable, like anything could come at us at any moment. I'd much rather be in a room, where we're hidden from view.

No one moves, and I remember: I'm the leader. They're accustomed to following me.

I hold my sword up, glad to see that my arm is no longer shaking, because it definitely was for a while there. For the briefest moment, I think about asking Chug to go first, but I see the way my friends look at me—with trust, with expectation. I can't show weakness or timidity now, because that might make them doubt me, or, even worse, themselves. With no other choice, I move into the next room, prepared to find another vindicator running at me, axe raised.

Thankfully, the room is empty of enemies, just a bedroom with a ladder up to a loft. I head for the closet while Tok scurries up the ladder.

"There's a chest!" he cries. It creaks open. "Ha! More loot! Here, Chug." Tok tosses down a diamond chest plate, which Chug quickly puts on, handing his iron chest plate to me.

"Maybe Tok should wear it," I say.

"No way," Tok calls. "Fighters get armor, runners get . . . um . . ."

"The runs?" Chug offers.

Tok makes a strangled noise. "Uh, no. Let's hope not. Runners get new boots, should they show up. Although my boots are fine. There's also some bread, a golden apple, another enchanted book, and a mysterious disc labeled only 'cat.'"

"Toss me that apple, bro," Chug says.

Tok climbs down, holding it close. "No way. It'll help someone heal faster when they really need it. It's not a . . . a snack food."

"All foods are snack foods if you try hard enough," Chug grumbles, but not unkindly, as he's still staring down at his new diamond chest plate, holding his diamond sword up to it. "I really love woodland mansions, by the way."

A feeling of dread shivers down my spine at his words. "It's been easy so far," I remind him—and everyone else. "But there will be more vindicators and zombies and skeletons, and eventually, we're going to find an evoker."

"We can take 'em down!" Chug cheers. "And then find more chests!"

Tok's eyes meet mine as Chug dances around. I can see that he agrees with me—we've been lucky, and it's bound to get worse. We have to clear out every evoker in this mansion if we want to save our town. But when Chug is in a good mood, he's more effective than usual, so neither of us will burst his bubble.

Outside the door, Lenna's bow thwacks. "Skeleton," she says, drawing another arrow. Before we can reach the door, she adds, "Got it. Ooh, and it dropped arrows." She rushes down the hall to collect the arrows, and I'm just exiting the room when I see a familiar form running toward her.

"Lenna, vindicator!" I shout. She rolls out of the way and into another room, out of sight. The vindicator tries to follow her, its axe at the ready, so I charge it with my sword. I get in three slashes and it topples without doing any damage to me, thanks to my new iron chest plate.

"Mal, help!"

In the next room, Lenna is frantically shooting arrows at a skeleton wearing a helmet and armor, and it isn't going down as easily as the last one. As she fires arrow after arrow, I run in and start hacking, my sword cracking against bone. We finally reduce it to a pile of ribs, and Lenna kicks the iron helmet over to me. I put it on, and even if I don't like how it restricts my sight, I'm definitely here for keeping my head safe.

Lenna's collected a full stack of arrows now, and the room is clear. I look around, hoping for a chest—and there is one! But it's empty. The rest of the room is, oddly, dedicated to mushrooms. When Tok and Chug join us, we throw several of the mushrooms into our pockets for later. There might not always be a dining room around, and we need to keep up our strength.

The next room looks like a blacksmith's outfit, but the charac-

ter who runs at us, axe swinging for our heads, is another vindicator. We make quick work of it, and I'm ready to leave, but Tok is
fascinated by the anvil.

"I think I remember how the book said to do this," he murmurs. "Lenna, hand me your bow."

Chug takes Lenna's post at the door as she gives Tok her bow
and stands nearby as if it's physically painful for her to be separated from her chosen weapon. Tok pulls the enchanted book
from the first chest out of his pocket and fiddles with the anvil,
bow, and book for several minutes until the bow starts to glow. I
don't actually understand anything about what's happening, but
he seems elated as he hands the bow back to Lenna. "Flame enchantment." She nods and runs back to the door, and Tok holds
out his hand to Chug. "Give me your sword."

Chug hugs his sword, looking affronted. "What? No! This is
my sword, bro! What if you break it?"

Tok rubs his temple, a familiar gesture. "I'm not going to break
it. I'm going to enchant it."

"To do *what*?"

Tok's grin, for once, echoes Chug's. "I'm going to enchant it to
do more harm."

Chug doesn't argue at all, just holds out the diamond sword.
The cats play with a dust bunny while Tok pulls out the other
enchanted book and does his work, and then the diamond sword
takes on an otherworldly glimmer.

Chug swishes it through the air. "Feels the same."

"Bro, it's glowing."

"But that's something you see, not feel."

They're dangerously close to quibbling, so I step in. "If you
don't want it, I'll take it."

Chug holds the sword closer. "First of all, how dare you?"

I can't help but laugh. Thanks to the food and our success, we're all in better moods. We move swiftly through the next few rooms, which are all bedrooms containing neither loot nor mobs, and soon stand before the stairs where we started. Lenna and Poppy linger a bit behind. Chug runs out the door, and I'm about to call him back when he suddenly reappears, looking relieved.

"Thingy's fine," he assures me.

I try not to smirk. "That's some pig," I say.

For a moment, we mill around, but I'm not willing to waste precious daylight being frightened of something I have to do either way. I head up the stairs, glad to know that Chug is right behind me with an enchanted diamond sword. The second floor seems to have the same layout, and we start clearing rooms. We find more bedrooms, a small library that makes Tok whimper with longing, another dining room that lacks anything good to eat, and a very odd room full of nothing but dark oak saplings. Like a well-oiled machine, we take down zombies and skeletons and vindicators and collect their loot—and Lenna loves how her enchanted bow sets its targets on fire. We find more armor and weapons, and I'm thrilled when I find a diamond pickaxe.

Except . . . there's something familiar about it.

"Stop," I say. Everyone stares at me, curious. I turn the pickaxe over in my hands, and there's a scratch here that's very familiar, plus a certain little triangle stamped into the butt of the handle, a triangle that almost looks like . . .

A cornucopia.

"Guys, I think this is my great-great-great-grandmother's pickaxe."

They crowd around me, gazing down at the object in question.

"You know, I thought this helmet looked familiar," Chug says, pulling an extra iron helmet out of his pocket. He points to a scuff. "I remember when that happened. It was a particularly ugly zombie."

Tok holds up a battered cookie. "And this is from Nan." He looks at us. "This is our stuff."

"But how'd it get here?" Lenna asks.

We gaze around the empty room like there might be answers, but nothing of this building speaks to the brigands who stole our belongings. There are no portraits, no plaques, no sign of my llamas.

"It doesn't matter," I say. "Let's not lose it again." I feel braver with the family pickaxe in my pocket and move out into the hallway as the boys briefly scuffle over Nan's cookie. Sure, this is disturbing news that raises more questions, but our task is still the same: Find the evoker and kill it.

We have a rhythm now, and the mansion is starting to feel very doable. Just like with any other endeavor, we started out making mistakes, learned from them, and got better. Lenna collects the arrows she shoots and loots what she finds on skeletons, and even Tok has a sword now, for all that he doesn't look like he knows which end is pointy.

I'm about to enter the next room when I hear an odd sound that reminds me of a horn.

"What—" I start, but something pulsating with gray and red fills my vision. A sword strikes me, and I stumble back. Another gray thing shows up, and they're hissing and battering at me. I slash out with my sword, but it's like trying to hit air. Lenna's arrows thwack again and again in a rain of fire, and both of the gray things fall, their swords clanking on the ground.

"Vexes," Lenna says, sounding older than her years.

I haven't taken much damage, so I refocus and step into the new room, sword up. I remember from Nan's book that vexes can be summoned only by evokers, and that their evoker won't stop sending vexes at us until we've destroyed it—or it has destroyed us.

I don't see any more vexes.

There are, however, two vindicators and an evoker.

Both vindicators run at me, and the evoker raises his arms.

22.

LENNA

 The moment I hear that horn, I know what's coming, and I know that even if it feels like we're ready, we're not. I run for the door with Poppy on my heels, slide in past Chug and Tok, target the nearest vex, and take it down with two fiery shots. Same with the second one. This enchantment is a real game changer! Mal is reeling, but she quickly recovers and does exactly what she needs to do: aims for the vindicators to clear my view of the evoker.

I've landed two shots on it when Poppy yelps and something slashes at my legs. I look down and see a spectral fang rolling past. My legs burn with pain, and I stumble. Poppy dances away, growling, daring the mysterious menace to come back and fight. In the time it takes me to refocus, the evoker has sent two more vexes. They charge at me, hissing, pulsating, swords out, but I just need one more shot at the evoker.

"What's happening?" Chug asks from the doorway, and I don't mean to look away, but I do. One of the vexes lands a hit, and it's like my whole body burns, it hurts so much. The world seems both sharp and fuzzy, and I begin to see why a sword might be useful. These vexes are so close that I can't launch an arrow. Poppy leaps and snaps and snarls, but they stay just out of her reach.

"Hit the little gray things!" I shout at Chug, dodging to the side to evade their swords.

Chug is pretty good when you tell him exactly what to do, and I force myself to focus on the evoker and let him handle the vexes. It takes me two more shots, but I take the evoker down and breathe a sigh of relief.

And then a sword slashes my back, and I fall flat on my face.

"If the evoker is gone, why didn't they go away?" Chug cries.

I look up from the floor to find Chug battling both vexes while Mal and Tok fight off the vindicators, their axes flashing in the torchlight. Mal's almost got her vindicator down, and Tok has an iron sword and is doing his best to distract his vindicator, even if he's not close enough or hitting hard enough to do any real damage. My back is killing me, and my whole body aches like my blood is on fire, but I drag myself to sitting. Poppy licks my face, which is kind but not helpful.

"They didn't go away because I didn't destroy them yet," I say.

I shuffle over to a position where I can shoot at the vexes without hitting my friends—no easy task, as I can barely stand and aiming an arrow from the ground is nearly impossible. Chug, who's already suffered multiple wounds, takes a hard hit to the head, thanks to a vex sword, and reels dizzily. Tok trips over one of the cats and falls on his back on the floor. I release an arrow toward his vindicator, and it flies wide and lands in the wall. Poppy whines and nudges me with her nose, and I have no way to tell her that it's counterproductive—and painful.

My head slumps forward, heavy like it's full of sand. This fight shouldn't be this hard, but it is. We shouldn't be losing . . . but we are.

"A little help?" Mal calls, desperately parrying the second vindicator's axe swings with her sword, now nicked and shiny with use.

"We can do this," I growl. "We have to. We're the Mob Squad, so let's kick some mob butt!"

I grit my teeth and take aim at one of the vexes harrying Chug. My arrow lands true, and Chug manages to hit it with his sword despite the fact that he looks cross-eyed and like he's going to throw up. Tok throws him the golden apple, and Chug eats it in seemingly one bite. With only one vex left, he shakes his head and grins like he was seeing double but the world is finally clear again. I scoot to a better angle and hit the vex with my second arrow, and the moment it falters, he smacks it down with his diamond sword. Mal charges her vindicator with a mighty slash — of her diamond pickaxe. The monster falls, dropping its axe beside her broken sword.

All that's left now is the final vindicator.

With Mal on one side, Tok on the other, and the cats acting like absolute loons, my choices are limited. I won't risk an arrow shot that could harm one of my friends. Chug turns to the fray and grunts; apparently he can't see a good angle, either.

Mal gets in a hit, but the vindicator is so close to her now that there's not much she can do, not with her back against the wall. Tok jabs at the monster with his sword, but not hard enough. With terrifying speed, the vindicator spins around and brings its axe arcing down toward Tok's head. Tok gets his sword up, but the vindicator is taller, stronger, more willing to do harm. Tok is gentle, respectful, creative—there's not a violent bone in his body. The axe is about to cleave him in two. I draw my arrow and release it, knowing full well it's a perfect shot.

Mal's stroke and Chug's jab land at the same time as my arrow and the vindicator collapses forward onto Tok, dropping its axe and two emeralds.

The room goes silent, and everyone but Tok spins in place, searching for the next attack.

None comes.

Tok crawls out from beneath what's left of the vindicator and curls up into a ball with his back against the wall. Both cats trot toward him and rub against him, purring, and he pets them, one with each hand, staring out into nothing.

"You okay, bro?" Chug asks.

"It tried to kill me," Tok replies, his voice high and tremulous.

Chug and I exchange a look; we both know this feeling. Surely Mal does, too.

It's the startling realization that there are things in the world that genuinely, maliciously want to hurt you.

And even more, it's the understanding that when you fight back and cause damage or destruction, it hurts you in a different way.

Chug slides down the wall to sit beside his brother, their shoulders and hips touching. Although I'm normally pretty skittish about these things, I take Tok's other side and reach out to pet Candor. Poppy curls up against Tok's foot and wags her tail gently. For a while, we just sit there like that, taking turns patting the cats and being quiet. Tok stops shaking, and his breathing goes normal again. Mal stands in the doorway, keeping watch while shooting worried glances at us.

"That was pretty scary," I admit, because it seems like it's okay to talk again. "The way they all just attacked at once."

"So that was your little gray flying dude." Chug shudders. "To tell you the truth, I'm not a fan."

It takes a few moments, but Tok finally offers, weakly, "Yeah, it really *vexed* me."

Chug's mouth falls open. "That should've been my pun!"

"Then consider this your *pun*ishment."

The chuckle starts out silent, but Chug is shaking—I can feel it through Tok's shoulder. Then the laughter is breathy and sputtery instead of Chug's usual guffaws. Smart, because we don't want to alert any more enemies to our presence here.

"Good one, bro," Chug allows.

"Thanks."

I can finally take a deep breath again, and I let it all out of my mouth in a big whoosh. I'm injured, but I'm pretty sure I'll be okay. It's Tok I was worried about. Sometimes invisible pain is so much worse than superficial injuries. He's thawing, coming back to life, and I'm glad. It's like we're in this weird club now, four friends who used to live safely behind a wall but are now out in the wider world, fighting real battles and taking real wounds. The thought of Jarro's usual jeers is laughable now. What are some boring little bully's words compared to fighting off multiple zombies and skeletons and vindicators and evokers and vexes?

We're so much stronger than we ever knew.

I'm so much stronger.

I can't imagine how I would react if I were magically transported to the dinner table right now and my parents and siblings took turns telling me everything I should've done today, that I should've been sweeping and sorting stone and being quiet and good. I'd probably laugh in their faces, pick up my bowl, and go eat outside, up a tree where they couldn't reach me.

Or at the base of the tree so I could share with Poppy. She nuzzles up to my side, and I stroke her gray fur. Once, I might've worried if my parents would let me keep her when we get back home. Now I know the truth: This wolf is mine, and I'm hers. We've fought together, traveled together. She understands me better than anyone in my entire family.

That's another funny thing—how sometimes the people who really see you, who really connect with your heart, aren't necessarily the people in your family but the people you find along the way. I lean my head against Tok's shoulder, and I look down and see that the brothers are holding hands. Mal smiles at us from the doorway, and I wish she could be here connected with us, too. But she's the leader, and she feels responsible for us, so instead, she keeps watch. We have a job to do, after all.

"*Oh,*" I say, and everyone looks at me. The world feels like it spins around me as the realization slots into place. "You guys—*we did it.* We destroyed the evoker that was sending the vexes that were poisoning our town."

Chug chuckles. "I guess I forgot about that part while I was trying not to die."

"Whoa," Tok murmurs. "We did it. We really did it. We saved the day!"

"We're heroes," Mal says from the doorway, grinning. "Even if no one back home ever knows it, we know it."

I try to stand up, but . . . that doesn't work so well. "I think we need some food," I say, because my entire body hurts.

"Yeah, I got axed. 'Hatcheted'? 'Sliced'? 'Vindicated'? I don't know what you call it, but even through diamond armor, I can feel every strike." Chug shifts and winces, and Mal's brows draw down. She pulls a few potatoes from breakfast out of her pocket.

"Eat whatever you need. If we don't come across another dining room, we can run back downstairs." She looks around the room, her eyes widening in surprise at what she sees. "Lenna, do you think Poppy could keep watch for a minute? I need to check this room out."

I appreciate that she asked, and I trust Poppy to sit in a doorway and growl if anything nasty shows up. I nod, and Mal calls the wolf over. Poppy sits where Mal points and aims her eyes, ears, and nose down the hallway. That frees up Mal to walk around the room, which we've all been ignoring in favor of fighting, recovering, and, now, eating. Someone hands me a cookie, and I realize I've never been hungrier in my life.

"Did you guys see this?" Mal murmurs.

"Mmrph hrmph," Chug says, stuffing a potato down his throat.

Tok stands, although he has to put a hand on the wall to steady himself. He probably doesn't need to eat like Chug and I do, since he didn't take any physical damage, but he's nibbling on a cookie anyway, and I know it'll make him feel better.

"Whoa," Tok says again.

Curious and fortified by the food, I join them at the big table in the center of the room.

"Oh!"

There's a cloth map laid out on the table, a huge one. Mal's map never really made sense to me, but I can kind of start to understand this one, if only because it's far more detailed and the main things on the map are a woodland mansion in a dark forest and a walled town.

Our town.

But there are other landmarks, too—a river with a log bridge, a village, and a mountain pass, to be exact.

The oddest part, though, is that there's a path that makes no sense. It leads from the woodland mansion directly to Cornucopia, but it doesn't follow the landmarks I would expect. It doesn't lead across the log bridge—that no longer exists. It doesn't even use the obvious mountain pass. Instead, it seems to cross over everything in a nearly straight line. The nonsensical path is drawn like a ladder, but it can't be a ladder.

"Oh my gosh," Mal breathes.

"What?" I ask, cocking my head in the hopes that it will help the map make more sense.

"Is that a ladder?" Chug asks.

"No," I say, finally understanding. I remember the last time I saw that pattern, the last time I was deep underground and looking for someone who'd disappeared under mysterious circumstances.

"Those are rails. The kind of rails you use for a mine cart underground."

23.

CHUG

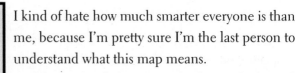I kind of hate how much smarter everyone is than me, because I'm pretty sure I'm the last person to understand what this map means.

"So those rails Lenna saw in that underground cavern connect this mansion to our town?" I ask.

"I think so," Mal says.

"That would explain how the vexes got to Cornucopia." Lenna traces a finger along their path. "But . . . you don't think it connects to my family's mine, do you?" She gasps. "Wait. Do my parents know about this? Is my family part of this?"

Mal shakes her head and pulls an arrow out of the wall, using it to point to the place where the line connects to Cornucopia, a straight shot from here. It's not in Lenna's family's mine—the mine is in a far corner of the town, far away from the rails, whereas the line leads directly into the center of town, the Hub.

"It looks like someone's house." Mal taps the end of the line. "But whose house?"

The map is big but not superdetailed. There are no handy-dandy words labeling houses or anything, just shapes. Near the Hub, all the houses are kind of crushed together. The baker, the blacksmith, the tanner, the weavers, the shops, the tiny cottages our oldest residents prefer—they aren't spread out like the farms are, and every year, some family has to build a new house to give their kids or parents some place to move to. It's a lot more crowded than I'd like, but I've also never looked at Cornucopia from overhead, noting how all the spaces are filling in. Even our farm got smaller a few years ago, when Aunt Becca got married and she and her husband built their own farm in the east field.

"And do they know there's a secret rail below their house?" Tok adds, because of course he's the smartest of us all. He steps up to the table, leaning in, and I'm just so glad that he's out of his shock trance. "See, right here? It looks like there's a place where the rail stops just outside Cornucopia, too. Behind these boulders." The spot he's pointing at has a little fork in it, like the rail splits. "And then here's our field—the first one that was poisoned." He points to the nearest farm, and I can tell it's ours by the square orange dots representing pumpkins. "Right by where the track branches out."

Lenna might not be sure if her family is involved, but I'm completely certain that my parents have no idea what's going on. They're not good actors, and I was stunned by the reality of Mom's tears this morning—wait, no.

That was days ago. I haven't even been counting. It feels like we left Cornucopia so recently, but for our families there, it must feel like forever. To them, we simply disappeared. They must be going crazy, worrying about us. And even if they don't know it back home, they're counting on us. We're their only hope if they want life to continue as the Founders, our ancestors, intended. I get so caught up in just staying alive that it's easy to forget why we're here in the first place.

We accomplished our goal: We ended the evoker so it can't send any more vexes.

But now that we know about this rail, our work is definitely not done.

"We need more food," I say. Mal gives me an exasperated look, and I barrel on. "Not because I'm feeling snacky. Although I am. Because we need to get healthy as quickly as we can so we can figure out what's going on here. Somewhere in this mansion, there must be more clues. Nan said the illagers weren't smart, that they couldn't talk or plan. But—"

"They're planning," Mal finishes softly.

I nod.

"Good thinking, bro," Tok says, and it might be the best compliment of my life.

Mal glances around the room. "Tok, see if you can find any more clues. Lenna, collect your arrows. Chug, keep guard. I'm going back to the dining room." Before anyone can protest, she darts out the door.

The strangest feeling comes over me the moment Mal disappears. It's like when your foot falls asleep and you can't stand up straight and you know that if you had to run, you'd fall flat on your face. Mal has always been there for me, and it's uncomfortable, having her out on her own, where I can't keep her safe. I move to the door, where Poppy keeps watch, my sword in my still shaky hand.

Lenna grabs her arrows while Tok examines the map from every possible angle. He peeks under the rug on the floor, looks under the table, pulls on the torches like they might secretly be levers.

"Nothing," he murmurs to himself, annoyed.

Thwack.

An arrow embeds itself in the doorway, and I duck back into the room. "Skeleton!" I call to Lenna. She nods, runs for the door, fires off two arrows, and races outside to collect whatever the skeleton has dropped. Poppy remains sitting as she's been commanded, but she whines the moment her mistress is down the hall. Lenna returns with more arrows, grinning.

"I'm starting to like skeletons."

I can't imagine a single reason she would ever say that sentence back home.

Mal is back shortly, and at first I'm disappointed that she isn't carrying food—but then she turns out her pockets, releasing a magical smorgasbord. This trick of Nan's is amazing! I reach for a chicken leg, relief flooding me at my best friend's return—and the promise of fresh food. I dig in, but everything tastes like dust and sticks in my throat. This was the hardest room yet, and for a minute there, I wasn't sure we'd all make it. The next room could contain yet more tulips, or it could be full of supersmart illagers making potions to hurl at us. I wasn't so scared before because I didn't know what we were up against. Now that I know what it's like to fight an evoker, I kind of want to crawl under the table and hide.

"Ready?" Mal asks from the doorway, sword in hand and armor on.

She looks fierce and confident, and just seeing her grin gives me the strength to nod and join her. Tok clearly doesn't want to leave the map—but then his face lights up in that way it does the moment he has an idea, and he rolls up the whole darn thing and carries it in both arms toward Mal. She understands immediately and somehow manages to stuff it in a pocket, and I'm not sure how she gets it in there, but she does.

"It's not blocking the food, is it?" I ask, and I hate how nervous I sound.

"Naw, the food's in the other pocket. Let's go."

We're back in formation, Mal and me and Tok and Lenna and Poppy, the cats pacing at Tok's side like tiny versions of some ferocious beast.

We clear the rest of the floor, which is blissfully lacking in evokers and has only a few vindicators who don't stand a chance. Most of the remaining rooms are bedrooms or empty, and the loot we do find goes straight into our rapidly filling pockets.

The top floor is more of the same. Empty rooms, a few zombies and skeletons, a vindicator here and there. We're ready for all of them, working together like we were born to do this. I have to drag Tok away from another library, but he manages to slide some books into his pockets to enjoy later. Finally, we stand by the open front doors. I run around the corner, toss Thingy a melon from the dining room, and smile as he happily devours it.

We've scoured the entire woodland mansion, but we haven't figured out what's up with the map, and we haven't found any hint at leaders or an organization. It's like a bunch of mean monsters randomly found a way to a protected home and decided to cause as much damage as possible. As frustrating and confusing as it is to me, it's clearly driving Tok and Mal crazy, not knowing what's going on. Things happen for a reason. This is just too dangerous to be any sort of coincidence.

"We must've missed something," Tok says, rotating in place as he looks up the stairs, down each hall, and out the open door.

"But we looked everywhere." Mal is frowning. She can feel it, too—there's something more.

"Well, look on the bright side. We got rid of the evoker, and now the vexes won't be able to hurt Cornucopia anymore." There goes Lenna, daydreaming again. It's like the old Lenna is here for just a moment, but the new Lenna's hand is tight around her bow, her mouth twitching.

It would be so easy to think it's true. That we've won the day, and our town is safe.

That we can just go home as heroes and know everything will be fine.

But we can all sense it—there's something else. Something we're missing.

It's not safe yet.

We can't go home now, and we all know it, but we want to go home so badly.

"There must be another way." Tok spins and spins, and I'm surprised he's not dizzy.

And that's when it hits me.

There's one direction he isn't looking, possibly the most important direction, considering our current predicament.

"Bro," I say, hoping I don't sound stupid, "maybe there's a basement."

Tok looks up, meeting my eyes. "A basement. A basement! Of course! Because how else can you get underground to those rails." He smacks his own forehead. "You're a genius!"

Three little words, but my heart flutters like a baby chicken.

No one has ever called me a genius before, much less smart.

Most people call me dumb.

Jarro called me an ignoramus once, but I'm pretty sure he got that from his mom.

Mal and Lenna are nodding, too. "There must be a cavern down there," Lenna says.

Tok starts walking down the left-hand hallway, following our original path.

"We're looking for carpets, then. A trapdoor. Probably in a room that was guarded when we first went inside. Don't bother moving furniture—I don't think anyone would trap themselves underground like that."

Since we've already cleared the mansion, our progress goes quickly. It's kind of fun, tossing carpets aside and hunting for anything that could reveal a secret passage.

"Got it!" Lenna calls, and we all run to where she and Poppy stand in the overdone, banner-filled bedroom, a rumpled carpet pulled back to reveal a trapdoor.

For a moment, we all just stare at it. We don't know if we're going to open it and find a long, terrifying fall, like when Mal opened up that last cavern, or if there will be a band of illagers waiting to attack us with axes and vexes and fangs. My fingers tighten on my sword. This feels right, like it's what we're supposed to do.

We have weapons. We have armor. We're healthy and full of good food.

Most important, we have one another.

"Are we ready?" Mal asks.

I nod, and Tok nods, and Lenna nods. Poppy gives a soft woof.

Grinning, Mal opens the trapdoor.

24.

TOK

 I don't know exactly what I was expecting, but I was expecting something bad.

More evokers and vexes, probably, as they're the most terrifying foes we've faced. But the open trapdoor reveals only an underground cavern like any other, with stone stairs leading down into the darkness and torches placed at cautious intervals along the wall, their flames indicating that someone has been here recently.

I don't want to set foot down there—I've never liked the concept of being underground, with all that weight overhead. I begin doing calculations and running disaster scenarios. But Mal starts down the stairs, and Chug follows her, and then it's just Lenna and me. I look back at her, and she offers me an understanding smile.

"It'll be fine," she says. "Or the cave will, at least. It looks like it's structurally safe."

I trust her, but we both know what she's not saying.

Even if the cave itself is fine, we're bound to find all sorts of mobs down there. With this much darkness, they can show up anywhere and everywhere. There might even be things we haven't seen yet, things we didn't pay much attention to in Nan's books because at no point did we anticipate having to go underground. I'm holding a sword dropped by a skeleton, but it's slippery in my grip because my hands are sweating like crazy. I have a helmet, too, and it's heavy and dull and smells of metal, and I know it'll offer excellent protection, but I hate how it restricts my vision. The cats sniff the air, make that weird, offended face, and follow Chug down the stairs, and then I either have to follow or cause a scene.

I hate that feeling, when everyone suddenly stops paying attention to the problem at hand and starts paying attention to me because I'm being cerebral instead of just doing what everyone else is doing. My reasons all feel like excuses, and they all boil down to fear. I'm just flat out more scared of things than my friends are—but then again, I know more than they do. I feel safer when I'm with them, but that doesn't automatically make everything easier. I'm constantly running mental statistics on all the myriad things that could go wrong, and it makes me freeze.

I'm doing it now.

Lenna puts a hand on my shoulder.

"Listen. This space is big, okay? This is not some dank little hole someone dug. It's either a large natural cavern or something someone put a lot of work into. There are torches, we have the cats to keep creepers away, we have swords and my bow and Poppy. It's no more dangerous than the woodland mansion was."

"We almost died in there," I say quietly.

"We almost died ten times in the last week," she agrees. "We almost died on Tommi's roof. But here we are. If we don't do this, if we don't go down there and put a stop to it once and for all, then everything we've done so far won't matter. We'll go home, after facing all these dangers, and they might still abandon the town and separate us. So we've got to get through this next part. This is just . . . one more thing to get through."

I can see what she means—we can't just leave. Just because we took down one evoker, we can't assume we've gotten rid of everyone who wishes our town ill—not after finding that map upstairs. If we're right, we'll find rails down here and a direct path back to our town. There's nothing I'd like more than to have a faster way home with fewer thieves standing in our way.

"Meow," one of the cats calls plaintively, urging me along.

I step down onto the stairs, and the stone is freezing. The air is just *different*—I can feel it, heavy and with a distinctive odor. I take another step, and another, and I almost drop the sword, my sweaty hand is shaking so badly. Another meow echoes up from the darkness, and I keep going. Cats do not belong in caves, and therefore anyone who hears them will know something unusual is happening. If I catch up, maybe they'll stop making noise.

Lenna is close behind me, closer than she's generally been on this trip. She's worried about me, and rightfully so. It's amazing, how well she picks up on emotions and energy. I can hear Poppy's claws on the stone, too, treading carefully. Soon I've caught up to Mal and Chug and the cats, who've stopped to wait. The stairwell is a tight spiral with torches placed closely enough that we're never in shadow. But everything feels like a shadow down here.

Once we're all together, Mal leads us deeper underground. It's the oddest sensation, how the world shrinks down to each separate step, the same as the last. We've been on the staircase a minute and an hour and a week, and I begin to wonder if I'll be here forever, walking in descending circles. How many feet have trod these stairs? I can't tell if this place is old or new, and I'd like to ask Lenna a thousand questions about stone and mines, but we need to be quiet. And we need to hurry, because if we meet someone on these steps, there won't be much room to fight.

There's a sigh of relief in front of me, and then I'm stepping onto ground that thankfully isn't a stair.

"How . . . is this possible?" Lenna says.

I'm not sure what she's referring to until she puts a hand on the wall and I notice that it's not raw rock but chiseled stone. We're in a small vestibule, plain but well-lit, and there's a door facing us. Mal pushes it open, diamond pickaxe at the ready, but we pass beyond without incident.

The space is strange and nonsensical, as if designed long ago by someone with a plan we can't quite understand. The floor and ceiling change heights, and there are doors and torches and chests planted at odd intervals. We open the chests, of course, and soon we're all outfitted in various bits of mismatched armor. I'm slightly disturbed by the fact that someone has been stockpiling so much armor and so many weapons, but we need to stay as quiet as possible, so I don't voice my concerns. I can tell that everyone else is thinking something similar, except for Chug, who's probably thinking about cookies.

Mal slows, and I realize that she must be lost. How could she not be? Unlike the woodland mansion or a reasonable house, this place isn't symmetrical. There are no hallways, no closed rooms. It's all topsy-turvy, and we've been rushing from chest to chest, our senses on high alert for danger. We haven't run into any mobs yet, but that's probably because there are so many torches. We haven't seen illagers, either, so it's still a mystery as to who planted those torches in the first place.

Lenna touches the back of my arm, and when I look at her, she tilts her chin at Poppy. The wolf is turning her head from side to side as if searching for something. I shrug, and Lenna points at Poppy's ears, which are twitching, and I understand: Poppy hears something we can't. When the beast takes a few halting steps in a new direction, Lenna follows her, and I tug Chug along, with Mal following. I'm sure they'd like to know what's up, but we understand each other well enough that they just go with it. Maybe they can see the excitement and worry on my face, or maybe they're noting how Poppy is excitedly speeding up.

A sound echoes down the hall, and it's not the groan of a zombie or the hiss of a vex or the grunt of a villager or illager.

It's a man's voice.

A human man.

"To think: Those simpletons have no idea," he says, smug and self-assured.

Lenna catches Poppy's collar before the wolf can barge in on the owner of that voice, which is oddly and impossibly familiar. Poppy's ears swivel as she strains toward a staircase leading down, but Lenna instead leads us toward a different staircase that's going up. I don't really understand her plan, but I follow her. We end up in a smallish room, almost a balcony, and it's looking down into a chamber richly outfitted with carpets, a chest, and a big bed.

Someone is pacing back and forth across the room, and I startle and stumble back when I realize it's a witch.

Or . . . is it?

The purple robe and hat perfectly match the witch we faced in the swamp, as does the big, orange, warty nose. But as the witch paces and gestures, muttering, I can tell that this is not some mindless monster that attacks on sight.

It hasn't even said hee hee hee hee.

"The debris is cleared off the rails now, so that's taken care of," the not-witch mutters. "Thank goodness for gunpowder, eh? The crops are expiring, exactly as I planned. The denizens of the town are so busy packing that they haven't noticed anything unusual — and they won't until we're among them. The fools!"

When the not-witch adjusts his nose, lifting it up to scratch underneath, I'm certain that we're dealing with a human being in disguise.

"There's something about that guy," Chug whispers in my ear. "Something familiar. I don't like him."

Witch or human, there's not much to like. Whoever this is, he's just admitted to poisoning our town's crops.

"To think — this wealth of riches has been beneath Cornucopia all this time, and no one up above has any idea. Such simple minds! Other than that one tiny mine, no one ever thought to dig down and see what might be waiting below. They've never wondered if there might be more to life, whether beyond the wall or under their feet. Soon, once I have amassed a few paltry blocks of obsidian, I will possess a Nether portal of my own. Nether wart and glowstone powder galore! No more begging for potions from that ridiculous old man in town who thinks he knows everything! And all we have to do is scare them out! Hee hee hee!" His laugh could almost pass for a witch's cackle, except his is full of emotion.

I'm sick to my stomach. Cornucopia is a tightly knit place where everyone knows everyone and takes care of everyone. Our families are all descended from the same Founders. We've all grown up together. And now I'm learning that one of our neighbors is a very bad person willing to harm people, animals, and crops just to get their hands on . . . well, whatever a Nether portal is. They're willing to sacrifice us all for personal gain, for unlimited access to potions, as if Cornucopia itself isn't valuable and wonderful in its own right. They want *things* instead of people and the fruits of hard labor, and it's disgusting.

And I still can't figure out why I know that voice.

It's not like I even know that many people to begin with.

"Uh, boss?" This new voice is familiar, too, scratching at the back of my brain. "You never said anything about attacking the town. You pay us to steal armor and weapons."

The fake witch spins dramatically and points at someone standing below our balcony, just out of view. "Oh, so your crew is acclimatized to highway robbery but balks at a simple little siege?"

"Pretty much," the mysterious voice says, and I put two and two together.

This is the head brigand, the guy who stole our llamas and chests and tried to eat Thingy. I put my hand on Chug's shoulder, but since he's not rushing down there to bop anyone in the nose, I have to assume he hasn't figured it out yet. But who is the fake witch?

"Fine. I don't require your services for this part. Go guard the mansion, and you'll still be richly rewarded when my portal is functional. With the log bridge toppled, my dark forest is safe from curious onlookers. I'll gather my waiting illagers and lead them to the mine carts, and we'll barge up into the Hub and do what you are too cowardly to accomplish. My naive neighbors have forgotten how to fight. They've forgotten that illagers even exist. They've forgotten that they don't know everything, and they've stopped trying to learn anything new. But soon I'll teach them a lesson myself. They'll leave, or they'll regret it, down to the last scalawag and rapscallion."

I can see the cogs of Chug's mind grinding, his brow drawn down. Mal and Lenna both look confused, like the voice isn't as familiar to them. Something in that last little speech is clawing at the back of my brain like Candor when she wants out of my closet.

"And best of all, I'll never have to taste another beetroot again."

I turn to Chug, and his eyes are as wide as mine.

We know who that is, down there in the witch costume, planning the destruction of everything we know and love.

It's our least favorite and most verbose neighbor, Krog.

25.

MAL

 I feel it, the moment Chug has decided to go fight the head brigand and whoever else is down there, planning to destroy our entire community. And I can understand why that's immediately where his mind goes. But Chug has probably forgotten in this moment that he'd be facing off with fully grown adults who have already shown that they're willing to poke kids with swords and hurt people and livestock to get what they want. The fake witch said he had illagers, and I know the brigands have weapons, but even if they're dangerous villains, we're not going to march down there and try to kill them like they're mobs. If we tried, we'd probably be the ones who ended up hurt. Or dead.

My hand lands on Chug's arm, and when he makes his move, I pull him back—as does Tok, who already has him by the other shoulder.

"That's Krog, and I'm going to kick his—"

Chug doesn't finish his whisper because I interrupt him.

"You can't kick his anything. He's an adult—and a person."

"And that other guy—he tried to eat Thingy!"

"Uh, guys?" Lenna says from closer to the balcony. "They're leaving now."

I see that Lenna's arrow is nocked, her bow taut, and I shake my head at her. No matter what happens, we're not going to hurt people. Mindless, violent illagers and mobs are one thing, but there's got to be a better way when it comes to human beings, even if they're the sort of human beings who steal and maim for a living—or call us Bad Apples. She lowers her arrow and glowers at me.

"He said he was going to get his illagers and attack the town," Chug whispers harshly. "And we could've already ended this!"

"Or met our own end. Attack Krog, and those brigands will attack *you*, even if they're not going to Cornucopia. This is serious. This isn't playing. Even if you hate him, I don't think you're ready to face off with Krog, bud. I don't think you're willing to kill a human being, much less hurt one." At my words, he blushes and looks away, ashamed that he'd even considered doing just that.

"So what then?" he asks, and they all look at me, and I realize that we don't have much time. All these days that we've been traveling and learning and fighting, we've been aware of why we left in the first place, of how badly we need to save Cornucopia. But now there's a real ticking clock.

If we don't act now, a raiding party is going to descend on our town. Our parents, our cousins, our livestock, my Nan—they're all there, innocently going about their lives, or at least doing harmless things like packing to leave instead of building up defenses. Krog is right—they don't know how to fight. They don't know what they'd be facing, the terror of taking on an evoker and its vexes as vindicators lunge at you with their axes. Our people don't have any weapons, other than simple iron farming tools. People really could die.

"We've got to get there first," I say. "We have to let the town know. We can't fight them alone, and we can't fight Krog, but we can tell the adults and let them decide what to do."

"The mine carts!"

We all turn to Lenna.

"We have to beat him to the mine carts and ride back to town before he can."

I break out grinning. It's the right answer. "Then we have to hurry."

After a few beats, I take off, knowing they'll follow. But then I stop.

"Wait. How deep do we need to go? You can tell how deep we are underground, right?"

Lenna ducks her head shyly, a gesture we all know well—but then raises her chin, her eyes steely. "Deeper than this. I remember what it felt like, in that cavern where I saw the rails. We're looking for another stairwell down. It'll feel colder. And just . . . deeper."

I want to lead—and I know they need me to lead—but this isn't something I know about. I've never been underground before this, unless you count digging into hillsides to make our shelters. Mining is fun, but I don't like being down this deep, and everything feels dangerous to me.

Thing is, I like being in charge, and I like making decisions, and I think I do a good job of that. Chug acts before thinking, Tok thinks too much, and Lenna is usually lost in her own world and needs to be called back. I'm the one who brings them together and makes them a team.

But maybe it's time for me to admit that sometimes being a good leader means stepping back to let someone else do what they do best.

"Take us there, Lenna."

Her eyes fly wide, and her mouth drops open to tell me all the reasons why she can't do that . . . until it snaps closed again and she nods and runs off, with Poppy loping behind her. I follow Lenna, Tok follows me, and Chug takes up the rear with his sword. Relief floods me as I acknowledge that this is the right decision and that Lenna is the only one who can get us where we need to go.

It's hard, though, not being in charge. I want to remind everyone to be quiet, want to gesture for Tok to keep his cats close and for Chug to be watching for attacks from behind, but Lenna's moving fast and we can only follow. Our armor clanks and our boots stomp, but I soon hear a noise that drowns us out completely: illagers.

"Hmn" and "Huh huh!" and "Hee hee hee hee hee" echo up the halls, along with the sound of many, many feet on stone. Lenna takes a sharp left and plunges down the first set of stairs she finds. Luckily there are torches everywhere. Unluckily, that means that if we run into our foes, they can see us just as well as we can see them.

The stairwell is a dead end, and we back up hastily. Lenna closes her eyes and sniffs the air before taking another tunnel. I begin to question whether I should be the one in front, if there's some better way to find what we're looking for. At the next junction, Poppy whines and sniffs at stairs going up, and I wonder if there's food up there or something else that calls to her.

When Poppy darts up the stairs, Lenna starts to follow, but I catch her arm. "What are you doing? We're supposed to go down, not up."

"Poppy's nose is better than any of ours. She'll take us the right way."

"How do you know? How do you know it's not just rotten meat she's after?"

Usually my stare cows Lenna, but this time, she stands her ground. "Because I trust her. You trust me, and I trust her. So let's go."

She jogs up the stairs, and I follow, with Tok and Chug behind me.

"Uh, is this right?" I hear Chug ask, and I flinch. He never questions me.

The stairs go up—and then they go straight down, twisting and twisting. I feel it—when it gets colder and things start to smell different, mustier and somehow bigger. After what feels like forever, the stairwell spits us out into a huge cavern, and I'm so grateful and excited and relieved that I want to shout and hug Lenna and give Poppy all the meat in my pockets, but we don't have time for that.

"There—the mine carts!"

Lenna points, and we full-on sprint for the line of mine carts waiting on silver rails that glimmer by torchlight.

"Hhn!" someone calls from across the cavern, and I don't stop running, but I do glance over and see a huge band of illagers heading toward us. They're some distance away, over by some chests, but they definitely know we're here now.

"Hurry!" I shout, because let's face it: The element of surprise isn't going to cut it. And besides, they're no longer surprised.

But Tok doesn't hurry—he slows down, rummaging in his pockets. When he pulls out a potion, my heart sinks. We need all the potions we can get for what's to come. And, honestly, his throwing arm is terrible.

But in a true show of brotherhood and an understanding of his own flaws, he hands the potion to Chug, who hurls it at the band of illagers. Pink liquid splashes them, and they start to move as slowly as bees caught in honey, just like Lenna did when the witch's potion splashed her.

Ah, yes—the other potion from the witch's hut, which we rediscovered in the mansion's chests. Slowness!

Tok and Chug redouble their efforts to join us, and Lenna reaches the mine carts first. She helps Tok and Candor into the first car and, without asking anyone anything or telling us what she's doing, sends it careening into the darkness.

"Whaaaaaat?" I can hear Tok screeching as Candor's "Meeeeeeew!" matches him in tone and terror.

Chug places Clarity in the next cart before jumping in himself, and Lenna sends him off right behind his brother. Of course, what he shouts is "Wheeeee!" because that's Chug.

"You next, Mal," she tells me.

I jump into the third mine cart and look at the illagers, still advancing on us, albeit slowly—dozens of them, some even riding strange, dark gray cow-pig things—knowing that the Slowness potion will wear off eventually. "You're coming, too, right?"

She snorts. "Of course. But I've got to do something first."

"What?"

Instead of answering, she does something to my cart, and it rockets into the darkness. Despite how tough I think I am and how tough I'd like to be, I scream.

26.

LENNA

 I shouldn't be laughing but seeing Mal's face as the mine cart took off was pretty hilarious. I guess I should've mentioned how fast they go, and that once you're in one, you have almost no control whatsoever?

At least Krog cleared all that debris off the tracks—or so he said.

Too late to worry about that now.

The illagers are still moving slowly, and I'm the only one who knows how that feels. So frustrating, so infuriating. I wish I could just pick them all off with my bow right now, but there are too many of them, and I have only so many arrows. Still, there's a whole line of carts left, and I need to make sure they can't follow us—at least for a while.

I know a lot about how mine carts work, as my parents rotated me through all the different aspects of their mining operation before deciding I was utterly useless. And the thing about mine carts is that they're quite sturdy . . . but the wheels come off pretty easily, if you know what you're doing. Keeping the illagers in my sights, I kneel and remove a wheel from each of the remaining carts and toss them all into the first cart. I help Poppy in, jump in myself, and soon I'm hurtling through the caverns at breakneck speed—with all the extra wheels. My parents never let me ride in a mine cart, probably because they thought I might like it too much.

And they would've been right.

I don't just like it—*I love it.*

The fierce whooshing of the wind, the unexpected depth of the velvety dark, the sounds of dripping or squeaking or moaning that zip past my ears. I know it's going to be a long ride, judging simply by how long it took us to get here from home. But then, we took a much more erratic path with plenty of stops, whereas this rail is a straight shot. I think of what we passed on the way and what I saw on the big map upstairs, and I imagine us zooming under the river—I can even smell it and feel the coolness. The village we visited wasn't along this line, but maybe a wandering trader ventures this far with a caravan of llamas. I'm certain I'm passing under grasses and flowers and trees, the life overhead utterly ignorant of my presence.

Poppy sniffs the air beside me, and I reach to stroke her head. I can imagine her eyes slitted to smiling, her ears blowing back in the wind. I'm glad she likes it instead of being terrified, because there's nothing I could do about that. I hope Tok's cats are faring as well.

It's easy to lose track of time, as there's nothing to compare anything to. There are smells, and the cart goes up or down a little, the air becomes colder or warmer, but for the most part it's just seemingly endless humming as the wind whistles past. I worry that we're going to plow into that huge pile of rocks—which I now know I rescued Krog from, only so he could continue his plans to harm the town. But no collision ever comes, and I don't hear any of my friends shouting up ahead. I have to assume Krog cleaned up well, carefully sweeping away all the pebbles and dust so he'd have an unimpeded shot at destroying Cornucopia.

Well, good luck, Krog. We're going to beat you, and your little beetroots, too.

Sometime later, although I have no idea how long that some-time is, I hear the heavy thump of a mine cart reaching the end of the rails. Two more thumps follow it, echoing down the tunnel toward me, and then my cart stops, too—and not gently. There are torches here, plenty of them, but my eyes are so accustomed to the pitch-black dark that everything is too bright and very blurry.

"Brakes," Chug mutters. "Carts need brakes. Or slow-downers. Or antinausea pills."

He drags himself out of his cart, and when I squint, I see him helping Tok get the cats out and then climb out himself. Mal has already hopped out of her cart and is adjusting her armor. Chug comes to lever Poppy out, and I get out on my own, although he offers me a hand. Maybe I would have accepted it last week, but I know what I'm doing now.

"That's a good girl," he says, patting Poppy, and then his face falls. I've never seen Chug look this upset, this stricken and hurt and angry and—ashamed?

"I forgot Thingy," he says softly.

"We can go back for him," Mal assures him. "Once Cornuco-pia is safe, we can take the carts right back and bring him home."

"But what if he's scared? What if he thinks I forgot him?"

Now Tok pulls his brother into a hug. "We didn't have a choice, bro. He'll be fine. The faster we take care of this problem, the faster we can take care of that problem. Don't beat yourself up."

Chug sobs heavily, his shoulders jerking, and Tok pulls him closer. Mal joins the hug, and after a moment, I do, too. I can't imagine how I would feel to be here and realize that I'd left Poppy behind. It dawns on me that for as long as I've known Chug—since we were toddlers—I've never seen him cry before.

"I'm okay," he says, his voice gruff, like he's trying to hide the fact that he's really not okay at all. He goes to pull away, but Mal pulls him back.

"You're not okay, and you shouldn't be okay." She rubs his back. "You're completely justified in being really upset. But it's not your fault, and we're going to make it right. We're going to fix it. All of us."

"That's right," Tok chimes in.

"We'll have him back in a few hours," I promise. "We'll take him some of Nan's cake."

"He'll like that," Chug sniffles softly, his earlier gruffness gone.

We stay with him while he gets all the tears out, then turn away while he sniffles and wipes his nose on his sleeve and re-adjusts his armor. When he turns back around, he has his sword in hand and looks ready to kick butt. "So, what do we do now?"

Back in her element, Mal points to a stairwell. "We go up there and tell the Elders. All the adults. So let's do it."

She takes off running, and we fall into our places. Mal, Chug, Tok, me, Poppy. This time last week, I couldn't run all the way to Mal's house without having to walk a bit, but now loping just feels like my natural stride. I have my bow in one hand, an arrow in my other hand. The last one out, I look back at our carts sitting there, at the empty cavern behind them, the silver rails disappearing into darkness.

I hope removing the cart wheels has bought us enough time, and I kinda wish I'd had time to remove all the wheels instead of just enough to slow our foes down.

The stairwell is pretty exhausting, zigging and zagging up and up and up. At least there are plenty of torches. I guess even Krog the faux-illager doesn't want zombies and skeletons in his midst, probably because they'd be able to sniff out that he didn't belong. I'm panting by the time I nearly run into Tok, who's stopped and is standing on a stair, looking up, the cats sitting calmly at his feet while they wash their fur, as if this is just extremely boring for them.

A few steps up, past Chug, Mal stands with her hand on a trapdoor. "Ready?" she asks.

"Ready," we all say.

Mal and Chug and Tok have their swords and I have my bow and whatever we find on the other side of that trapdoor, I have to believe we're ready to face it.

With a mighty heave, the trapdoor flies open . . .

In someone's house.

Thankfully, it's empty.

We climb up into a small, dark, stuffy room, the windows thick with dust. A ragged carpet is rumpled up nearby, suggesting that it probably spends a lot of time hiding this very trapdoor. It smells old and musty in here, and nothing moves.

"Where are we?" Mal asks.

"A house in the Hub." Tok runs a hand along one wall, which is made of rough stone. "An old one, I think. Look at the odd dimensions, and the old-fashioned ceiling."

The home looks like a relic from the past. It's all done in the style our grandparents liked, which has fallen out of favor with our parents' generation as they moved out to live on their own farms.

I walk to a mantel, which has small clay figurines on it, three of them, little cones with sculpted heads. I pick them up, one by one, to read what's written on their bottoms. I can't help grinning when I find what I'm looking for under the smallest one and hold it up for my friends to see.

"Krog," I say. "This must be the house where his parents lived when they got older and moved off the beetroot farm. Their Founder's house." Every Founder had a house in the Hub, and it's always inherited when the next generation passes on. Krog is an only child, and he doesn't have any kids of his own.

"But Krog stayed on the farm after his parents passed," Chug says, his brow rumpled. "He doesn't live here."

"Well, he had to keep farming beetroot—who else would want to do it? I guess he came here, got curious, dug down, found the cavern, and decided to use this as a base of operations while he kept farming."

"He asked our dad if he wanted to buy the beetroot farm once," Tok says. "I was inventing something in the hayloft and overheard it. But Dad hates beetroot."

"See, it's not just me!" Chug exclaims.

Mal silences him with a finger to her lips. "We could talk all day about why Krog is doing this, but we don't have much time. We need to go tell the adults."

I look around the room, barely lit by the scant light filtering through the windows. "But first we need to put something heavy over this trapdoor. They'll fix the carts eventually, and it needs to be really hard for them to get out."

Mal grins, and I feel this wonderful rush of pride to know that I've done something useful. We heave over a dresser and a bed, planting them right over the trapdoor, the bed's leg pressing directly down. Satisfied that Krog won't be able to pop out easily, we head for the front door.

"We should be a little less obvious with our weapons," Mal says, probably because she's noticed how lethal Chug looks holding a diamond sword and frowning.

And she's right—there are plenty of people in our town who have never seen a single weapon. They probably don't even know they exist. When I first saw Nan's sword, I thought it was just a really long, weird knife.

As much as I hate how it feels, I shove my bow and arrows in my pockets and try to look innocent. How am I supposed to look harmless? I don't know how anymore. I've forgotten.

Mal leads us outside, and . . . wow, it's depressing.

Every door is open as families build and load carts and worriedly run around. Mal heads straight for the Hub and into Stu's shop. The shelves and walls are nearly bare, but there's a new display of weapons—inferior ones. Wooden swords and axes, mostly.

"You bad apples know you're not allowed in here—" he starts, but his eyes go wide as he takes us in. "Is that . . . diamond?"

Mal slashes a hand through the air to silence him—to silence *Stu*! An Elder!

"Krog is bringing a band of illagers to attack the town. There are evokers and vindicators. They have weapons and potions. Some have armor. There's a cavern with a mine cart under the town and an entrance in Krog's parents' house. He sent the vexes to make us leave so he could keep all the loot and get to something called . . ." She looks at us in confusion. "The Nether?"

Stu's blue eyes go wider, but it's not fear or worry. It's anger.

"You don't even know what half of those words mean!" he shouts. "The adults are taking care of things, and you're, what? Manufacturing crazy conspiracy theories? After disappearing for days and taking up valuable energy? What are you trying to do, stir things up more so you can steal from all the loaded carts parked outside?"

Chug looks at him like he's the one who's crazy. "Uh, I'm wearing like a thousand diamonds right now. Pretty sure stealing someone else's stuff isn't going to help. Now, do you want to save the town from a bunch of illagers or what?"

Stu raises a trembling hand, pointing his finger at the door. "No more lies. Get out! We should've separated all of you bad apples years ago! But it'll happen soon, you mark my words." When we don't budge, he walks around his counter, shooing us with his hands. "Go on now. Go tell your parents where you've been. You should all be ashamed."

We look to Mal, who is absolutely stricken. Mal doesn't lie, and the thought that she would lie, that she would steal, is unthinkable. And insulting. Even if the rest of us are bad apples — a brawling troublemaker, an inventor who blows things up, a daydreamer who spins tales — Mal is the good one, and everyone should know that.

Except now that we've been gone for days and made everyone frantic with worry, I guess they don't.

Mal's shoulders fall.

She puts a hand on the door and pushes her way outside, looking defeated.

27.

CHUG

 It's afternoon somehow, and we're all standing around in the sunshine in a circle, silent. I have never felt this weird in my entire life, and that's coming from a guy who once wore a chicken as a hat.

Around us, our neighbors are hurrying, talking, packing, frantic. But we're still and quiet and stunned.

They should believe us.

Why didn't Elder Stu believe us?

Sure, we have a reputation for . . . well, not causing trouble. Not on purpose. But not being normal. Not just putting our heads down to fit in. We're different, and we've always been different. But maybe that's not so terrible. Maybe we're not bad apples— we're good pumpkins.

And Tok says I'm awful at metaphors.

"Who cares what Elder Stu thinks?" I say.

"He's the head Elder," Mal mumbles, her voice soft as she

looks down at the ground. "Everyone follows him. Everyone believes him. And he doesn't believe us."

"Yeah, well, who cares?"

They all look up at me when I say that, maybe a little too loudly. "Look, so Elder Stu doesn't believe us. Who gives a poot? Stu has never set foot out of this town. He was born behind this wall. He's never fought a zombie. He's never faced a witch. He's never dug his own shelter or scrounged for his own food. But we're the Mob Squad, and we've done all that *in the last week*. And now that we've been out there, out beyond the wall, I actually think he's maybe not the nicest guy. I mean, the guy's never told anyone how a crafting table works so he can continue to charge high prices for his wares."

Tok's jaw drops. He apparently hadn't considered that. It feels pretty nice to have figured out something that my brainy brother hasn't.

"Thing is, Elder Stu is the same as everybody else here. But the four of us have always been different. And do you know who else was different?" I pause and drink in the expectant way they're looking at me, like I actually have something to say and it's not stupid at all.

"The Founders were different."

Their eyes glow with understanding, so I go on.

"The Founders left wherever they were before, and they came together, and they made something great. Because, yeah, there should definitely be a door in the wall and people shouldn't be so secretive and stingy with their family secrets, but Cornucopia is pretty amazing. Being different is what made the Founders special, and it's what makes *us* special." A new thought dawns on me. "And, hey. Know who else is different? There's one person in this town I know will believe us. Because she already does."

"My Nan," Mal whispers.

I nod.

It takes a moment to sink in, but then the old Mal is back, eyes burning and jaw set. She turns and starts running. We all follow her, because this is what we are now: a unit, a family, a machine that has exactly the right pieces to work together. The street is crowded with people and stuff, and we have to dart in and out and zig and zag, but it's particularly gratifying when Poppy brushes Jarro's mom's leg and makes her scream.

"Lenna! You stop right there."

I inwardly groan. I know that voice. It's Lenna's oldest sister, Letti, who thinks she's an adult and has been bossing us around forever. I want to keep running because I know Letti is bad news and will only slow us down, but I know full well that Lenna—even the new, more focused, more confident Lenna—can't resist following Letti's orders.

We all stop and turn back, flanking Lenna. Poppy's head is under one hand, providing support, but Lenna's other hand is a tight fist.

"You've been gone almost a week. Mom and Dad are worried sick. Everyone is." The older, snottier, pointier-nosed version of Lenna looks us up and down, disgusted. "I guess you guys were hiding to make us waste time looking for you? And now you're wearing costumes for more attention? Honestly, this is so embarrassing. We're going home right now." She puts her hands on her hips and raises her eyebrows.

This look would've cowed last week's Lenna, who would've hung her head and waved goodbye to us as she slumped off to get yelled at. But this Lenna doesn't let her head hang. She doesn't budge.

"No."

Letti is taken aback—I guess Lenna has never challenged her before. Which makes sense, as Letti is terrifying.

"What did you just say?"

"I said no, Letti. I'm not going home right now. We're doing something important."

Letti steps forward aggressively, and Poppy growls. As if she's just noticed the full-grown wolf, Letti does a double take and steps back warily.

"What is that thing?"

"Her name is Poppy, and she's not a 'thing.' She's a wolf."

With an audible gulp, Letti looks around like she's searching for help. "How'd it get in here? Get away from it. It's dangerous."

Lenna's hand stroke's Poppy's sleek gray head, and Poppy's tail thumps once, but the wolf remains vigilant against the person acting very much like an enemy.

"She's with me, she's not dangerous, and I'm leaving now. Bye, Letti."

Lenna turns her back on her sister and starts walking. Letti's jaw drops, and I have to smother a laugh. After all the insults she's hurled at us over the years, it's fun to see the tables turned.

"Lenna, don't you dare walk away. I am giving you a direct order."

"And I'm not following it."

"You're going to get punished."

At that, Lenna turns around and gives her sister a death glare. "Oh, punishment? What, is my whole family going to treat me like an idiot? Oh no. How terrible that will be. Look, I'm actually doing something important here, Letti, so go home and snitch. It's what you're best at." Lenna turns back around and walks a few steps before calling over her shoulder, "And a group of illagers is about to raid the town, so you might want to round up all the pickaxes at the mine."

With that final nugget of disdain, Lenna takes off at a sprint, and I shout "She's not kidding. Everyone should get ready for a fight!" before following.

After our time spent outside the wall, the run to Nan's house feels so short. It's hard to believe we stood here just a few days ago while Nan showed us a whole new world. Her cottage hasn't changed a bit, but we certainly have.

Mal knocks politely and fidgets while she waits for Nan to open the door. Seeing us, the old lady grins, her eyes dancing.

"You're alive!" she crows. "All of you!" She looks down at Poppy and laughs. "And you found a friend. Oh, I miss wolves. They decided it was too cruel to keep them within walls, but I'm glad you found one. Who's a good girl? You are, you are!" Sensing a friend, Poppy licks Nan's hand and wriggles to receive so much attention.

"Nan, the illagers are on the way," Mal says. "A raiding party."

Nan looks up, frowning. "On the way? But you were supposed to get rid of them."

"We found the woodland mansion and cleared it out, but then we found a secret trapdoor that leads to an underground cavern with mine carts. Krog was there. He's dressed like an illager, and he's leading them here. It was his plan all along to run us out of town. And he wants to build a portal—"

"To the Nether, no doubt," Nan finishes, her face a mass of angry wrinkles. "Always knew that Krog was no good. His parents were odd. It's good that you didn't kill him, I suppose."

We glance among ourselves at the wistful way she says that last bit.

"We tried to tell Elder Stu, but he didn't believe us," Mal continues. "We realized . . . no one would. It sounds impossible."

"But I believe you, and I know it's not impossible." Nan sighs heavily and heads into her house.

Mal looks at us, but no one is certain what's supposed to happen next. Do we go inside, even if she hasn't invited us? Is Nan giving up?

"Well, come on in," she calls peevishly. "We're going to need weapons. Unless you've brought enough for everyone?"

"You mean it's not *snacks* you're calling us in for?" I grumble, but I'm smiling.

I'm glad to be inside Nan's cottage again, and not just because there are several fresh pies on the counter. She starts opening every closet and chest, pulling out swords and random bits of armor and a weird, heavy bow that looks like it could shoot down the sun. Lenna reaches for that, her eyes alight. I want to tell her that I'm proud of her, that she was awesome facing down her sister, but I don't know how to put that into words, so I just say, "Yeah, that's definitely yours."

As we pack our pockets with a lot more weapons than anyone's great-great-grandmother should have lying around, we tell Nan our story. She nods seriously, gasps in surprise, hums with worry, growls when she hears about the thieves, and laughs when laughter is appropriate. Her eyes go soft when Mal talks about the llamas, so I tell her about Thingy, and I guess she can tell how upset I am about having to leave my pig behind because she grabs my arm and leads me over to the pies, saying that food will keep my strength up. I do not argue.

Tok is over at Nan's crafting table, turning out as many simple iron swords as he can. Lenna is making more arrows out of supplies that Nan thankfully has on hand. The old lady's eyes twinkle when she looks at them, nodding her approval.

"You're a bunch of good apples, you know that?" she says, and my heart feels like it's glowing so brightly the whole world could see it.

I begin to wonder how we'll know when we're ready, if there's some secret number of swords and arrows and—whoa! Shields?! Cool!—that's enough for us to go out there and win. With Mal packing and Tok and Lenna crafting, I honestly feel kind of useless.

Nan appears at my side, holding out a detailed drawing of nine people. Four women, four men, and one tiny girl sitting on a skeleton horse. She points to a burly man holding an axe on his shoulder, his arm around a much smaller woman with stick-straight black hair, and I recognize instantly the cleft chin that runs in my family.

"Your great-great-great-grandfather Chuk was a fighter, too," she says softly. When she holds out the framed image, I take it like it's the most breakable thing I've ever held. And I've held a lot of eggs.

"I've never seen this before."

"How could you? It's mine. And it's the only one like it. We met a caravan on our way here, and one of the guards was an artist. He drew it for us in exchange for a milk cow." She sighs. "These are the Founders. And me."

Mal and Lenna and Tok come over to look at the image, too. There, holding a familiar diamond pickaxe, is Mal's great-great-great-grandmother, Nan's mother, who has the same freckles, and grin, and red hair as Mal and her mother and, probably, long ago, Nan. I can recognize Lenna's great-great-great-grandfather by his

246 DELILAH S. DAWSON

cloud of curly hair and dark skin and her great-great-great-grandmother by her mousy, worried look. The last couple, Bria and Wil, are the only ones none of our group are related to, but of course we know their story.

"They meant well, you know," Nan says. She's fixed us all a cup of cocoa and sits down at the table. She tries not to show it, but clearly all this work is exhausting for her. I sit, too, so she won't feel so alone. "The Founders all came from different places. They'd each experienced terrible things—I heard them talk about it sometimes, around the campfire at night, but whenever they saw my eyes flash in the firelight, they went quiet. They met in a caravan and found kinship, and so they decided to build Cornucopia, which they hoped would be much safer than where they'd been born. Building the wall was the hardest part, the work of a lifetime. Lev and Lil mined the stone and placed it while the other families cleared trees and built homes and planted crops. They wanted a place where no one had to worry."

Nan snorts and sips her tea.

"I guess they got it. But that doesn't mean the wall was the right decision. If one person like Krog can drive us all to panic and flee, then what good is the wall anyway?"

"I think the wall is great," Mal says softly. "But I'd like it better with a couple of doors."

Nan reaches across the table to hold her hand, and tears spring up in my eyes.

After a moment, Nan pulls her hand away, finishes her cocoa, and stands.

"Well," she says, matter-of-factly. "Let's go beat the snot out of Krog."

28.

TOK

I wish my grandparents were more like Mal's Nan, but they spend most of their time sitting in a dark, stuffy house in the Hub, complaining about why no one ever visits, which is why no one ever visits. Nan, on the other hand, has one of my freshly made swords in hand, testing the swing of it. She looks tired but furious. I wouldn't cross her.

Each of us packs our pockets with weapons and armor. We head outside, and she closes the door with my cats inside to keep them safe—no creepers here!—and stares up the path through the forest with a weary sigh.

"Wish I had a horse," she grumbles.

"Or a pig!" Chug chimes in.

She looks at him sharply. "How strong are you, son?"

Chug puffs out his chest. "I once carried that pig across a log over a river."

Nan nods. "Good. Then carry me into town. I weigh significantly less than pigs, if I remember correctly."

Chug obligingly turns his back and squats, and then my tough, proud, angry brother is trotting down the path with an ornery centenarian crouched up there like a chicken jockey. We all follow, and I'm struck by how odd it is, being back home after I've been on a journey that's changed me so much. Everything here feels smaller—cramped even.

It doesn't take long at all for us to get into town, even though last week walking out to Nan's cottage felt like traveling to the ends of the world.

"Take me straight to Stu," Nan commands, and Chug nods and keeps trotting, a little out of breath but determined not to show it.

It's not long at all before we're on the paved walkways leading into the most crowded part of Cornucopia. Chug has to navigate around wagons and chests and angrily bleating sheep. He stops in front of Stu's Store and helps Nan down. She brushes off her vest and pants, pats her hair to fix a few errant curls after her ride, and storms in the door with Mal hot on her heels.

"Why, Nan! It's been too long," Stu calls, stepping out from around his counter to bow to her. He wants us to think that he's pleased to see her, but I can tell he's nervous by the way his eyes keep darting from Nan to us to the wide glass windows through which curious onlookers can be seen gathering.

"Don't you sweet-talk me, Stu." Nan bustles right up to him like an angry chicken and pokes him in the chest with her finger. "Did you call my great-great-grandchild a liar?"

Stu shoots an angry glare at us before giving Nan his biggest smile. "Well, now, if I believed every preposterous thing these bad a—" He clears his throat. "These kids have said over the years, we'd all be in trouble. They have a reputation around town for getting into scraps and making up fantastical stories. Can't always go believing children, can we? Such imaginations!"

Nan grinds her finger into Stu's chest, making him swallow hard. "If she told you someone was coming to attack the town, are you saying that would be preposterous? After someone destroyed the crops and jeopardized our livestock and food stores? Is that how you define 'preposterous'?"

Stu's mouth drops open, but he recovers quickly, stepping back to straighten his robe and give Nan a stern look. "It *is* preposterous. No one in Cornucopia would seek to harm our town. I'm the eldest of the Elders, and it's my duty to keep our people calm and safe, and I can't do that if any random child with a stray thought sees monsters when they stare too long into the dark."

"If a child sees a monster in the dark, there's probably a monster!" Nan shouts. Then she clears her throat and smiles that smile little old ladies use when they're about to stab you with a knitting needle. "Have you asked Krog if the allegations are true?"

I grin.

Oh, Nan's clever.

"Ask Krog? You want me to just walk up and ask him if he's destroying Cornucopia?"

"I do, yes." Nan takes her place beside Stu, grabs his arm, and drags him outside, but in a way that makes it look like he's chivalrously squiring her.

"Krog doesn't live downtown," he reminds her, trying to dig in his heels and failing. He's honestly not that much younger than she is, and he's definitely not as spry. I'm starting to realize that Nan is made out of iron wrapped in beef jerky.

"Krog recently inherited his parents' house in the Hub," she reminds him, just as tartly. "Let's go see what's going on there."

We've reached our destination, and Nan marches right up to the door and knocks. No one answers, of course.

"Krog? Hello?" she calls. "Shout if you don't want us to come in." Two seconds pass before she shrugs and opens the door, muttering, "He had his chance."

"You can't just break into someone's house!" Stu says, mortified and standing on the doorstep like he's waiting for an invitation.

"It was unlocked." Nan steps inside, and Stu has no choice but to follow her, as do we.

It's exactly the same as when we left it just a short time ago, the rug still tossed aside to reveal the furniture we piled messily over the trapdoor, hoping to make it that much harder for Krog's plans to come to fruition. Nan waves a queenly arm at it, and Chug and I remove the dresser and table.

"Oh, a trapdoor. How curious. I wonder if it leads to . . . an underground cavern, just like the children suggested?" Nan tugs on the door, but it's too heavy for her. Chug reaches down and pulls it open easily.

"This isn't how things are done," Stu sputters. "Krog clearly isn't here. If you really wish to talk to him, we can go to the beetroot farm and find him. I'm sure he's out in the fields, utterly oblivious to these accusations."

Nan stares down into the hole at the stone stairwell lit with torches.

"Or, now that we've discovered something that should be impossible, we could just take a teensy little peek down there and see if there are mine carts and a rail. You know, to see if the kids really are lying or not. Considering our entire town's future depends upon it."

Staring down into the hole, Stu trembles. I'm not sure if it's because he's old and frail or if he's scared of the dark or if he just really, really hates being wrong. He's so accustomed to being the oldest, the wisest, the one in charge. It must be really hard, realizing that even if we're lying, there's still something going on in the town that he doesn't know about. No one is allowed to dig into the stone except for Lenna's family. I never thought to question this rule—but I guess Krog did.

"I'm not going down there," Stu says. "It's unsafe."

"Actually, it's quite safe," Lenna tells him. "Plenty of support in the stairwell, loads of torches."

"This shouldn't exist." Stu shakes his head, but even he can no longer deny it.

"Sure, and neither should zombies and skeletons and evokers and vexes," Nan says mockingly. "I know you didn't forget the rhyme they used to teach us. *If you do not wish to sob—*"

"Stop that right now!" Stu barks. "You were among the Elders when we decided that was no song for children! That it would make them question things—"

"I voted against you! Children definitely deserve to know what's worthy of their fear. And they should be questioning everything!"

Nan's voice is shrill and ragged as they face off. Curious faces peek in the open doorway. We children have been forgotten; it's just Nan and Stu now.

"You've given them a wall and denied them a world, Stu. I remember what it was like out there, how big the sky was. I remember horses and llamas and pigs and wolves. I remember the thrill of trading with villagers and fighting zombies. And I'm sorry that you were born after the wall was finished, but pretending that all those things don't exist is not the way to a brighter future. *These children* are our future. They've been beyond the wall. They've fought and learned and crafted—yes, Tok there is a skilled crafts-man now, so there goes your monopoly. You can never again tell them their dreams are foolish, because they have truly lived, in a way you never have. So listen to them, you old fool. Listen, and tell the people to take up weapons, because Krog is coming, along with all the mobs from that song you're so determined to forget."

"How dare you—"

"Shhh!" Lenna holds up a finger and points at the ground.

I can't believe Lenna—Lenna!—just silenced the Eldest Elder. That was an incredible speech by Nan, and I want to clap, and I was even looking forward to Stu's spluttery rebuttal, but I hear a noise that I definitely shouldn't be hearing, a noise that makes the hairs rise on the back of my neck. Stu hears it, too, cocking his head at the trapdoor, his eyes wide.

"Hee hee hee hee hee."

It burbles up from the darkness, that snicker, along with the sound of shuffling feet and the hiss of vexes.

When Stu just stands there like a fool, Nan sighs and reaches into her pocket, handing him a sword of his own.

"Looks like I win this round," Nan says succinctly. "Preposter-ous, isn't it?"

29.
MAL

 I'm so proud of my Nan that I could spit, but the illagers are about to burst through the trapdoor, so I slam it shut and drag the bed back over it. Chug and Tok replace the dresser, and at first, we feel pretty satisfied with our work.

Then the vexes appear, hissing and flashing red.

Because, oh yeah—they can travel straight through walls. And trapdoors.

"This isn't possible!" Stu cries, flailing around with his sword like he's trying to hit a piñata rather than destroy a vex.

"I think we're past the point of letting you be the arbiter of the possible." With three quick hits, Nan takes down the vex, but of course two more appear.

Lenna is firing arrow after arrow, and Chug and I have our swords out, but Tok just stares down, eyebrows rumpled in that way that means he's thinking.

"We have to open the trapdoor," he finally says. "Or else the evokers will just keep sending more vexes. The vexes will never end until we take down the evokers."

Chug groans. "So we just open the door and let these jerks invade?"

"It's better than spending the rest of our lives fighting vexes. The evokers won't stop. You know that."

One of the vexes smacks him with a sword, and Tok gasps and grabs his arm. This, of course, only makes Chug angrier.

"Fine! Mal, help me with the dresser?"

I don't like this plan, but he's right. I look to Nan, and she gives me a firm nod. Chug and I heave the dresser off the trap-door.

I pause before reaching for the bed. "Elder Stu, will you please go tell the town what's happening? You're the only one they'll believe. And Tok, maybe you could hand out weapons."

He nods, and Chug and I empty our pockets on the floor as Lenna keeps shooting at the vexes. Our piles of weapons grow, and Stu's jaw drops.

"Who taught you that trick?" he barks. "With the pockets."

"I did," Nan barks back. "I reckon once that secret's back out, you won't sell nearly as many chests, eh?"

For once, our Eldest Elder is speechless.

"Go on, Stu," Nan says. "Go spread the word."

Without a word, Stu stuffs his pockets with weapons—proving he *did* know the trick!— and hurries out the door, happy to avoid the vexes even if he has to face the town. Tok collects the rest of the weapons and follows him. With our most vulnerable friend safely out of the room, Chug and I push the bed off the trapdoor, and he reaches to throw it open again. We stumble back, swords ready, both of us taking spots in front of Nan. I know she has skills with that sword, but I also know she's ancient and exhausted.

She's fought her fight.

This one's mine.

Of course Krog's not the first one up the stairs—three vindicators barrel out, axes ready, grunting. Chug and I engage them, working as a team as Lenna keeps harrying the vexes with her flaming arrows. Poppy knows just what to do, rushing in to yank at the vindicators' robes with her teeth as she growls. We each take down a foe, but more vindicators rush up from the darkness to replace them. One goes after Lenna but only meets Nan's blade.

"I'm too old for this," she complains.

The next vindicator hits the floor and I turn to look at the open door. Townspeople should be rushing in to help, or at least running around the street, flailing and shouting, but nothing is happening. Did Stu give up and run home to hide? No, Tok wouldn't have let him. Maybe Stu did tell the people, but the people didn't believe him.

More vexes fly out, and one lands a hit on my back before Lenna can nock another arrow. The cry of pain flies out of my mouth before I can stop it.

"Outside. Now." Nan doesn't wait for agreement before she bustles out the door. Chug and I break at the same time, following her, and Lenna comes last.

Out in the street, people are walking toward where Stu stands on the dais, shouting about enemies and weapons. Tok holds out swords, but no one is stepping forward. A few of the other Elders stand nearby, whispering among themselves.

"Vexes!" Stu shouts. "And evokers and vindicators! They're coming up through Maddie and Tobi's house. I saw them! We have to fight!"

"Those are just old stories," Elder Tiber says. "To scare us when we were wee."

"The reports of vexes are all hearsay. The fabrications of attention-seeking children and farmers with failed crops. There has to be a more realistic explanation," Elder Zach adds.

"It's those bad apples!" This from Jarro's mom, Dawna, of course. "They probably made up this whole stunt just to cause trouble." The smug, "I told you you'd suffer" grin she shoots at me and Chug makes me madder than any vex could.

But when an actual, literal vex flies out into the street, flashing red and wielding its sword, that grin disappears.

"Yeah, this is all us," I shout with an epic eye roll. "We just loooove trouble."

"Now, do you want a sword or not?" Tok gestures at the pile of weapons.

A telltale "Huh hn!" makes me spin around as a vindicator sprints out the door, axe raised. I can't pay attention to the towns-people anymore—I have to fight. Either they'll take up their own weapons and join us or they'll run away.

Oh, no.

Would they do that?

Could they possibly believe that hiding in their houses, ignoring this problem will just make it go away?

More vexes swarm out the door of Krog's house, followed by their evoker. Ghostly white fangs ripple up from the ground, hitting Dawna in the leg and making her scream. She whispers to Jarro, who runs away toward his house. Much to my surprise, Dawna reaches for one of Tok's swords, takes her first swing at a vex, and, incredibly, lands a solid shot.

I take a stinging hit to the shoulder and refocus on what I can do with my own weapon. Chug and I move into our best position, fighting back-to-back as the vexes come for us. Lenna aims at the evokers, knowing that as soon as they're gone, so are their pesky vexes and fangs. Iron flashes, inches away from my face, as Old Stu takes down the vindicator that nearly felled me. I should be scared, but I'm not. I'm fighting. And it feels good.

Even if I can't tear my eyes away from the vexes long enough to see what the townspeople are doing, I can hear the clanks and clangs and grunts as swords and axes find their targets. Following in Dawna's footsteps and heeding Stu's words, the people of Cornucopia are taking up their weapons and facing the monsters they've been forced to forget. I nearly trip over an emerald, my boot kicking away a helmet. The more enemies we destroy, the more loot they drop. I just wish my neighbors had the good sense to snatch up the armor and enchanted swords scattered on the cobblestones.

"Mal?"

I break away from the vex when I hear that voice—my mom.

She's peeking around a corner, and she beckons to me. I want to go to her. I want a hug. I want safety. I want her to tell me everything will be okay. But . . .

"Kind of in the middle of a fight to the death, Mom," I say, redoubling my efforts against the vex and taking it down with a violent slash.

"We've been so worried about you."

"I'm fine." A vindicator lands a solid hit on my armor, making me stumble. "Well, okay, maybe not *fine* fine, but fine enough."

"This isn't safe. Just come on home and let the adults handle this, okay, honey?"

I can't look up again, can't risk taking any more hits. "No."

"Either pick up a weapon or go home, Mara," Nan grumbles. She's fighting off her own vex, sweat running down her face under the diamond helmet she's swiped off the ground. "Your kid's a hero. Don't get her killed."

My mom gasps like she's just realized this is a possibility. I can't look at her, but I can imagine her watching me, her heart in her eyes, thinking that if she's just reasonable enough I'll put down the sword and walk away.

But I can't. The town needs me. It would be nice if the adults could fix this problem, but I'm the one who's been training, the one who's in shape, the one who knows this sword like it's an extension of my arm, the one with a Founder's diamond pickaxe in my pocket. I can do this, and I'm not hiding anymore, whether behind the wall or behind my front door or behind the façade of the perfect daughter who does everything she's told.

I snatch an iron helmet off the ground and toss it to my mom without looking. "You've got Nan's blood, too. You're probably pretty good with a weapon. Go sword or go home."

I hear a tentative rasp of metal on stone, and then a determined grunt, and my mom has picked up a sword and joined the fray, fighting back-to-back with Nan. I grin, a fierce joy singing through me. I take down the next vex and have a moment to look around. Hope surges through my chest to see so many of my neighbors fighting these monsters.

Even though most of them have never held a weapon before today, they've chopped wood and hammered over forges and slung a blade to harvest wheat. Like my mom, like me and my friends, adventuring runs in their blood. The people of Cornucopia are descended from the Founders, and the Founders built this place with blood, sweat, tears, and, I'm learning, quite a bit of hostile mob destruction. Even the Elders have taken up their weapons and are doing their best to strike back at the monsters who would harm us.

But wait.

That reminds me.

I see vexes and evokers and vindicators, but there's one robed pest I'm missing.

I look around, hunting for the illager who doesn't quite fit.

I find him hiding behind the dais, peeking up every now and then like the coward he is to toss splash potions.

Krog.

I nudge Chug's shoulder and point at that fake witch's nose peeping over the wood.

"Let's go get him," I say.

30.

LENNA

 My entire world is the curved wood in my fist, the taut string against my fingertips. I'm the only one with a bow and arrow, the only one who can pick off the dangers without taking a direct hit. Once I've found a barrel to hide behind, I barely move . . .

Until I reach down to my arrow stack and find nothing.

The problem with vexes is that they fly and then disappear, so it's not like pulling an arrow out of whatever is left of a zombie or skeleton. My arrows are spread all over the Hub, sticking out of walls and skittered over stone and lying among piles of armor and dropped emeralds.

I look to Mal and Chug, just in time to watch them nod at each other in that uncanny way they have and run toward the dais where the Elders make their proclamations. My main goal was to keep the mobs from attacking them, but there are a lot fewer mobs now, and they're focusing their energy elsewhere. That gives me time to replenish my supplies.

I dart out, zigging and zagging to pick up every arrow I can find. Poppy is fighting her own fight—she's particularly clever about tugging on the jackets of vindicators to distract them from their axes. I'd be worried about her—I *am* worried about her—but she's a wild thing who's chosen to join the fray, and she's taking a wolfish glee in it, bounding here and there to ravage our attackers.

As I reach for an arrow, someone grabs me around the middle and drags me backward into an open door. I flail and shout, but there's so much chaos, so much noise, that no one really notices. My elbow catches someone in the face—I feel the pop of their nose at the solid hit, and they grunt and drop me.

"Ow! What was that for, idiot?"

It's my sister Letti, and as I scramble to my feet and face her, she drags a sleeve across her now bloody nose.

"For grabbing me. I didn't know who it was."

"Why would anyone else grab you?"

I gesture to the scene outside. "Because there's a fight going on, and I'm actually pretty good at fighting, so the bad guys would like to see me fall."

She looks down her dripping nose at my bow and fistful of arrows. "I didn't know you were good at anything." I hate how doubtful she seems, like I still might be mistaken about my own skills.

"I've been traveling the real world for a week," I tell her. "Digging out shelters, crafting my own tools, foraging food, fighting mobs. If I weren't good, I wouldn't be here. Now leave me alone—I'm going back out there to help."

I head for the door, but she grabs my shirt and yanks me again.

I . . . do not like being yanked around.

"You can't go out there. I told Mom and Dad that you were back, and they told me to bring you home. You're in *so* much trouble."

I snatch my shirt away and square my shoulders. "Letti, honestly. Who cares about 'trouble'? We're under attack. Every second I'm not out there, more vexes—"

She rolls her eyes. "This is for the Elders and Hub folk to deal with. This isn't our problem."

Classic Letti.

She's just one of those people who think that her problems are more important than anyone else's, and that other people aren't worthy of our help.

And I don't believe that.

I never did.

"This is our town, Letti. This is our life. This is my problem. It's your problem, too, which you would notice if you weren't so focused on me and my punishment. I'm not going home right now."

She moves to block the door. "Yes, you are."

All my life, she's told me what to do. When she could've been kind, she was curt. When she could've asked me what was wrong, she told me to stop crying and be normal. When she could've taught me how to hold a pickaxe, she told me to go bother someone else. And she always told me it was for my own good, but now I realize that it's because I was inconvenient, and she cared more about not being bothered than she did about me.

"No," I say, quite simply.

And then I whistle, and Letti looks at me like I'm the idiot she's always assumed me to be.

"What was—"

Poppy appears, and when I point at Letti's tunic, my wolf friend grabs it in her teeth and wrenches backward, tail wagging. Letti flounders and grabs for the door, but she's not very strong or agile, and she's being dragged by a full-grown wolf. I wait until she's clear of the door and run outside, wedging myself behind a wagon where I'll have a good shot at the remaining vexes. There are still two evokers left, and once my arrows start flying, the crowd rallies and redoubles their attack.

"Lenna!" my sister calls from the sidewalk as she holds the torn hem of her shirt. "You're going to be in so much trouble!"

"I don't care!" I shout back. "I'm used to it!"

Letti turns and runs home.

Deciding to ignore her, I hunt for my next flying target.

31

TOK

Outside, the fight rages. But inside Stu's Store, he and I work at our crafting tables, creating swords and axes and shields and armor as fast as the townsfolk stagger in empty-handed to request them. Part of me feels bad that I'm not outside, doing the hard work, putting my life on the line like Chug and Mal and Lenna to keep our town safe.

But as I glance up to see Old Stu wipe sweat from his brow as he crafts a sword—a process, I note, that takes him much longer to accomplish than it takes me—I begin to see the value of what I'm doing here.

Unlike Chug's diamond gear, all we can give the people are simple objects made of humble materials. Iron can crack. Wood can splinter. A vindicator can tear up a shield. Unprotected, unable to fight, the people come here and take our creations in hand and smile gratefully.

What we're doing—it's valuable. It's special.

And it turns out I'm a lot better at it than Elder Stu is.

"Never had kids," he says as he picks up two broken swords to create one stronger weapon. "Never found me a wife. Thought being an Elder was my calling." He glances over at me, one tufty eyebrow up. "Forgot to pass on my skills. Where'd you learn to craft like that?"

"From a book." I inspect the shield I've just created and lean it up against the wall so that whoever needs it can grab it.

"What book?"

"Something Nan gave me. It was stolen by brigands outside the dark forest. Wish I had another one." And I do. I never found Nan's book in any of the woodland mansion chests.

I start on an axe, but Stu just watches me. Normally I would mind—my dad used to stare at me when I was trying to bring my inventions to fruition, but it was kind of like the way you'd stare at a cow trying to climb a tree, like it was an interesting effort but doomed to failure. This time, I don't mind. Stu is watching me . . . like he might be learning something from my technique. I did figure out a clever way to recycle some of the diamond chips to make a stronger and more effective axe.

"I have a few books," Stu says, a little cagey.

My head jerks up. "About crafting?"

He nods. "If we get through this, you can borrow some. Not take 'em with you," he hurriedly adds, one hand up. "Valuable things, you know. But you could come here and read. Try things out. I could teach you."

At this point, I could probably teach him, but I'm sure there are subtleties and tricks I don't know, and I really want to get my hands on those books.

"I'd like that," I say.

Stu smiles, a brief and rare thing that I've never seen before in any way related to me or my friends. Then he goes back to looking surly as he reaches down for the next broken sword. "We're running out of materials. Can you make a run out there, see what you can find?"

I don't want to—I like it in here, and I love crafting more than anything. But it's a fight, and my job is to fix and repair weapons, and I can't do that if I'm standing in an empty room without any raw materials. I nod, finish up my axe, lean it against the wall, and pause at the door to look around outside.

The fight has grown more concentrated. There are a couple of evokers left, and they're using their vexes and fangs to keep our side from getting anything done. Chug, Mal, and Lenna are nowhere to be seen. As Stu anticipated, raw materials are everywhere—broken weapons, things our fallen enemies have dropped, wagons reduced to chunks by—

Wait. What could possibly reduce a wagon to chunks?

I hear a snort and look up to find a huge beast snarling at me. It's like a cow crossed with the biggest, ugliest rock I've ever seen. It paws at the ground with an enormous hoof and charges.

I drop all the materials I've collected and run. My mind stops working—an unusual and unique sensation—and I panic and put all my energy into not getting trampled by the beast. I pass townsfolk, but no one steps in to stop the creature or help me; they're all fighting battles of their own.

"Chug! Mal! Lenna!" I scream, because even if I don't know what will keep me safe, I know they'll try.

But for the first time in my life, my brother and friends don't answer.

The beast surges at me, and I dodge, and it rams the corner of a building with its head, causing rock to rain down. I guess I know now what happened to those wagons, and I'm very certain I don't want it happening to me. Clearly, as long as I'm just running away in a straight line, it's going to have an advantage.

Think, brain, think!

Funny how it can keep me up all night imagining seemingly impossible machines, and yet the one moment I desperately need it to do something clever, my brain flat out goes completely blank. I can barely even remember how to get around the Hub—it's so twisty and crowded down here, all dead-end alleys and broken stairs—

Wait.

That's it.

I remember that alley where Jarro and his cronies cornered us on the day the first vex showed up. I jump up on the fountain, balance around it, and take a new direction, running all the faster now that I have a clear goal. I grab a fallen sword as I charge through what's left of the battle, my path serpentine as I leap over piles of rubble. The beast follows, sometimes so close I can hear its grunts and smell its foul breath.

When I see the blue door I'm looking for, I take a sharp left down an alley between two of the tall, leaning buildings. Just like I remember, it's wide enough for the beast, and it follows me without slowing. I have to be careful here. I may finally be able to hold a sword without slicing myself, but no one has ever called me nimble, and what I'm going to do will take some finesse.

The alley takes another sharp turn and narrows, the scent of rotten fruit filling the air. If this monster was related to cows or pigs, it would definitely stop to investigate that pile of melon rinds, but it's entirely focused on me. I just hope—

Yes!

I find the right spot—an ancient, half-rotten set of steps that leads up to a door set high in the wall. Last time, when Jarro was chasing me, Chug had to give me a boost to the lowest stair, but a lot has changed since then. I step onto a broken box and catapult myself to the bottom step, pulling myself up with my new-found strength. The beast follows on my heels but can't quite stop, and it runs headfirst into the stone wall below me with a heavy crunch that takes a chunk out of the blocks. It can't turn around because the alley is too narrow, and it isn't the kind of animal that can back up quickly or effectively. I kneel on the step over its head, broken sword in hand, hating what I have to do next.

Without a sound, I drop down and land on the beast's back, hoping it's as easy to ride as Thingy was for Chug.

It is not.

The creature screams and throws me, and I skid on my back across the cobblestones. It hurts, but I don't let go of the broken sword. I'm all too aware that it's all I have left.

I look up, and all I see is a ton of stinky beast butt.

I raise my sword and do what any kid would.

I stab it.

32.

CHUG

 Mal and I have almost reached the dais—and Krog— when something flies through the air and crashes against her chest. Liquid drips down her armor, hissing a little. It's bright purple, more sinister than a healing potion. Tiny purple droplets fleck her chin. Mal's jaw is dropped, her eyes wide. We don't know what this potion is, what it will do. All the potions in our town are helpful and rare and expensive, crafted only for emergencies by Elder Gabe. But this is surely a potion meant to harm, and it's the one thing we don't know how to fight.

She gasps, and it's like . . . I don't know how to describe it. Sometimes a pumpkin plant starts to die, and we don't know why. Its leaves turn yellow and then brown, its vines withering and its fruit shriveling.

Mal looks like that.

Her cheeks are sinking in, there are purple hollows pooling under her eyes, her lips are going dry and cracked as I stare at her in horror.

"Mal! What is it?"

"Some kind . . . of poison," she creaks. "You've got . . . to . . . get him."

I glare at the dais, where Krog is hiding and apparently hurling potions at children like a coward. There's a broken shield nearby, and it's not perfect, but it's enough. I leap and kneel, coming up with the shield and holding it before me as I barrel directly toward Krog.

A potion sails past my head, crashing on the cobbles. Another one strikes the shield, and a few drops land on my hand, but that's not going to stop me. I'm running like I did when I carried Thingy across that log, not caring what happens to me as long as I get to stop Krog before it happens.

That fake witch face pops up from behind the dais, and his arm rears back, hurling the next potion. I'm too close, I'm holding the shield all wrong, I can't stop it, it's hurtling through the air, end over end, it's going to hit me and burn off my lips, and—

An arrow smacks into the glass, knocking the potion harmlessly to the ground. I don't have to look back over my shoulder to know that Lenna is here and I'm not alone.

Well, Mal's here, too, but I know she can't fight. She can barely talk.

I reach the dais and leap onto the wood in a smooth roll that's gonna leave a magnificent shoulder bruise. On the other side of the wooden structure, Krog is spinning to run away, his fake witch robe billowing behind him. He may be an older guy, but he's lean and muscled, thanks to life on the beetroot farm. I know from personal experience that he's a fast runner, and that when he finds a kid in his field, he can generally catch that kid by the collar and carry them home like a sack of pumpkins.

This time, I have to be faster.

He runs down the street, and I know where he's headed: his parents' house, where the trapdoor is.

Maybe he didn't win today, but he can keep at it. He can collect more illagers and send them into the town. He can create more potions and sneak back in. Sure, we can reseal that trapdoor, but he's a smart guy with resources. He can pop up through someone else's floor or mine, up through the ground into his own beetroot farm, probably. He can use the entrance outside the wall.

If we don't stop this guy, he's going to keep threatening Cornucopia until we really do leave, or he's at least going to make our lives miserable and put us on constant guard against what he might do next.

"Lenna, shoot him!" I shout, realizing just how desperate the situation is becoming.

"I'm out of arrows." She appears at my side, loping along with Poppy. When did she get so fast? "Is Mal okay?"

"I don't know. Potion. Didn't look good."

Up ahead, Krog skitters between two buildings, and we take the same turn into the narrow alleys of the Hub. I don't like it here. I never have. Everything is too close, like the buildings could collapse at any moment.

"We've got to take him down," I say.

"We do," Lenna agrees.

"Boof," Poppy adds.

I don't know this part of town that well, except to know that it smells bad and there aren't a lot of places to hide because there's not a lot of room. I'll have to turn sideways and suck in just to squeeze through some of the narrow alleys. Krog takes another turn, and I'm terrified we're going to lose him, when we're the only thing that stands between him and his evil plan succeeding and all of us getting split up after we've worked so hard to save everything we love.

But when we come around the corner, Krog has stopped. He's reaching into his pocket for what I assume is another potion, but I don't stop to see what's made him pause. I run full speed at him and land a solid hit with my sword.

Except . . .

It doesn't really do much.

It's like my arms are made of noodles. I can barely lift the sword.

A hit like that should have laid him flat on his back, but it barely made a soft thump. Krog turns around, fake witch brows drawn down in annoyance. When he sees me standing there, confused and barely managing to hold my diamond sword up off the ground, he grins the grin of evil old men everywhere who think they've won.

"Potion of Weakness. Wondrous, isn't it? I—"

We don't get to hear him gloat further, as he topples forward, eyes wide, and crumples to the ground. Behind him stands Tok, holding a broken iron sword in both hands and looking just as surprised as Krog.

"I should've known—" Krog starts.

"Hit him again, Tok!"

Tok does, and it's nice to finally hear Krog shut up.

"Here, take my diamond sword." I try to hold it out to my brother, but I can't even lift it now.

He shakes his head.

"He's not a mob. We aren't trying to kill him."

"Maybe . . . just a little bit?"

Tok and Lenna both give me warning glares.

"No," Lenna says firmly. "This is definitely something for the town to decide."

As Krog tries to stand, I scoop up some of the potion from my chest plate and wipe it on his forehead.

"Potion of Weakness," I say in a mocking voice. "Wondrous, isn't it?"

While Tok stands over Krog with his sword, Lenna pulls a lead out of her pocket and uses it to tie Krog to an old door. Krog tries to wiggle away, but the tip of Tok's sword scares him into stillness. I want to help, but I can barely move. I want to nap so bad, and even more than that, I want to eat like ten chickens, but I can't do any of that until I know that we're all safe.

Me, Tok, and Lenna just stand there, admiring our trussed-up villain— and it occurs to me that everyone else in town is off fighting the mobs and has no idea we're here.

"Stu!" I shout. "Elders! Anyone! We've caught the bad guy!"

It takes them a few minutes to find us, considering how twisty the alleys are back here, but soon Stu, Nan, and several other adults stand over what appears to be a witch.

"Behold!" I say, reaching down to whip off Krog's fake witch nose. It's stuck on with something, and I'm still really weak, so Lenna has to help, and it's not as dramatic as I'd hoped. But there is a collective gasp when ol' Krog is unmasked. Lenna yanks off his witch hat, too. It feels good, witnessing the moment he knows he can't wriggle out of what he's done.

"Where's my Mal?" Nan asks, noticing us.

I gasp when I realize that she hasn't joined us. "Back by the dais. She got hit with a potion."

"What kind?"

When I say, "Poison," Nan starts running.

33.

TOK

 My bones are still ringing from getting bucked off a malodorous beast, but the moment Nan breaks into a run, we follow. If a lady that old and tired is sprinting, there's got to be a problem. I guess there was so much going on that I didn't notice Mal was missing, and my shoulders climb toward my ears with shame, to think she might be alone and in danger. I'm sure my brother feels even worse.

Chug, Lenna, and I naturally glomp together as we run. It's funny, how we used to mostly run away from problems we'd caused with our mischief but now we're running to *solve* much bigger problems. I'm a little out of shape but stronger than I was — and Chug is pretty weak thanks to that potion, so I help him along.

It's not a long run back to the dais, because the Hub is not a large place. We pass piles of loot dropped by the evokers and vindicators that Krog brought into town to . . . well, what did Krog want them to do? Not kill us. Just drive us away faster, I guess. But they *could've* killed us. There are injured people here and there, leaning against buildings or sitting on steps or wagons. Gabe, the elder who makes potions, is distributing vials of magenta liquid, his face pained. He charges such high prices for them that it's got to hurt, giving them out for free. Hopefully he has one that will help Mal, but we've got to find her, first.

On the far side of the dais, Nan stops, and when we skid to a halt around her, it's hard not to just start crying. Mal is on her back on the ground, and she looks like a piece of old, rotten wood. Her skin is gray, her hair is dull and greasy, her once bright eyes are sunken in and empty. Her lips are shriveled and dry and cracked, and her arms look older than Nan's, scrawny and weak.

"Poison," she whispers as Nan gestures for Chug to help Mal sit up.

"You," Nan says to me. "Smart boy. Go get me some milk."

I was just about to run to Gabe, but I turn back in surprise. "Milk? Not a potion?"

Nan shakes her head. "Potions can't always solve potion problems. We need milk. And get some for your brother, too."

I nod and sprint for Mal's farm. I'm not the fastest or the strongest, and I feel like Nan should've picked someone else for this important errand, but I can tell that Mal doesn't have much time left, so I put everything I have into moving my body. My legs pump, my arms swing, my heart pounds. Town has never seemed so large, not since I was a toddler. I skid past the outskirts of the Hub and onto the road that leads to Mal's farm. I wonder if her parents even know what's happened here. The way our town works, they could be outside working, doing normal cow things, and have no idea that their downtown neighbors are fighting for their lives. That *Mal* is fighting for her life.

Mal's fence is in sight, and I put a hand on the gate and vault over like I'm being propelled by some outside force that makes me more confident, more graceful. I know where they keep the covered buckets of milk, so I skip the house and head straight for the barn.

There—six pails lined up, each covered with a cloth as the farm cats prowl and beg.

A cow sees me and moos in surprise, and Mal's dad looks up from his milking stool.

"Tok?"

"Mal's in trouble. Nan said to bring milk. They're at the Hub."

I don't wait for the inane questions I know he'll ask. I just grab two pails of milk and run.

Well, except milk sloshes everywhere, so I adopt a rolling run-walk and smoothly speed away from the barn.

"Tok, wait!" Mal's dad calls. "What kind of trouble?"

So he *doesn't* know what's happening in the Hub. And I'm not going to risk Mal's life by explaining. I ignore him and walk as fast as the sloshing milk allows.

Walking this way—it's taking forever. I feel so slow and ponderous and useless, like literally anyone could do a better job at what I'm doing. I felt this way a lot, before our adventure outside the wall, and it's not particularly pleasant to feel the negative thoughts creeping in again.

I'm doing my best, I remind myself.

Chug might run, but he would spill the milk.

Lenna might be faster, but she would've stopped to explain everything to Mal's dad.

Maybe I'm the best person for this job.

Maybe I'm doing it exactly right.

I focus on my legs moving smoothly and quickly, on my aching fingers holding the handles of the milk pails. I zip past the fences and into the Hub, directly to where everyone is waiting for me. Mal looks even worse than before, like she's somehow both melting and drying out. Her eyes are closed now, bulging behind lavender eyelids. Nan tries to take the bucket from me, but it's too heavy for her.

"Help her drink, boy." She looks around, frowning and on the edge of panic. "Is there a cup?"

No one moves, so I dart into the nearest open door and return with the first cup I find; whoever owns it can have it back later. Nan dips it into the milk and holds it to Mal's desiccated lips. She tries to pour it, but most of the milk dribbles down Mal's chin. I grab the cloth from the top of the other milk pail, dip it into the creamy white, and poke that into Mal's open mouth. A few drops must find their way past her lips, as she swallows and then starts to suck on the cloth. Nan takes over, dipping the cloth in the milk and dripping the milk into Mal.

We all wait, breathless, terrified. Cornucopia has always been a safe place, and the worst thing that's ever happened here are a few broken bones or cuts that were easily healed through potions and good food. The only people who ever die in Cornucopia are the very old. I don't even know what we would do if a child—

If Mal—

Tears prick my eyes, and I dash them away. When I look at Chug, he's flat out crying. He can't wipe away his tears while holding Mal up, so he just lets them flow, and I realize in that moment how very strong my brother is, and how very proud I am of him. Lenna sits on Mal's other side, quietly sniffling. Poppy is lying down next to Mal, her head on Mal's leg, her eyes on Mal's face. Mal's mom is there, and her dad finally finds us.

The milk in the first bucket is half gone. When Nan holds up the next cup, Mal turns her head away and closes her eyes.

34

MAL

 Everything hurts.

Everything hurts in a way that I can't quite understand. It's like being sunburned on the inside, like I'm drying out, all my blood turned to ash.

And then there's . . . milk?

It's the first thing my parents gave me as a child, fresh milk from our own cows. Sweet and cool and . . . clothy? I spit out the rag in my mouth, and the cool metal of a cup touches my lips. I drink and drink and drink, and I begin to feel my fingers and toes again. My blood is replaced by milk.

As a girl who grew up on a cow farm, this is almost funny. I try to laugh but can't; my throat is still too dry. So I drink some more.

Milk fills me. I begin to sense things—shadow and light, the pressure of an arm around my back and a warm body against my leg. I hear whispering—scared whispering. Is it for me? Did I do something wrong?

I can't quite remember.

The next time the cup returns to my lips, I turn away.

I'm getting pretty sick of milk.

Everything around me goes terribly silent.

"Mal?" someone says.

It's Chug.

"Mal, you can do it," someone else says. That's Tok.

"Come back to us. Please." And there's Lenna.

I cough a little and blink, but my eyelids are so heavy.

"If I stick around, can I have something besides milk?" I say, and my voice creaks like I'm older than Nan.

I feel the collective sigh of relief, and when I open my eyes again, everyone is staring at me—like half the town. Lenna and Tok and Nan are nearby, and Chug is holding me up. Stu stands a bit away, blocking a flock of curious townsfolk, all bruised and beat up.

"Mal, honey?"

A shadow resolves into my parents—my vision is still pretty blurry. My dad bombards me with questions—What happened? Where have you been? What's wrong with you? What did you kids do this time?

And Nan gives him a stern talking-to about paying less attention to gossip and trusting me more.

"They saved the whole darn town!" she barks, shaking a finger at my parents. "You should be thankful."

And they are—my parents are both crying and trying to hug me, but Chug is still holding me up, and I'm pretty sure I'm not able to sit on my own yet.

"It's fine," I tell them. "I'm going to be fine."

And I am. I can tell. Because the way I felt before? It wasn't fine. As soon as the poison touched me, I could feel it seeping in, sucking the life out of me. If it wasn't for this bucket of milk—I'd probably be dead.

My parents back away a little, and I shift in Chug's arms, trying to get more comfortable. Everyone is staring, and it's making me uneasy. As if sensing this, Nan growls, "Now go on and take your potions and clean up. If there's a single evoker left, we'll all be sorry. And get Krog in jail."

"I think we've been storing cobblestone in the jail," Stu says, fidgeting. "We've never used it for people before."

"Then clear it out. There's a first time for everything. Think, man! Honestly, if it weren't for four kids, a wolf, and an old woman, you'd be in a whole world of trouble."

When Stu blushes and bustles off, I grin.

"How about some more milk?" I ask.

35

LENNA

 Once we're certain Mal's no longer in danger, things get odd. No one really knows what to do. When Nan shouts "Enough!" the onlookers disperse. Gabe hands out more potions, Stu makes sure the jail is cleaned out and Krog is locked in it, and Inka brings cool, sweet melons for everyone who's been fighting so hard, the last ones harvested before the vexes arrived. Once Mal can stand, Nan makes Chug drink the entire other pail of milk, which he considers a dare. The Potion of Weakness had made it almost impossible for him to hold Mal up all that time, but he'd refused to complain or let anyone else take his place.

We search everywhere, but we don't find any more illagers. The trapdoor in Krog's house gets sealed, just in case anything else tries to come up. The Elders do their best to make sure all the loot is distributed evenly, which causes some fights and complaints, especially by Jarro's mom, but that, at least, is an adult problem.

As for me and my friends? We did our part.

Nan is barking orders at anyone holding still, but she doesn't tell us what to do—she just winks at us and makes a shooing motion. We kind of drift, unsure where to go.

If we just go home to our houses, we'll all have to deal with the same thing: our families. Now that we're back and safe, they're free to be angry that we left. They'll be glad to see us, but it's a lot of work, explaining things. And for me, my experience feels so personal. I don't actually want to tell my family—much less defend myself from whatever Letti has told them. The boys probably feel the same way about their folks. Mal's parents have always been more understanding, but she's always been a better kid. I'm very well aware that the last time I spoke to a family member, I told my older sister off.

My parents won't care that I helped save the entire town.

They won't see how far I've come, what I can do, how strong I am.

They'll see me only as disrespectful and a shirker.

And they'll tell me I have to get rid of Poppy.

Without talking about it, my friends and I drift out of the Hub and toward Nan's forest. When I was little, I was so scared of it, but now it's a relief. This place is as close as I can come to being outside the wall. If I had my way, Mal would dig a shelter, and Tok would make beds, and Chug and Thingy would go fishing for salmon, and Poppy and I would keep watch, and we'd all settle in and laugh and tell stories.

As it is, we sit under trees, our backs against the bark, our legs stuck straight out in the grass.

"So that went well," Mal says.

We can't help laughing.

"We won." Chug picks a flower and inspects it. "I can't believe we won."

"And the whole town knows it," Tok adds. "Not that our parents will believe them."

"They don't have to," I say quietly. "We know the truth. And Stu does, too. And Nan."

Mal looks to the cottage, nestled at the far side of the forest, up against the wall. "I can't believe she's been out here, all this time, with a window to the world."

"And so many books." Tok shakes his head. "And we lost them. All that knowledge—gone."

"Oh, I bet she knows everything," Chug says, tossing his flower at Tok. "I bet there's nothing in the whole world Nan doesn't know."

And that's when I have an idea.

A way I can move forward.

A way I can continue as I am instead of returning to who I used to be.

A place where maybe I could belong.

"Mal, do you think your Nan might take me on as an apprentice?" I ask.

CHUG

And so everything turned out pretty okay.

We saved the town from Krog, and Krog is now in jail. The Elders aren't sure what to do with him long term, but that's none of my business. At least I got to smack him with my sword, even if the Potion of Weakness made me feel like a bee punching a mountain.

The biggest issue was the crops. Krog's vexes had destroyed nearly three quarters of everyone's harvest, and all the farmers were getting ready to just pull up everything and start over. But can you guess what happened? Nan had a book on potions, and Tok figured out how to make a potion to save all the plants. It was like magic, watching all the mushy black pumpkins and their gray, crispy vines reinflate and turn orange and green again.

Well, it wasn't *like* magic, it *was* magic. Because we know magic exists, now.

The next big thing that happened was that we told our story, and with Nan's backing, people listened. We stood on the dais and laid out our entire journey, from crawling out of Nan's window to visiting the village to finding the woodland mansion and everything in between. Every time someone tried to correct us — or scold us — Nan glared at them. And we had Poppy and Thingy to back us up — because of course we had to zip back to the woodland mansion in the mine carts to collect my pig. Nan says pigs are the tastiest of animals, but I tell you right now I'm never going to taste one.

We took the Elders down to the mine carts, and they oohed and aahed. No one could believe such a giant cavern was under our town all along, and no one knew what to do with the half-built Nether portal, so they dismantled it. The woodland mansion was completely empty, but it was fun, watching grown-ups look completely flabbergasted.

"See? We told you so," I said, and it felt great, after all the times they'd complained about us over the years, calling us bad apples and accusing us of lying or general mischief.

And then the impossible occurred: The town voted and decided to open up the wall. It was getting pretty crowded in here, anyway, and some of the younger families were interested in spreading out. Nan gave a big speech about how keeping important knowledge from the new generations had almost destroyed us, and how life happens outside the walls, too. She shook her finger at the Elders and reminded them that knowledge is to be shared, ignorance isn't always safety, and life is to be lived.

And it worked.

There's a gate in the wall now, and it's always manned by a sentry in case someone else with Kroggish thoughts decides to threaten us, but there are houses outside, too, with gardens and trees and even a few wolves Lenna taught folks how to tame.

And that's maybe the best part—Lenna is so happy now.

She'd been scared to go home and get yelled at, but Nan went with her and gave her parents—and all her siblings—an earful. She told them how smart and capable and helpful and brave Lenna is, and when anyone tried to argue, she shut them right up. See, Nan loved the idea of having an apprentice, so she told Lenna's family that Lenna would be staying at her cottage from now on. Nan said it was to help her get around and learn her lore, as Mal's parents need her on the dairy farm and she needs to pass on what she knows. When Lenna's parents argued that they needed her at the mine, Nan pointedly looked at all Lenna's siblings and told her parents they had enough to share.

I wasn't there, but Lenna said it was amazing, and that she had to try so hard not to laugh.

Once her family realized that Nan was probably right, they stopped whining about Lenna and focused on what they really like, which is apparently cold, hard stone. It suits them.

As for Tok and me, our parents were as angry as we thought they'd be about us running away but surprisingly supportive once they heard the full story. Tok is now one of the most important people in town, as he can craft pretty much anything with his crafting table or the brewing stand he brought back from a trip to the village. He's happy as a pig in mud because he doesn't have to work on the farm anymore, and I'm happy because I work with him, selling the things he makes in our shop and showing folks how to use swords and ride pigs. Clarity and Candor had some superadorable kittens, and they love to sleep in the sunbeams that shine through the shop windows.

Mal is still at home, and I guess of all of us, her life has changed the least. She still wakes up at dawn to take the cows out to pasture. But as soon as her chores are over, she's running past the Hub and toward the gate, out to New Cornucopia, where Tok and I have our shop outside the walls under the endless sky.

Maybe one day when we're the Elders, we'll tell the story of how we saved our town, even when none of the adults believed us—or believed *in* us. And we'll remind that new crop of kids, bad apples and good apples alike, that they are descended from adventurers and crafters and fighters, and that they, too, contain that spark of adventurous spirit.

All I know is that once you've seen what's beyond the wall, you can't look back.

Life is better with pigs.

TOK

What?

Why are you still here?

Look, I'd love to talk, but I'm working. Remember that machine that could hurl pumpkins? I'm finally going to get it to work.

Chug already told you how it ended.

Go on, now.

Go find your own adventure. Go find your own Mob Squad. And take a kitten when you go. Cats are good luck.

ABOUT THE AUTHOR

DELILAH S. DAWSON is the *New York Times* bestselling author of the *Star Wars* novels *Phasma* and *Galaxy's Edge: Black Spire* and the *Star Wars* story "The Perfect Weapon," as well as the Blud series, the Hit series, *Servants of the Storm*, and the Shadow series, written as Lila Bowen. With Kevin Hearne, she cowrites Tales of Pell. Her comics include *Star Wars Adventures* and *Forces of Destiny, Firefly: The Sting, Marvel Action Spider-Man, Adventure Time, The X-Files Case Files*, and *Wellington*, written with Aaron Mahnke of the *Lore* podcast, plus her creator-owned comics *Ladycastle*, *Sparrowhawk*, and *Star Pig*. She lives in Georgia with her family and loves Ewoks, porgs, and gluten-free cake.

whimsydark.com
Facebook.com/DelilahSDawson
Twitter: @DelilahSDawson

ABOUT THE TYPE

This book was set in Electra, a typeface designed for Linotype by W. A. Dwiggins, the renowned type designer (1880–1956). Electra is a fluid typeface, avoiding the contrasts of thick and thin strokes that are prevalent in most modern typefaces.

DISCOVER MORE MINECRAFT:
LEVEL UP YOUR GAME WITH THE OFFICIAL GUIDES

- ☐ GUIDE TO COMBAT
- ☐ GUIDE TO CREATIVE
- ☐ GUIDE TO ENCHANTMENTS & POTIONS
- ☐ GUIDE TO FARMING
- ☐ GUIDE TO MINECRAFT DUNGEONS

- ☐ GUIDE TO OCEAN SURVIVAL
- ☐ GUIDE TO THE NETHER & THE END
- ☐ GUIDE TO PVP MINIGAMES
- ☐ GUIDE TO REDSTONE
- ☐ GUIDE TO SURVIVAL

MORE MINECRAFT:

- ☐ EPIC BASES
- ☐ EXPLODED BUILDS: MEDIEVAL FORTRESS
- ☐ LET'S BUILD! LAND OF ZOMBIES
- ☐ LET'S BUILD! THEME PARK ADVENTURE

- ☐ MAPS
- ☐ MINECRAFT FOR BEGINNERS
- ☐ MOBESTIARY
- ☐ THE SURVIVORS' BOOK OF SECRETS

Penguin
Random
House

DISCOVER MORE MINECRAFT:
Have You Read Them All?

- ☐ *The Island* by Max Brooks
- ☐ *The Crash* by Tracey Baptiste
- ☐ *The Lost Journals* by Mur Lafferty
- ☐ *The End* by Catherynne M. Valente
- ☐ *The Voyage* by Jason Fry
- ☐ *The Rise of the Arch-Illager* by Matt Forbeck
- ☐ *The Shipwreck* by C. B. Lee
- ☐ *The Mountain* by Max Brooks
- ☐ *The Dragon* by Nicky Drayden

Penguin
Random
House